I0584109

LIGHTS OVER THE SENTURION MOON

JON VASSA

Black Rose Writing | Texas

First printing

This is a work of fiction. Names, characters, businesses, places, events, and
incidents are either the products of the author's imagination or used in a
fictitious manner. Any resemblance to actual persons, living or dead, or
actual events is purely coincidental.

ISBN: 978-1-68433-945-7
PUBLISHED BY BLACK ROSE WRITING
www.blackrosewriting.com

Printed in the United States of America
Suggested Retail Price (SRP) $20.95

Lights Over the Senturion Moon is printed in Sabon

*As a planet-friendly publisher, Black Rose Writing does its best to eliminate
unnecessary waste to reduce paper usage and energy costs, while never
compromising the reading experience. As a result, the final word count vs. page
count may not meet common expectations.

LIGHTS OVER THE SENTURION MOON

CEPH

CHAPTER 1

The smell of rotten flesh is unmistakable. No matter the size of the carcass, the stench still hits you right behind the eyes. As I climbed the feeble steps, that familiar hint of death greeted me. A lingering musk that beaconed me to a red-painted door at the end of the hallway.

I jiggled the handle a few times and then attempted a couple of soft knocks, knowing it was useless.

She's dead, I thought. *What are you being polite for?*

After waiting several seconds for a response, I rammed my shoulder against the door and broke inside with little effort. It didn't take long to spot her sitting on a dirty cot; eyes wide open and a needle dangling from her black veins.

A sense of deja vu rippled down the back of my head to the tips of my toes. I'd seen this before—unnatural black veins and a half-used needle lingering in the victim's arm.

I threw the back of my hand up over my nose and stepped further into the room. It wasn't just the dead body that got to me, but the years of neglected filth and accumulated trash left to ferment.

How her face had changed.

Taking out an old picture her father had passed me, I instantly saw the stark contrast between the two. Bright blue eyes versus dull greyish orbits sunken deep within her bony skull. Vibrant hair springing with life as opposed to the tattered grease encased in dander upon her head.

I kicked a few cans out of the way, accidentally stepping on a glass pipe while reaching the girl. There, I kneeled beside her to check her pulse—more out of habit than any actual hope that she might still be ticking.

No such luck. She lay as dead as her parents' wishes and my wishes at a pretty bonus at the end of this case. Clients rarely sent me any extra credits unless I brought back their hopes and dream, in one piece, and what more alive.

I fixed my hat upon my head, dug into my jacket for a white glove, stretched it over my hand, and dragged the needle out of her cold skin. There was a drop of liquid left inside the syringe—a cloudy white liquid with a shimmering blue tint congealed in the middle.

Funny how creative chemists are, whipping up glittery mixes for girls like this to jab into their arms and check out of the hotel early. With all the effort I can muster, I do my best to keep out of narc cases—I prefer to avoid the tangle they seem to breed.

Everyone always wants to find a source, as if there's a single chemist in some secret hideout standing over a giant black cauldron mixing up this rubbish, and then sending out phials for anyone close enough to get their hands on it. And if we found them? Then, what? Their cousin resumes the operation until we bust them, and then their cousin's cousin until there's no end?

I placed the needle on the floor and snapped a picture of the girl. As I backed out, I was thankful for the fresh air and felt encouraged to exit fully from the building. Why does it have to be drugs? Couldn't she have been kidnapped because of her father's political leanings or sour business dealings?

I left the building and stood outside on the vacant street for a while, thinking to myself. The winds blew around me as if they couldn't be bothered by much this evening. Sheets of newspapers were scrapping inches above the pavement with nothing to catch them.

This town used to give me real proper cases. Once, I found myself at a lofty mansion, where the electricity went out moments before an old lady was suffocated under her pillow. Of course, the only people in the house at the time were all key suspects. It was a wild three days that left a nice crescent-shaped scar near my collarbone. Or what about the months I spent tracking down a serial rapist only to find him sitting comfortably in his office with the name Doctor printed on the door and a welcoming smile on his face.

A car passed by on the main road a good twenty meters away and quickly faded into a wake of silence. I spied down the dim street, eyeing the abandoned buildings along the road, and saw a tall factory burning orange flames out of its chimney at some distance behind them.

I knew I needed to make the call. He told me to call him as soon as I found her, no matter the time of night. But still, I lingered.

The streetlight across the road was dying out, flickering on and off, while illuminating a pile of rubbish on the ground. Was that myself? Flickering out into oblivion as the rest of the world basked under halogen bulbs and talked about how bright their future seemed?

I raised my arm near my face, clicked my wristwatch, and spoke into it. 'Found your daughter. Let's have a chat if you're awake.' I sent the message.

I spotted an old, worn mutt dragging its black paws along the pavement, occasionally stopping to sniff at the scattered piles of rubbish.

The cops would be the next to call. They seemed to appreciate a heads-up when you found a missing person. Go figure. I pulled out a cigarette from my jacket and bit down on its filter. While the dog snapped its head up over the trash, its eyes fastened on mine, wary of my every move.

My wristwatch alerted me to a new message. *Can you stop by the house?*

I exhaled a plume of smoke and stared at the black dog, who was staring back at me. 'Of course I'll stop by,' I said while getting ready to respond to his message.

•　　　•　　　•　　　•　　　•

The engine rumbled as it cut off. Moonlight cut through the clouds, illuminating the outline of a nice house before me in one of the few remaining suburban areas left in this town. Concrete is the new gold, I've been told. Why build a dwelling that's only two stories high with timber and clay shingles when you can cram yourself into a nice shoebox in the city for the same price?

Smoke drifted from my teeth and danced for a while under the moonbeams. I finished my cigarette and stepped out of the car. The house's lights were off, but beside it, barred by a small gate, lay an old gamekeeper's home with an orange light shining from its window.

I picked the gate's lock, pushed it open, and walked through the garden, creeping towards that orange-glowing window. The moon shone a faint blue glow on atop the old gamekeeper's shack as the winds pushed a black shingle on and off the window. Fixing my jacket, I walked up two stone steps, knocked at the door, and then stepped back and waited. It opened almost immediately. I saw a sliver of moonlight painted across the old man's eyes. His fingers slid out through the crack in the door as he held onto the painted black frame.

'Yes?' he said. 'Can I help you?'

I rubbed the corner of my eye. Every client has a different reaction when it comes to this moment.

'That depends.'

The door slid open further. 'Vince? Why didn't you tell me you were coming?'

I could smell the alcohol on his breath. 'What did you assume my reply meant?'

He paused to measure me over once more, then raised his wrist watch toward his face, pressing the red blinking notification. Without any concern for me or the cold nip outside, he stood there, reading the holographic message I had sent him over an hour ago.

'Your wife's asleep?'

'Excuse me?' He looked up from his watch.

I grunted to myself. 'You want to talk out here or what?'

His eyes shifted back and forth as his fingers retracted. And, slowly, the door creaked wide open.

I stepped in and lingered underneath the dim orange lights glowing inside.

'Nice place,' I said. 'You ever thought of renting it out?'

Wherever his mind was, it wasn't on my words because no niceties returned my way. He remained fixed in place, staring at the floor, not yet fully closing the door. I noticed his thin fingers resting on the handle and the skeletal wrist that emerged from his loose suit. His bones made him seem more like a child playing dress-up in daddy's clothes rather than a grown man with a thriving business uptown.

I scratched my chin as I looked at him. His eyes were scanning the room as if he had something to say but couldn't quite stack all the bullets in a row. He looked up at me with concern.

'Why don't we sit?' He gave the door a final shut, then gesturing into the room, indicating for me to go inside.

I nodded and went to a brown armchair right under the dim light. He lingered behind for several seconds before entering the room. He picked up a bottle of amber liquid, considered it for a moment, then placed it on a table near my chair.

'You're sitting in my seat,' he laughed, with his back to me.

'Everyone takes news differently,' I said. 'So how about humoring me for a while.'

His back was still facing me as he went to an armchair opposite of mine. I could tell he was digging into his coat, struggling in the process to drag something out. Then, he sat facing me, aiming a gun in my direction.

'Where's my daughter?' he said.

'Let's make this easy on the both of us. You know what I'm going to say.'

He clicked the hammer back and pursed his lips, then gave me a thin smile. 'Mr. Sturgis, when I paid for your services, I specifically requested that you bring my daughter back to me alive. Was that not clear enough?'

The air grew dense in the room. I reflexively reached for my jacket to get a cigarette, then stopped when he tensed in his seat. I laughed, putting my palms flat in the air and then back down to my lap.

'How much do you make a year, Mr. Sturgis?'

The calculation trickled along the gears in my head. 'Pardon?'

'You've seen the house,' he said, 'the cars and the lavish rings on my wife's fingers. And now you're contacting me without bringing my precious child home?'

'I'm not asking—'

'Yes, you are! I eat hucksters like you for a living.' The gun wagged at me. 'And this is always how it plays out. There's some kink, and you need more money, and this time, it's triple the cost!'

'No one's saying—'

'What game are you playing at?'

Licking my lips, I squint an eye at him.

'You want to make things easy? Huh? Then, why don't you cut the bullshit and tell me how much you make a year. That way, I know, without a doubt, you're playing me before I rip you a new one.'

'And, again, that information is personal.'

'In the context of this situation, do you honestly feel that's important right now? I'm going to ask you once more nicely... how much do you make?'

Shrugging my shoulders, I opened my mouth and said nothing.

'You're a fraud,' he said. 'When we discussed this, I told you to bring her back alive. Not to come crawling back here to siphon more cash out of me!'

'Obviously, I'm pretty bad fraud if I'm not asking for any more money.'

'Shut your mouth,' he said. 'Shut your friggin' mouth!'

'Did you know what she was on?' I glanced at him. 'That she took her first hit of white dust alongside your pool? During one of those fancy parties you like to throw.'

'You're a liar and a con artist!' He stood up, shaking the gun in my face. 'I want to see my daughter, you sick pup!'

Digging into my jacket, I took out my cigarettes and set the pack on my lap. He made sure to flash the gun within my sight to remind me of its presence.

'Toss me a lighter, will you?'

His eyes went wide. He showed me the barrel once more, snarling through his teeth.

I refused to meet his eyes. I just hoped this wouldn't take the entire night.

Then, after a count of fifteen in my head, he slowly lost his edge. He reached into his pocket and threw a lighter to me. I caught it and lit my cigarette.

His face began to droop. The gun's barrel quit staring me down. I dragged on my cigarette, watching the embers glow at the end, and then let out a heavy breath full of smoke. I reached into my jacket, the cigarette hanging loose from my lips, and took out the photo he had given me and tossed it onto the floor.

'I get it,' I said. 'There's nothing easy about this.'

He snarled at me with his perfect white teeth. He gained no reaction from me. I simply waited.

After a while, he bent down to pick up the photo, still in a grimace as he snatched it up. Then, he started to look it over, shaking his head with spit forming at the edge of his mouth.

'So?' he said. 'The hell are you giving me this for? I already know what she looks like.'

I then reached inside my jacket and pulled out the most recent photo I had taken before I called him or the authorities. I threw it onto the floor and took in another breath of smoke.

His face froze into a still panic. He gulped, sweat beading on his forehead, and bent down to pick it up. His lips quivered as he gripped the picture. His nose pinched up into his cheeks like there was a foul smell inthe air.

I tipped my ash into a metal dustbin nearby, then took another drag. 'I'm not saying it was your fault,' I said. 'Or hers.'

He kept shaking his head, staring at the photo.

'You were right about the boyfriend,' I said. 'He introduced her to the crew at his apartment the night she went missing. But he wasn't the one who got her hooked on the harder stuff. She was already dosing herself long before they started dating.'

The man backed towards his chair and dropped into the seat. His gun tumbled to the floor as the photo fell onto his lap. 'That son of a bitch...'

'He didn't know any better,' I said. 'Neither did she. They both expected to have a good time. And from what I've gathered, they were both lied to in the process. It's unfortunate, but whatever this new drug is—'

He gritted his teeth and hissed at me through them. 'Get out of here.'

I paused a moment. 'Sorry?'

'Leave. Now.'

I snubbed the cigarette in the metal bin and stood up, looking around the room.

The man glanced up at me. 'You know where the door is.'

'Fair enough,' I said. 'But let's at least stick to our original agreement, yeah?'

A sense of realization fell over him. He stood up and went to the table where his bottle sat, grabbed a large envelope, and threw it across the room at me.

I caught it near my face with a smile. 'You can let me know when you want the full story then,' I said.

He jabbed his finger towards the door. 'Get the fuck out of my house!'

'See you around.'

I stepped through the room and out the door. The moon had a few clouds rolling over it. I walked past the garden and out towards the driveway. I got to my car and ruminated over a few thoughts before I started up the engine. When I glanced up, I saw his wife standing outside the front door in a red velvet bathrobe.

Tapping my watch, the engine rattled into a painful start. I clicked the gears and inched it along the front steps. She looked around for a moment as if someone might be watching her from the shrubs, then she wiped her nose and climbed into the passenger side of my car. She looked me in the eye and started to cry.

'She got tangled up in something bigger than herself,' I said. 'But it wasn't at all her fault.'

'I know it wasn't.'

I tapped my thumb on the steering wheel, thinking of the girl. She resembled her mother. They had the same complexion, but both getting pale for very different reasons.

'She's not coming home, is she?'

I shook my head. 'No.'

'Was she alone?'

I closed my eyes for a second and saw her daughter on the dirty cot in my mind. 'When I found her.'

She sniffed into her bathrobe. 'My poor baby.'

I licked my lips and glanced up at the stars hanging coldly in the sky.

The lady sniffed into a piece of her robe near her face. 'They strangled her?' she said. 'They did, didn't they? I had a dream they were hurting her. They had their hands around her neck and smiles on their faces. I couldn't get to her, though. The window was locked on the other side, and I couldn't reach her. But I tried! I yelled for anyone to help—'

'No one stole her,' I said. 'And no one strangled her either.'

Using the heel of her palm, she went about clearing the tears from her face.

'She was chasing a lie,' I said. 'Some people promised her a journey that only a select few have ever experienced on this planet.'

She was quiet.

'But I doubt she felt anything when she passed. This black death can be instant.'

She stared at me with her shimmering white eyes. Then, before I could stop her, she quickly opened her bath robe to expose her naked body. Her breast sagged on her chest while she traced a line on her belly, running her finger along an old scar amongst her stretch marks.

'My dream was to have a natural birth,' she said. 'I paid for classes and books and anything I could get my hands on to do it right. But they forced me to take their drugs. They made me take them.'

'Uhh, Mrs. Yuuth - '

'We almost lost her when she was born,' she said. 'The only way to save her was to cut her out before the umbilical cord choked her to death.'

Averting my eyes, I stared out of the windscreen. I lost sight of the scars and focused on the moon that was currently being overtaken by thick clouds.

She continued sniffing and left her robe wide open. 'And now what have I got?' she said. 'A bunch of scars to show for a child that I failed to protect?'

The night was too calm, too peaceful, and too indifferent. I tapped my thumb on the steering wheel as she began to cry in her hands again.

'This is all his fault!' she yelled. 'He told me to get the birthing drug, he forced me into it, saying there would be no harm! But look at where we are now? She never had a chance - she's been drowned in chemicals before she even entered this world!'

'I'm certain the hospital wouldn't—'

Grabbing clumps of her hair, she yanked at her head and started screaming. I took hold of her hands and pulled them away gently, placing them back by her sides.

'You're the same as everyone else,' she said. 'Everyone telling me I'm crazy. That I'm a dumb bitch who doesn't understand how science works! Is that it, Mr. Sturgis? Is that what you're saying?'

'I'm not saying that.'

'I know how this world works and whose money is going into the pockets of these immoral researchers!'

Leaning back into my seat, I knew this wasn't going to take me anywhere soon.

'We pump our kids full of this crap from the moment they're born,' she said. 'And then we act all surprised when our schoolyards resemble the back alleyways in our city's loins.'

'You knew of her habits then?'

'How could I miss it?' she spat. 'She's always been hooked on some drug or another!'

'Then, why did you lie to me earlier?'

'This is his fault!' she shouted, pounding her fists on the dashboard. 'This all his damn fault! I told him not to put drugs in my body when she was coming out and now look at this mess we're in!'

Silence filled the car. The echoes of her shouts still reverberated in my chest. My mind began to file this away, in some cavern deep inside my brain where I keep plenty of things that should have been tossed out long, long ago.

Glancing at my watch, I knew it was going to be a long night. She fell into her hands, crying. Crying. And crying. Leaving me in the dark, without a word to say.

CHAPTER 2

Twisting my keys in the lock too easily told me that the bolts were already loose, and the door unlocked. I reached to my side, taking hold of my gun, and nudged the door open, pushing my pistol inside first.

'Good morning,' said a woman's voice.

I lowered my gun and rolled my eyes. 'I told you to get rid of that key.' I shut the door behind me.

'Get a real lock from this century,' she said. 'Then, you can keep me out.' She sat at my fold-out table with her legs crossed, gently swaying her top foot in circles. 'Why did you call Reche about the girl instead of me?'

I slipped my jacket off my arms and threw it onto the sofa-bed. I went over to my small kitchen and poured last night's coffee into a dirty mug.

'I've asked you not to do this anymore,' I said. 'Don't come in here and leave the door unlocked like that. You know what - just don't come in here at all - stay the hell away from this place. Alright?'

'Are you making a fresh batch?'

I snorted.

'Can you get me some? In a clean mug.'

Pausing for a second, I lowered the dirty mug back down to the counter and grit my teeth.

'Thanks.'

I opened the coffee machine and dumped the old grinds in the sink. I then poured my leftover coffee into the machine's water slot before shoveling a new scoop of powder into the filter.

She stepped into the doorframe, leaning in to watch me. 'Why did you call Reche about this?'

Searching the cabinets, I found the cleanest mug I could find and held it under the tap to flush out the bits of dust inside. Her glare burnt through the back of my skull without me even catching her gaze. I put the mug down, as clean as it was going to get, and turned around to face her. She was dressed for work with a black shirt and leather jacket. She'd cut her hair too. It was shorter now. Same color, though. Straight and black.

'Reche is in charge of missing persons if I'm not mistaken,' I said. 'There's the logical progression there. I found a missing person and called the guy in charge of the department.'

She leered at me with her dark brown eyes. 'You knew I was after this drug. Why didn't you give me the heads-up first? That was a real jerk move on your part.'

The coffee was beginning to drip. Not fast enough, though. 'I didn't want to wake you. It was pretty late when I found her.'

'You never told me you were on such a case. You should've tipped me off earlier... And getting that close to the Black Death.'

I found an old pack of cigarettes in one of my cabinets. I opened it, pulled one out, and lit it on my stove's conduction burner. 'Listen. I'm not having anyone take over my cases. This one was private, all right? The last thing I need is the whole department sniffing around like a bunch of morons.'

She stepped in further, leaving less room in the kitchen. She picked up her mug to wash it herself with soap and hot water. 'I'm not going to bring in everyone,' she said. 'You can tell me this kind of things. Jeez. You know me better than that.'

The coffee maker hissed, and a beeping sound rang out from its speakers. I filled her mug first and then mine. It smelt bitter, like battery acid ready to eat away at my innards.

'I had no clue she was on the stuff,' I said. 'This is only my second time running into it. I'm not doing this on purpose. You make me out to seem like I was trying to track it down myself. I was merely out for a stroll last night and happened to find the girl's syringe half-full of the gunk.'

'But you called Reche instead of me.'

'It's nothing personal. I had my own things to deal with last night. Before I even thought you might be curious, I'd already put in the call.'

She opened the little fridge, making the kitchen even more cramped, and shuffled her hands inside. 'You haven't used any of these packs since I left?' She lifted a square packet of dried cream.

'I forgot they were in there.'

She shut the fridge, ripped open the dry milk packet, and dumped it in her mug. She ripped open a second one and poured it right in after the other.

'You and I need to spend more time together.' She ripped open a third packet. 'I want to know what you found and what circuits you were on to. You know, there was another case of this Black Death a week ago?' She rubbed her forehead a few times. 'If we don't cut it off, and do it soon, this whole town's going be turned upside down.'

'Not everyone's a junkie out here.'

'That's six confirmed cases. Six, Vince. I really hope the media doesn't find out about this, or there's going to be a huge demand for it all of a sudden.'

I exhaled a drag of smoke out of my nostrils. 'I doubt any of the guys I talked with would lead you to the source. Most of them are keeping their distance from the stuff, and any mention causes them to panic. Believe it or not, they're afraid of it seeping into their own dens, Mae.' I took another sip.

She snorted, then backed out of the kitchen with her mug. I followed behind her. She sat down in my chair again, crossing her legs, stirring her coffee with a rusty fork.

'Well, it's coming in from somewhere, and we'd better get on it fast before it takes over the market. I pray that no one famous dies from it.

Then we're toast. Everyone and their mothers gonna want to try this new blend.'

'These things always blow over,' I said. 'Didn't we have the same issue in twenty-nine? What was it, the Moxie Singe? And now isn't that drug everywhere?'

'It's not deadly like this.'

'That's what they always say,' I said. 'Forgive me if I have a hard time taking this seriously.'

She blew the steam from the top of her mug and gingerly took a sip. 'You know, I can hire you on a project basis. You'll be under my watch. But it's steady pay?.' She took another refined sip.

I went over to the side of the room, snubbing out my cigarette in a graveyard full of them, and then pulled the brown curtains back. The sun was rising higher now as everyone outside rushed to their cars in order to file into traffic with the rest.

'You wouldn't have to report to anyone else,' she said.

I watched a line of ants marching along the side of my windowsill. They were dragging crumbs and bits of food to their queen to fatten her up, so she keeps laying those slimy eggs.

'I don't like narcs,' I said. 'Once we nab this drug, there'll be a brand new one on the market that we've gotta chase down next and then another new drug after that.'

'You've never been squeamish before.'

'We never worked that closely on these matters before, partner.'

'Ha. Ha.'

I turned my nose up at her and sipped my coffee.

'Oh, come on, Vince. You don't have anything else lined up at the moment. It'll be a steady fix. Plus, you can see everyone down at the department again.'

I had more coffee as I listened to the train rattle by my window. It was filled with people, all going around the tracks endlessly, never seeming to get anywhere.

She stood up, drawing closer to me. 'You feeling sick?'

'Nah.'

'Then what?'

She yanked the other curtain fully open, blinding me with light, and showing clear all dust and cigarette holes in my apartment.

'Jeez.' I threw my arm over my eyes.

'It could be a good opportunity. You might even be offered a permeant desk uptown if you do this right.' She swiped dust off the glass and rubbed it between her fingers. 'What more you can queue for a civil honor flat. They're building another block, up in a good part of town. Where the trains run underground, hovering, not clacking like these old frontier engines.'

'I hate narcs. You start losing your mind when you deal with these people. Everyone's paranoid. No one knows the difference between reality and hallucinations. And there's always someone with a gun, unaware it's aimed at their own head. There's no class to it and if I truly felt these things would change... then maybe... but they don't.'

She breathed a sardonic laugh. 'You're full of it, Vince. I feel like I'm losing my head just talking to you.'

I turned to look at the door. 'Well, you'd better get out quick then.'

She sipped her mug with leisure as she watched another train plow by the window. The floors trembled a jitter. 'God, I really feel as if I've walked through some time warp when I come out here. The mayor said he was going to tear up these old tracks. Put in a bunch of new, sleek trains.' She touched the window, as if poking the rattling train passing by. 'And I hope he can. Before this Black Death rolls over the place.'

CHAPTER 3

I had a few messages on my watch when I woke up.

Hey Vince. You mind coming down to the station later? We want to ask you a few questions about this girl. Oh, and I talked with Mae. She said you might be coming aboard for a stint. . .

Reche

I clicked to the next one.

It's not like you know who your next clients are going to be. You may be right back, face to face with narcs again, without even knowing it. Seriously Vince. Take the offer. Move out of that shithole and come join the rest of us.

I clicked to the next.

Dear Mr. Sturgis,

I hope you will forgive me for my outburst last night. A man like myself has his hopes and dreams tucked close to his chest and feels that even in the bleakest of situations that he can still obtain them. But please understand when you burst that hope last night, I found my reality very difficult to manage. Perhaps we can talk this over more civilly in the future. But as of now, I need some time.

Mr. Yuuth

I checked the last one.

Dear Mr. Sturgis,

I've been watching your work for some time now with great interest. Especially your more recent cases that made headlines in Ceph. If you have the time, I'd like to arrange a meeting with you?

'What is with these rich guys. Always in a hurry.'

There is an old abandoned bridge outside your city limits, due south from your home; that would be an ideal place to meet tonight, around midnight? I hope to hear back from you soon, as this matter is quite pressing.

Best regards,

Elix Nouir

Groaning to myself, I stretched my arms and back, raising my hands high to the air, then grunted as I released the tension in my body.

'Another dumb politician trying to cover their ass... At least they pay in cash.'

I tossed the covers off myself and reached for a pack of cigarettes on the table. After lighting one, my thoughts took on a life of their own and turned me down a dim detour of the room I found that young girl in last night. She was vibrant, I'm sure, at one point. A beautiful smile and plenty of charm, before fantasy land hooked its lines into. These things happen, though; no matter wealth, charm, looks, or state of being. It's the chance we take in living, that we might wake up one day and realize we don't enjoy this existence any longer.

Slipping on a pair of socks, I set my feet on the floor, avoiding the shocking cold tiles, and stepped into the tiny kitchen. The coffee was still warm from earlier when Mae demanded a new batch. I threw the fridge open, picked out some eggs, and cracked them in a pan.

When I finished my breakfast, I went out into the mid-afternoon sun. It didn't heat our section of the planet that much this time of year. I was thankful for that fact, especially after the brutal summers we've had over the past three seasons. Maybe the people on this globe will wise up and quit taking the easy way out, relying on old sources of energy hanging around from the frontier days. Maybe Mae had a point about stepping into the current century, where we don't have to burn so much rubbish and chop down nearly as many trees.

As I went to my car, I found a note asking me if I had insurance to leave to my loved ones when I died.

'That's a good way of getting yourself killed,' I said, crumpling the paper and hopping into the car.

I drove into the traffic for a minute, then headed in the opposite direction, avoiding the congestion. Bringing my wrist under my chin, I spoke out a message to send. 'Reche, I'll stop in tomorrow if that's okay. I have some things to take care of right now. I'm a bit behind due to this case.'

I sent the message and began the next. 'My clients are fairly consistent and pay on time, Mae. I'm not strapped for anything, and maybe I like living near the old train stations. It keeps me grounded.'

I started the next one. 'I understand Mr. Yuuth. This is part of the job. I deal with it all the time. Whenever you're ready, you know how to reach me.'

I stopped at the light. A giant truck careened through the intersection, dragging a large brown tanker behind it, full of god knows what.

The light changed. I pressed on the gas, lifting my wrist back up to my mouth. 'Nouir? Fair enough, you like to keep things private.' I stopped again at another light. More trucks went by, with some punks on their motorcycles zoomed between them like buzzing flies. 'Some bridge due south. If you plan on coming alone, then send me the coordinates, and I'll see how I feel around midnight.'

Message sent.

I turned the car down into the underground highway and made a few sharp turns, going lower beneath the city. I stopped my car outside a dim restaurant where no light dwellers ever went. There were cloth awnings hanging over the place with rips stringing them apart, and holes big enough for bats to nest inside them.

There was a bouncer at the entrance with jewels adorning his thick fingers and a black suit buttoned tight around his meaty neck. He licked his back tooth as I approached the venue. 'Mr. Lemoshe isn't seeing anyone tonight,' he said.

'Did I ask to see him?' I said, sweeping a poisonous spider off my shoulder. 'Is that the only reason I could be here? Get real thicko, I heard you had a bit of foreign jazz playing tonight, who gives a whoop about Lemoshe.'

An eyebrow raised at me.

'You gonna let me in?'

He cracked his knuckles, opening and closing his hand into fists. 'Mr. Lemoshe asked me to keep people, such as yourself, out of his place tonight.' He cleared his throat and flared his wide nostrils as he exhaled. 'Seems fairly straightforward.'

'What about this new curry you have been stewing recently. That's new, right? And if it's a seasonal thing, then I'm flat out of luck.'

'Tough.'

'Come on. Breaded, deep-fried fish, laying atop a plate surrounded by a warm gravy. Sounds nice to me. And exactly where else am I going eat something like that in this town and at this time of day?'

The guard cleared his throat and kept his sights over my head.

'You look as if you've already had a few servings yourself,' I said. 'But look at me, skin and bones. Don't you think I could use a good meal as I smooth out my nerves with some live jazz? This has nothing to do with Lemoshe. Tell him he thinks too highly of himself.'

The bouncer cleared his throat again, annoyed this time. 'I'm going to crush your skull down so far into your ribs - '

'Just ask him if I can have a meal! Don't be so damn stubborn. I know you got a blockhead, but there's no need to be so dense even if you have little to work with upstairs.'

He grabbed me by my shirt and lifted me towards himself. 'Lemoshe said he doesn't want to see any private dicks inside the club tonight. You want to be walking out with holes in your side or a permeant dent in your head?'

I took hold of his wrists, trying to leverage myself while grinning back at him. 'I heard that big guys are often the most touchy.' I then puckered a faux kiss in the air.

He let go of my shirt, tossing me back along the pavement.

Sitting on the asphalt for a moment gave me a second to recoup. I made no rush at picking up my hat and brushing off my shirt. He kept his gaze straight ahead of himself. Snorting at him, I slipped a cigarette in my teeth and then lit the thing.

His eyes were on me as I stood back up.

I heard the music stringing inside. The upright bass was drawing rhythms out into the underground, shaking loose every bat and rodent. I kept my eyes on Mr. Sensitive, my face glowing orange and smoke running out the cracks in my teeth.

The guard pulled his cuffs back over his wrist and began fixing his jewels upon his digits.

I went to my car, sat on the hood, and flicked my cigarette towards him. It fell short. I then put my writs up to my mouth to dictate a message.

'Lemoshe, what the hell is this? You'd better call this dumb bull off before I find my own way into this restaurant. Is your memory going soft? You don't remember me anymore or what I might've done for you and your son?'

I sent the message.

The band started another song. I could hear the drummer tapping his snare to let the pianist ride out a nice riff. The upright seeped in the rhythm with a peppered cymbal, lightly gracing the background without bringing down the melody. I lit another cigarette and watched Mr. Sensitive. I even offered him a smoke. He refused.

Then, the doors opened. A tall man with his hair pulled back into a ponytail spoke with Sensitive, and then went back inside. The bouncer cracked his neck, then threw his big paw on the door, holding it open for me.

I slipped off the car's hood and started walking down the red carpet into the smokey den, the music now clear as day. I stopped for a moment to scan the place. There was an open booth to the side that looked comfortable enough. I sat myself and waited for the server to come by.

Everyone clapped for the band. I brought my hands together, my cigarette hanging from my mouth, and my hat tipped down over my eyes.

The server came to my table. 'Can I get you a drink?'

I stubbed out my cigarette and pointed to a table on the other side of the room. 'What is Lemoshe drinking tonight?'

The server turned over his shoulder with trepidation and then back to me. 'Bourbon,' he said. 'It's the Prime Minister's select. Only forty-five barrels ever made.'

'Lemoshe bought each barrel, no?'

The boy swallowed before he spoke. 'I'm not sure.'

I sighed, glancing at the tables around me. 'Fine. Get me a glass, then. And bring me a plate of curry.'

The boy nodded with his young, innocent face. 'Which curry?'

'You've got more than one?'

He stared at me, nervous at my question, but god only knows why.

'Kid, just get me the one with the fried fish.'

'Yes, sir.'

'Hop to solider.'

He raced away.

Leaning back into the booth buried me in the corner, hiding me from almost everyone else's view. That's one thing I admired about Lemoshe's sense of design. He knows how to build privacy in a public space. Or, at least, knows the right designer to threaten into understanding his vision.

The band continued to play; they were lost in a song now, stuck in an infinite loop that they might never break away from. I moved a little shaded candle on my table with a listless aim, back and forth, here and there, watching the hot wax shift inside it.

The boy came back, setting a serviette down on the table and then the glass atop it. I picked it up and had a sip.

The song ended, and I thought about clapping but stopped when I noticed a large man walking slowly across the room to where I sat. He was a rotund fellow with a dark mustache etched upon his upper lip and hair greased back atop his head. The man slid into my booth at the other end, with a cigar in his hand and a young waiter carrying his bourbon beside him.

'Evening,' I said.

Lemoshe tapped his index finger on the table, making the server put down his glass, and then waved the boy away. He sat across from me, measuring me up for some time, and then spoke.

'I said no dicks tonight.'

'Who? Me?'

Lowering his head, he grinned to himself. 'Funny guy.'

'What's with this new menu,' I said. 'You're holding out on me, Lemoshe. I had to hear the word from whore up on the twelfth street, you know? I'm hurt. Real hurt friend. And, now, you've given me grief when all I want is to eat a nice meal in peace?'

Twisting his glass on the table, he lost his smile and spoke in a real serious tone. 'What do you think about two broken femurs?' he said. 'Does that hurt? Because all I want tonight is some privacy. But that doesn't seem to be the case now, does it?'

'I thought we had a deal, Lemoshe. You let me keep my bones intact and, in return, I seemed to help your eldest boy out of a whole heap of pain. You think those pigs upstairs aren't still watching this place? That they wouldn't think twice to send the hounds again?'

With a smirk, he lifted his eyes, but not to mine.

'We're going clean from now on,' he said. 'So from tonight forward, you won't need be stopping in here anymore. Got it?'

I took a sip from my bourbon and lit another cigarette. 'I'd be careful if I were you,' I said. 'There's a pretty nasty drug floating around the city nowadays. And being friends and whatnot, I thought I might tell you that some of your boys might have a finger or two in the vat.'

Lemoshe gave a snide laugh, took a sip of his drink, and set it back down. 'Black Death,' he said. 'You got my shivering, Vince.' He bent his head down to study my reaction.

I exhaled more smoke into the misty room. 'Second case I've run into.'

He shook his head, holding his cigar near his face, his elbow propped up on the table. 'Get a grip,' he said. 'Hybrids are everywhere on Ceph. We had you boys, freaking out about the Ninth Blitz two years ago, and what happened? Nothing. Nothing happened other than a few kids had one too many hits before their thumpers quit ticking. You don't see me jumping when hyped-up fads roll into town, do you? If it's not this, it's something else a year later. Big deal.' Chuckling a little, he drew his cigar to his mouth, lingering it near his lips.

'I'm not disagreeing. But you'd better tell your lot to be careful,' I said. 'The police are desperate this time. And one other thing, whether you're clean or not, what do I care? But keep this in mind, you won't be getting any return customers with this kind of jab if you just so happen to be pushing.'

Lemoshe finished his glass and set it down on the table. He glanced over his back at the band as they finished their song. The pianist nodded at him, same with the upright bass player. Clearing his throat, he brought the young waiter to the table, who snatched up his empty glass and rushed to the bar to refill it.

'You think we're chums?'

'No. I'm still grateful both my legs aren't in splinters.'

Lemoshe had another drag of his cigar and let the smoke out the corner of his mouth. 'I had this group flown in straight from the motherland,' he said, as a thick vein crept up the side of his neck. 'They'll be going on some tour after tonight, though.'

I looked up at the band and examined them for some time. They looked like foreigners. Especially the pianist with his bright jacket.

Lemoshe tapped the table with his big forefinger. 'You enjoy your night,' he said, beginning to stand. 'And a word of advice. You might want to find a new country to visit for a while. Because even if you and

I are buddies now, that doesn't mean everyone else has forgotten your face in town.'

I lifted my glass a bit. 'Yeah. I'll think about that.'

He got up and strut back to his own booth, rubbing his hands together, and then snatching his bourbon from the young waiter. I leaned further back to watch the band and waited for my curry to arrive.

CHAPTER 4

An hour before midnight, my watch buzzed with an encrypted set of coordinates that only I could access. It wasn't uncommon for celebrities or even city hall persons to go about their communications in such a manner. The only thing that stuck an odd nerve in me was the form of the coordinates and how it seemed to block any other access or tracking measurements in my watch at the time.

With a fair amount of reluctance and just enough nudges from a thin bank account, I still found myself following those coordinates driving along the mag-highway to a desolate exit ramp that ushered me onto a paved road, split by large cracks and decorated with sprouts of desert grass.

Further south, I drove, passing by the city limit's sign, cruising deeper into the desert on the single lane road, not another car in sight. A slight veer in the road whipped past me too fast to make my necessary turn. I skidded the car to a halt then circled it in the dusty landscape, tossing up plenty of rocks and dirt before I caught the veer the second time around.

The bridge slowly outlined itself in my headlights. Parking at the side of the gorge, I stepped out of the car and peered over the sheer drop below. A sign warned me to be careful not to fall in the giant canyon in the earth, and I replied back by thanking it for stating the obvious.

As I walked onto the bridge, I saw no one else upon it. I thumped a knuckle on the metal rails at the side, listening to them reverberate down the long line. I'd never seen this bridge before. It must've been an old remnant of the frontier when humans first colonized the planet. I'm sure they were proud of the old red arch hanging over the deep canyon below.

Keeping my left hand on the cold steel gun at my side gave me a shallow sense of comfort, especially while I walked in the dark patches between the wide-spaced lights dangling overhead.

My finger slipped around the trigger when I saw a blip crawl into one of the distance lights at the other end of the bridge. A figure stepped through a bright patch, then disappeared, emerging closer into the next illuminated spot.

I paused to gauge him from afar. There wasn't much to tell other than his height and outer garments. He was tall and wore a dark trench coat, a black brim hat that shaded his face, dark gloves on his hands, and sleek boots to match them. He lifted his head an inch, showing me his sharp chin and beaky nose.

Using my right hand, I managed to pick out a cigarette and light it while keeping my left fastened to my gun. Walking along that dark bridge sent a shudder down my spine. The dull lights hanging above bore down upon me like a spotlight sweeping over its prisoners in the yard. And worse, when I glanced below my feet, the pitch-black canyon reminded me that there was only one way for me to know how far it really dropped at this time of night.

We both reached the same central light and halted at opposite ends of its perimeter. We studied one another for a prolonged time. Then, as if we'd planned it, the two of us marched in unison, meeting in the middle, under the orange ray cast onto the bridge.

He'd angled his hat to keep his face shrouded in darkness as he spoke. 'Mr. Sturgis?'

I nodded. 'Yeah, Nouir?'

The man stood up straighter, increasing his towering height even more. 'Are you recording any of this? Visual or audio?'

I shook my head with a faint laugh. 'You can't be serious.'

The man fixed his gloves with a poise I'd only seen in five-star joints. 'Why not?' he said. 'Everything I deal with is serious. This is no joking matter, Mr. Stugis. Do you understand that?'

I let out a breath of smoke, feeling like I'd stepped back into my old principal's office when they still gave kids such as myself the cane for misdeeds.

'Go on then,' I said. 'I'm listening.'

'As you know, my name is Nouir. And as you may not know, I work with classified projects that require the utmost secrecy in order to function.'

I scanned around us a moment. 'All right, what's your point?'

'That exactly. I deal with a tight measure of security that requires a certain precision and fluidity. You see, Mr. Sturgis, I've brought you here tonight to offer you a proposition, one that will put your unique skill set to the right use.'

The word proposition eased my finger from the gun's trigger. Not the word's meaning or that I might be able to bump up my rates this go round, but anyone using such a word when contacting me rarely ever had a weapon on them, and, if they did, I seriously questioned their ability to use it.

'Go on then,' I said, circling my hand in the air.

'Currently, my agency is wrestling with a very problematic situation, which requires us to enlist with someone who's low-profile and yet capable of handling extreme situations that only arise in your profession.'

I flicked my cigarette over the bridge. 'I'm all ears, pal.'

The man paused for a moment. 'There is a planet a great distance from Ceph that has two large satellite moons with inhabitants upon both, presumably. The odd thing about this system is that the primary moon, which orbits the mother planet, also has its own independent moon orbiting itself.'

'Sure, I've heard of it.' I swiped my nose with my finger's joint. 'A planet with a moon that has its own moon. You know we've got a decent city here. We're not a hoard of bumpkins putting buckets on our heads and smashing them against the wall. We're sat down and educated too, yeah?'

The man lifted his head again, showing me his gleaming eyes. 'That isn't what I was getting at. This is merely a backdrop. A way to ease you into the situation. To help me gauge your reactions to the proposed mission.'

'I won't pay for transport,' I said.

'That wouldn't be expected of you. No, if you were to sign up, you'd be well taken care of financially.'

I shook my head. 'I don't work under constraints,' I said. 'If you're looking for information that nobody wants to talk about, I'll handle it. But you leave the method up to me.'

The man drew in a poised breath and let it back out. 'That wouldn't be a problem – in fact, it would be preferable.'

'All right.'

'It's rather unfortunate that I cannot brief you on the details until after you've agreed to take on the project. I can tell you that I'm hoping to uncover the reasons as to why two individuals have died. There are enough clues I believe that will point you in the right direction, but I cannot describe the situation before I have your oath.'

I took out another cigarette and lit it. The moon was yellow tonight, with a haze running over its face. The city lay behind me, bright with concrete structures and in different lights. I took a strong drag and let it out.

'What's the pay?'

The man lifted his head, showing me a glimpse of his pencil-thin smile. 'You don't need to worry about that, Mr. Sturgis. I know how much you are paid, and I feel there is no use in giving you a figure, as it would seem like a joke in comparison.'

'Oh, shut up. Maybe this schtick works on the greenhorns that'll jump at any fruitless promise out there. You can tell me anything you want, by all means, have at it, but until I see a figure and sign a contract, you aren't phasing me over a damn thing. Especially not from some snob with a fake accent.'

Rubbing my eye, I began to laugh at him. No one ever talks with this much secrecy, even the gals who want to know where their husbands have been sleeping at night.

The man reached down into his pocket, took out a triangular glass gadget, and rested it in the palm of his hand. He tapped it gently, turning on a hologram showing a large figure.

'This is the amount of credits we will pay you to accept the mission.' He tapped it again. 'This will be the remainder transferred to your account when the case is finished.'

My cigarette dropped from my fingers onto the bridge floor. I wasn't laughing anymore. Because there was very little funny about how many zeros were behind the first two numbers.

Quickly, he clicked it off and put it away. 'Now, Mr. Sturgis. What do you say?'

CHAPTER 5

I drove back to the city with my head in a spin. He gave me twenty-four hours to make a decision. He didn't seem happy about the matter, but he still gave me that much of a window to think it over. When I reached my apartment, I parked the car and climbed up the stairs outside my door. The neighbors across the hall were experimenting with their subconscious music that often gave me the chills and once a bad case of diarrhoea.

Wanting to get away from the noise, I shoved my keys in the lock and felt the bolts loosened again. I let out a snort as I lifted my gun and tapped the door open.

'It's me,' she said.

I stepped in, put the gun away, and closed the door. 'I thought you hated this place. Why do you keep coming back here?'

She didn't respond.

I went over to the kitchen and pulled out an old bottle of vodka. I unscrewed the top, threw a glass down on the counter, and poured it graciously.

Mae went to the kitchen doorframe to watch me. 'Have you thought about the offer?'

'Nope.' I opened the freezer, dropped a few ice cubes into the glass, and had a sip. 'I saw Lemoche tonight.'

'Does he know anything?'

I shrugged. 'Won't find that out until we get to the end of this, will we?'

'So, have you thought about the offer?'

I added some fizz to my glass and gave it another stir. 'I haven't had time to think it over.' I pushed out of the kitchen and sat in my old brown armchair near the window.

She walked to the other chair, hitting the dust off of it before she sat. She let out a big sigh. 'What have you really got to do? Take the offer, Vince. You need the work.'

An attempted sip of my drink turned into a healthy gulp, then as if on automatic, my body tipped the rest down my gullet and slapped the glass on a table near my chair.

'Is that so? I've nothing to do,' I said. 'You're not the only person looking to hire me right now.'

'I don't believe that.'

I cocked my head to the side, picked up my glass, and jiggled the ice cubes, then glanced at my wristwatch.

She stared at me from across the room. 'Lemoshe? He doesn't want to hire you. The man wants you dead.'

'Not anymore.'

'Well, maybe you cut a deal, but... Lemoshe?'

'I never said it was him. I said I saw him earlier.'

'Vince, you know Phats and Blind Eddie are walking tomorrow night. And you think Lemoshe wants to hire you?'

I swished my hand at her, thinking of Phats and the last time I saw him. I wondered if he still had that long-handled meat clever or if he'd have to purchase a new one on the outside.

'Plus, you just finished a case. You don't get hired like that. Why don't you level with me here? Tell me, what is this really about?'

'Yeah, okay, I'm lying then. You got me, sheriff. There is no other case.'

Squinting one eye at me was her way of asking for more, that or waiting for the punchline. 'You're serious. What job is this? You didn't tell me anything.'

'That's because I just found out myself.'

She rubbed her hands together. 'How much are they offering you? We can see about getting a little more for your time and efforts.'

Laughing, I tipped the drink back, remembering only when I put it to my lips that ice was all that remained. I then grunted as I set it back on the small table.

'Little more?' I said. 'What are you going to give me, one of those dogs you use? And then are you going to talk with Phats and Blind Eddie to leave me alone?'

Her eyebrow raised. 'Is that what you really want? A dog?'

I turned my face to the side. 'No.'

'Are you serious about this other case? We can try to match their pay. I mean that, honestly, you know I do.'

'Don't bother,' I said. 'I'm not taking the case anyhow.'

'Was it narcs?'

I shook my head, put a cigarette in my lips, and lit it. 'No, I don't actually know what it was. And I don't think I should be talking about it either for some reason.'

There was a silent wind drawing between us. It tossed old newspapers down the gutter, clogging up the flow of sewage, waiting for someone to dislodge them.

'Stupid anyhow.' I lay my head back on the headrest. 'It's all stupid.' My eyes closed, and I fell asleep. Not by my own choice. It merely took over.

•   •   •   •   •

The sun was shining bright through the window, poking me out of rest. My vodka glass was still on the table, and Mae had long since left. There were a few messages waiting for me on my wristwatch. I sat up and clicked through them.

I have to know by tonight what your decision is. Might as well join us if you're not taking this other mystery case. The department isn't all talk like some people, they can back their contracts with cash, and they have ways of protecting their officers from newly released criminals as well.

Mae

Deadlines seem to enjoy overlapping over one another for some reason. I moved up from the chair and thought about breakfast, then thought about the empty fridge. Leaving the house wasn't a tough decision to make. I got in my car and drove to a diner a few blocks up the street. Had some coffee, eggs, and some lab grown bacon.

The waitress attending my section held a pot of coffee up in the air and lingered at my table. She wore thick blue make-up on her eyelids and bright red lipstick on her wrinkled lips. Nothing seemed to change in her daily beauty routine, never a fluctuation in color or density of make-up on her face, which made it all the more puzzling for myself when I noticed that she never wore the same pair of shoes. Ever. Not one day to the next.

She spoke with a raspy voice. 'Coffee?'

I moved my mug towards her, and sneaked a peak at her bright green shoes for the day. Classy. But I couldn't help wondering, where did she get so many different pairs?

She started to pour the coffee, keeping a firm eye on me. 'You haven't been sitting with the wrong crowds lately, have you?'

I pushed the remaining eggs on my plate, making sure they touched every inch of it, for no reason more than being caught in a trance of thought.

She finished pouring.

'I sit in the wrong den all the time,' I said. 'At some point, I feel like I need to start paying rent or helping out with utilities.'

'You keeping your nose clean?'

I took a sip of the coffee and laughed. 'Always.'

She raised an eyebrow at me, then spied over my shoulder as if she saw a new species of bird in one of the booths back behind me.

'Let's hope that's true,' she said.

I finished the coffee and thumbed out some cash notes to leave behind. As I stood up, I caught a glance of several familiar-looking faces, all staring at me two tables down.

'Morning,' I said, touching the brim of my hat.

Lemoshe scanned the diner lazily before responding. 'You're up early.'

I walked closer. 'You frequent this place now?'

Pushing his plate aside and flicking his hand back caused the crowd in his booth to shift out of their seats and gather in a semi-circle around me. They were all giants surrounding me. Mr. Sensitive was amongst them, fixing his rings upon his meaty fingers, looking like he wanted to imprint one of those jewels upon my face.

Finishing his last bite at his own pace, Lemoshe took his time wiping his mouth and then eventually slid out from the booth to join us. He came over to me and lay his hand on my shoulder like we were good pals.

'Where you going this morning? Let me give you a ride.'

Mr. Sensitive flipped a couple of crisp bills on the table as if they were nothing more than sheets of paper, while Lemoshe gave me a nudge in the opposite direction towards the door.

I walked alongside him and out the diner. 'I'm headed up to central station,' I said. 'They've asked me to verify some facts up at the department. Is that the kind of place you were hoping to swing by today?'

Lemoshe gave a small chuckle that wiggled the loose fat under his chin. He stopped by his black limousine and took his time, pulling a cigar out of a golden case, even offering me one.

I declined and pulled a cigarette out of my jacket, offering it to him in return.

He put the cigar between his teeth, and Mr. Sensitive was quick to light it with a match.

I had to light my own. It's okay, though. I prefer my independence.

One of the other men pulled the back door open, waiting like a bellhop for us to get in.

Lemoshe nodded towards the back as he squeezed his body inside. Mr. Sensitive pat me on the shoulder with his jewel-encrusted fingers, and when I hesitated, he shoved me inside.

I fell into a leather seat across from Lemoshe. Mr. Sensitive slid in the vehicle, scooted me along the bench, and then wasted no time making some drinks at the mini bar.

The door shut, and the car rolled out of the lot with a gentle hum.

Lemoshe took his drink, and I mine. We sipped whiskey as the traffic lights blinked different colors outside. The red held the car back. A giant tanker flew through the intersection, glistening in the sunlight, as a few smaller vehicles surrounded it like a pack of hyenas.

The car was filling with smoke. Mr. Sensitive opened the sunroof a crack to let it mix with the haze outside.

Lemoshe pinched his cigar between his fingers and pointed out the window. 'You seen these new billboards,' he said. 'You think they'd elect a guy like that for mayor? His neck's too thin, and his eyes are too far apart. No one's going take that man seriously.'

I twisted my cigarette in a glass ash tray then glanced at the billboard. His slogan was nice - if it was true. *A clean city means a clean life.*

'Who needs to clean up a city when it's fine the way it is? Do people actually vote for these jokers?'

I shrugged. 'Either he'd put me to more work or kick me out of a job.'

We passed through another intersection, gliding along the streets beginning to hover over the nicer sections. There was another billboard at the next stoplight.

Lemoshe tapped the window with his cigar between his fingers. 'See now, that's a mayor.' He twisted his mustache with his vacant hand, looking at the prospective mayor.

The man had a great deal of girth in his figure. A nice full head of hair with a confident grin, letting everyone know that he knew something they didn't. *Let's make our city NUMBER ONE!*

How cheap. But then, who wouldn't like to take the gold medal once in a while. Even if it was by default on this nearly barren continent.

We pulled down along the coast beside the docks. The limo kept its smooth pace as two guards spoke into their wrists, opening a metal gate for us to go in further. We glided past the fish market, where everything was on ice, or dangling from a giant hook. I caught sight of a large wild tuna, being auction to the highest bidder.

Good to know some species survived transplantation from the homeworld.

I watched another man using a great big hook the size of himself, stabbing into a cold tuna body and dragging it along the wet floors. We continued down towards a processing plant, slipped inside the giant factory doors, and parked next to a forklift.

Lemoshe finished his drink and popped his cigar into his teeth. His small eyes glanced around the windows then he waved his hand to be let out. The doors opened. He squeezed out first, and then I followed, with Mr. Sensitive close behind.

It smelled of seawater and rotting kelp in the plant.

Lemoshe walked to a set of stairs that led to an upper office overlooking the bay.

Mr. Sensitive left his jewel-encrusted hand on my shoulder, making sure I didn't lose my way.

We went inside the office, where Lemoshe plopped himself behind a large desk and stared vacantly out the window. The men slammed the door shut behind us. They then dragged a black body bag towards the middle of the floor and dropped it like a lump of clay.

I had a guess as to what was inside.

Lemoshe twirled his cigar between his fingers, now staring at its grey end. 'I assume you know about Phats and Blind Eddie?' He continued looking at the cigar, mesmerized. 'They're walking tonight.'

'So I've heard.'

'You know that band I flew in last night wasn't cheap.'

'I can imagine.'

Then after a slight pause, Lemoshe sliced his forefinger in the air.

Mr. Sensitive bent down and unzipped the black bag to reveal a pale young man inside. His eyes were open, looking glassy and staring out to nowhere. Same as the girl I found the other night. Not to mention the obvious black veins creeping up the side of his neck.

Lemoshe let out a billow of smoke with a hiss. 'How's your love life these days, Vince?' He twirled the cigar again. 'You keeping a regular lady at the house or paying for a fun time on the side?'

'Life's been too busy to worry about either.'

'Too busy?' He sniggered. 'I think you mean too poor, right? Because I know many busy men and women, and they still seem to find the time for their flings. It just becomes an extra expense more than anything.'

My eyes were focused on the young man in the body bag.

'Any ladies stopping by your place by chance? Ex-partners or, I don't know, women enlisted on the government payroll?'

'What do you want?'

He paused to glance at the boy on the floor. 'Why did you have to bother me last night?' Lemoshe sucked air through his teeth. 'This was a good kid. Honest. Loyal. Always on time with his deliveries. Same as his father. What a shame, though.'

I pulled a cigarette out of my jacket and lit it.

Lemoshe continued staring at the young man. 'How'd you enjoy the fish curry? Was it worth the visit?'

'I'd say so.'

'You put yourself in an odd position,' he said. 'You might make a man think he's being watched, especially if you're sleeping with some gal on the force who's adamant about this new drug hitting the circuits.'

I rubbed my eyebrow with my forefinger.

Lemoshe licked his bottom lip. 'I've got two types of people in my life. Friends. And friends that stab in the back. You hear?'

'How can you tell the difference?'

Lemoshe chewed on his cigar. 'Friends help me out in a pinch. They send the cops to someone else, like Phats or Blind Eddie, for example, or keep my record sparkling clean down at the bureau.'

'I'm not good with narcs,' I said.

'You're good with whatever you want to be.' He looked at Mr. Sensitive and motioned his head for him to come over.

The large man lumbered over to the desk and set a black bag on the table. He then ripped it open, showing it full of crisp hundred-dollar bills.

'How you like narcs now?'

Still wasn't as much as Nouir offered. But keeping my feet on this planet was a nice incentive. I snubbed my cigarette out on the heel of my shoe.

Lemoshe moved his cigar to the other side of his mouth. He waved Mr. Sensitive away with his finger. 'The way I see it is this, either you are my friend, maybe even family one day, working to help me out, while I keep Phats and Blind Eddie on their side of the fence, or you're scuttling along somewhere else while things get hot up in town. Both options would keep me happy.'

I rubbed my thumb along my knuckles.

'But then a man such as yourself, if you were teaming up with the police by accident, then Phats and Blind Eddie might be free to do as they please. Because I want you to hear this part and hear it well; anybody who's got information on this Black Plague and is kissing behind closed curtains with ladies on the force, are the types of people I'd need to be rid of to keep my operation running smoothly.'

Lemoshe looked down at the body and waved his hands with annoyance as if a swarm of flies had been buzzing around him. The guards zipped the body bag up and lugged it off the ground.

'Consider this an opportunity do yourself a favor.'

I watched them leave out the door and then looked at the sun hanging behind a cloud of haze outside the window.

Lemoshe stood up from his chair, walking towards me. 'You call me at midnight,' he said. 'And tell me what you're thinking. Because if I don't hear from you by midnight. . .' He hit me on the shoulder.

I stood up, fixing my hat over my brow. 'We'll be in touch.' I then looked at the two remaining guards. 'Now, who's giving me a ride back?'

Lemoshe grinned.

CHAPTER 6

The limo dropped me at the diner and drifted back out of the parking lot into the dull traffic. I fixed my jacket and decided it was a good time for lunch. I checked my messages as I sat in the booth, waiting for the green-shoed waitress to take my order.

Reche here. You still stopping in at central later? Mae said she talked with you again last night? We're out of the office now. If you stop by, make it after five.

'You're one lucky fella,' said the waitress. 'Or one well-connected man.'

I raised the brim of my hat up from my brow. 'A bit of both these days. How about some coffee and a reuben with extra sauerkraut?'

She kept her face puckered as she tapped a holographic chart at the end of the table. When the order was placed, she turned on her heels, like a former ballerina, and went back into the kitchen.

Soon, my coffee arrived, and within seconds of it landing on the table, I heard the front door's bell pealing like a call for my own death. Mae legged it to my booth and slipped in across the table from me.

'Just ordered?' she said, picking up a menu.

I let out a billow of smoke. 'Yeah.'

The waitress glided to our table. 'What are you having?'

'Coffee with a tuna sandwich.'

'No tuna. The coast is fished out, and imported cans shot up over the weekend. We have local fish, though. Erie's bass, white fin strousee, and some blue cod.'

'Can you fry the strousee on a sandwich, with a slice of cheese?'

'Local cheddar suit you because we don't serve any imported brands?'

'Fine.'

The lady tapped the order into our table and left. A holographic bill showed at the side, listing each item we'd ordered.

'You hate this diner,' I said. 'You hate this area. Why are you around here so much now? Missing me?'

She said ha as she pulled a serviette from the side of the table. Her coffee came. She doused it with cream.

'You thought any more about my offer?'

'Would you believe it if I told you I got a third offer this morning? There's some heavy competition out there for me. Who knew finding one girl would make me so popular.'

She sipped from her mug. 'Oh, is this another mystery offer? Are you trying to impress me or something?'

I shook my head and stubbed out my cigarette.

'From Lemoshe.'

She poured more cream into her mug and began to stir it. 'You're bluffing. What does he want you for? He has plenty of body guard and a bulletproof vest.'

'Maybe he's weary of this Black Death too.'

She paused from her stirring. 'He's in on it?'

I shrugged. 'Who knows? This could be a clever distraction. Pay me off to sniff around while chasing my tail as he dumps his supply in the city's water.' I moved my hands back as the reuben came, followed by the fish sandwich. 'He seemed unusual, though. He's never this pushy. But you know how hard it is to figure what card he's playing next.'

She circled her plate to the other side and picked up her sandwich. 'You think he's being honest?'

'I don't know. If he's not in on it, then it could be serious for his business. It's already taken one of his delivery boys.'

She swallowed her bite. 'How do you know?'

'He showed me. Same black veins and glassy eyes as the girl I found.'

She lowered her sandwich slowly to her plate. 'How old's the body? Is he going to report it?'

I shook my head, taking a bite of my sandwich. 'You think he'll report that one of his drug mules died?' I wiped my mouth and continued chewing. 'If he's serious about hiring me, then it's to keep everything under wraps, and handle the supplier in however he deems fit.'

'What is he offering you?'

'Free tuna.'

She rolled her eyes and took another bite of her sandwich.

My bread was beginning to fall apart, but I still managed to hold it partially together.

'How much?'

'Enough to keep me happy for a while.'

She sighed. 'Of course. Take the dirty route. Money over values.'

'Any my own neck when two unhappy campers walk free tonight.' I wiped my fingers with a serviette. 'Plus, I haven't made any decision yet. And last I remember, the department isn't as clean as a porcelain bowl either. It only takes one asshole to muck it all up.'

She put her sandwich down. 'Vince? Would you mind? Jeez.'

I went back to my sandwich. The waitress filled my coffee and asked if I wanted a slice of pie. 'Horseberry,' I said. 'And Mae? Peach? Apple? Bittergourd?'

She wiped her mouth and glared at me. 'You have violet rhubarb?'

'Another local dish,' said the waitress. 'Are you one of those terraform students? Studying our plants and what have you.'

'No. I was born here, is all.'

The waitress nodded. 'Me too.' She then glanced at me then back to Mae. 'You shouldn't be hanging around this boy. He's up to no good, you know.'

I took a final bite of my sandwich.

'I know,' said Mae. 'That's why I have to keep an eye on him. Push him in the right direction every now and then.'

The waitress raised her stenciled eyebrows at us both and then went back to the kitchen.

I lit another cigarette, waiting for the pie.

'Lemoshe is offering you a one-shot deal,' she said. 'You get the money, and it's over. Who's to say he'll really keep anyone at bay once you finish. Whereas if you do a good job with the department, we can see about passing you on a few more cases or have a stab at one of those offices uptown.'

The pies slid across the table. I took out the cleanest fork I could find and severed the triangular tip from the rest. 'Yeah. I get it. Thanks for making it clear. Sometimes, this adult world gets a bit too complicated for me.'

'You're such a child.'

'Don't expect much from me then.'

I left my cigarette to burn in the ashtray as we finished our pies. I tried to pay for the bill, but she was certain I was poor or something prejudicial like that and clicked her watch before I could lay down any cash.

The sun was dropping over the tall buildings outside, and the haze was getting stronger as traffic congested in the streets.

'I'll let you know tonight. Around midnight?'

She opened her car door, leaving it to hang. 'The department won't interfere with your work. I promise. So remember that in whatever decision you should make.'

I smiled and went to my own car. 'See you around.'

CHAPTER 7

The sun was back behind the earth when I left the central police station. The stars were trying to poke through the dark blanket in the sky. And I spotted a few air taxies carting important folks from one rooftop to another.

When I reached my car, I saw another pamphlet advertising life insurance in case of my own untimely demise. Before I tossed it in the bin, I caught eye of a number scribbled on the back and felt my throat getting cold. The number just so happened to match my apartment's address and beneath it my mother's house before she found greener pastures.

I quickly drove back down south through the city. There were kids walking unsteadily on the streets, hopping from bar to bar, their groups growing larger and smaller as the night passed.

It was almost nine by the time I reached my home. I pulled out a cheap bottle of whiskey and poured myself a nice drink. I swirled the cubes inside my glass, letting the flavors melt just right.

When the clock struck eleven, I got in my car and decided to take a drive even further south. I reached the old bridge hanging over the canyon and stepped out of my car. I paced up and down for some time, basking in the orange lights dangling above the bridge.

I checked the time: *11:59*. I lifted my wrist up under my mouth and started to dictate a message, but I stopped when I saw a dark figure walking down the opposite end.

The man walked slowly, his heels clicking on the old bridge and echoing down into the canyon.

'Evening,' he said.

'Evening.'

'You've thought it over?'

I rubbed my jawline, trying to catch a glimpse of his face, but he kept it concealed. 'How far away is this planet?'

'It will take you over a week to reach.'

I sighed to myself.

The man remained still.

'I've gotten a few other offers recently,' I said. 'I'm no good at handling narcs, though. And I'm not so certain I'll be able to see the end of the case. Does your case have anything to do with the Black Death?'

The man lifted his head, allowing a slice of light to shine upon his eyes. 'I'm not allowed to say,' he said. 'Until I have your word.' He put his head down an inch.

I grit my teeth as I considered. I looked over the bridge at the endless drop, wondering for a second what it'd feel like to smash into the ground – would I feel the pain of bones shattering into fragments, or would it be a quick darkness that brings me into an eternal void?

The man pulled the triangular piece out of his jacket again. The same holographic number appeared over it. 'I need an answer,' he said.

That was a big downpayment.

He eyed me with the blue glowing numbers right under his face.

'How do I know this is legit?'

The man's face kept stoic. 'You won't.'

I exhaled with a bitter pant, looking at that number again. 'I don't know if I'll be any good on another planet. I've got my roots here. My contacts and reputation.'

The man raised his eyebrows a sliver. 'I need your answer.'

I hissed through my teeth and rubbed the back of my head. 'Shit,' I said. 'You haven't given me anything to go on, just a big number.'

The man didn't say anything more.

'Do you even know of this new drug called Black Death?'

'Sorry.'

'Yeah, me too. It could be a fluke, or it could really fuck this town up something awful.'

'I need your decision.'

Closing my eyes, I gritted my teeth harder and tried to make the right decision. Phats and Blind Eddie were probably already released by now. Could Lemoshe or Mae truly hold them back from finding me? My doubts were larger than my sense of optimism. Even if I stayed, I'd be pinned between two fronts, demanded upon to give vital information on the other. That's a good way to find yourself sleeping in a dirt coffin.

The man sighed and began to lower the triangular piece.

I lifted my hand and stopped him. 'You'll get me off Ceph for a while?'

'For as long as it takes.'

'Fine. All right. I'll take it then.'

The man tapped the triangle with his thumb, and the number became zero.

'What happened?'

'The credits have been transferred to a private account, which can only be accessed by you. The rest will be transferred once you have completed the task.'

I bit my lower lip. 'I want to see this account.'

'You will if you don't mind following me.'

I watched him for a moment. 'I need to send a few messages first.'

'Can they be done along the way?'

I nodded and walked with him to the other side of the bridge, wondering if I'd done the right thing or not.

•　　•　　•　　•　　•

We climbed into a decent-sized airship, one of those personal crashers that people had a great deal of trouble navigating when they first appeared on the market. I assumed it was one of those crafts that could leave the mesosphere. Good for orbiting the planet, using as a small camper home, or getting picked up by a larger vessel, but not much else.

As he led me to the lounge area, he started to pull his trench coat away and slip his hat off his head. He had a thin face, with a long sharp nose and uneven teeth. His eyes were incisive and made me even more curious to hear what he had to say.

'Would you care for a drink?'

I nodded. 'Something strong.'

He went to the back of the cabin and brought back two glasses of scotch.

I snatched it from his thin, gangly fingers and stirred the giant round cube inside with my thumb. I started feeling bad for a moment. Like the kind of pit you get when someone's been let down. I tasted my thumb then took a sip from the glass. It burned from my throat down into my chest, filling up that black pit of guilt for a second.

'Mr. Sturgis. Would you be ready to leave Ceph tonight?'

I bobbed my head. 'Are you asking me, or is the ticket already arranged?'

Nouir had a faint smile on his face. 'There are a few ground rules we must go over before we get you to the spaceport. First, you've never been contacted by anyone to investigate anything on the satellite world of Senturion. If anyone asks, you are taking a holiday to see the magnetic lights that fill the skies once a month.

'Second. If you are to land into any kind of trouble that might compromise our cover or make it seem as if you are a private investigator, then you will be left to your own devices. We cannot take the risk of having our operation blown.'

My heart thudded loud in my ears.

'And third. You are not to attempt contact with me during your time on the planet. You will send no calls, ask for no information, nor do anything out of line for a tourist. Is that clear?'

I took another sip, thinking he'd forgotten to pour me a full glass.

'Fine,' I said. 'Not like I get free bail down here.'

The man paused to measure me over a second longer. 'Yes, but you were born here. This is your homeworld. And I'm well aware of your connections with key members of your government's law.'

I licked my teeth and smacked my tongue. 'How am I to give you this information when I'm back then?'

'Don't worry about that. We will contact you when you arrive at the nearest planet.'

I took another sip. 'I've taken on a lot of shady work before.' I laughed. 'You'd better pray those credits are legit.'

'Mr. Sturgis. That should be the least of your concerns right now.'

I finished the glass and shook the rock inside. 'Can I get another?'

He stood up and took the glass with his long fingers, and went into the back. I thought about leaving the ship. I even stood up and went near the exit.

Nouir came back into the room and handed me a fuller glass this time.

I took a healthy gulp and began to pace the floors.

His eyes followed me as I paced.

Blowing a laugh out my nose, I felt my legs growing soft and then reminded myself of Phats and Blind Eddie. Were they still mad at me? Then another reminder cropped up quite conveniently. A bank statement with enough credits to purchase me a meal or two at the roadside market, but little else.

'Are you familiar with the Senturion?'

'Familiar. . .'

'It's better if you're not.'

Rubbing my eye, I tried to concentrate my attention on his words.

'There are enough rumors surrounding the planet at this point that even we are unsure of what's fact and what's myth.'

Maybe they weren't that mad at me. Would they be so bold to touch a police detective if I patterned up with Mae again? Or would they feel more timid if they saw I was in Lemoshe's pocket?

A red holographic projection emerged from the floor. I saw three planets clustered about each other and another lonely fourth planet much further away.

'Senturion is part of a unique planetary system,' he said, shooting a green laser upon the biggest planet in the cluster. 'There is Kaivus, the largest of the three and the only planet that orbits their central sun.'

The laser then shined upon the second planet. 'And this here is Senturion, Kavius' only natural satellite.' The laser then touched onto the third. 'Then there's Eroth, the second moon which orbits Senturion instead of Kaivus.'

My eyes met his. Then, I walked beside the holograms and pointed at the fourth lone planet. 'And this one?'

'That's Ceph,' he said.

I gazed at my planet and sensed a pang of longing for some odd reason. Like I might not see it again.

'And what do you want me to do exactly on Senturion?'

'I want to you find out why a prominent diplomat killed herself after working on the planet for over a decade.'

I scratched my ear.

'Have you ever heard of a Miss Tsuki Kage?'

'No.'

'Very few embassies are allowed on Senution or Kavius. Tourists have only been granted access in the past two decades, which still requires a hefty visa. And not a soul, other than select Senturion officials, is granted access to the moon of Eroth. It's a known fact that various spacecraft have gone missing or been efficiently gunned down when treading too close to their precious moon.'

I eyed him.

'But Miss Kage, as I said, was one of the rare diplomats to be stationed on Senution, and for a long time at that. She seemed to live a pleasant enough life there until she began sending cryptic messages to her homeworld, and was then scheduled to return on a private vessel. Miss Kage never made it aboard that vessel though, as she was found hanging in her apartment the night before the ship landed.'

Calculations trickled away my other worries and concerns for a second. I'd trained my mind for years to block everything out when it came to work. And now it's one of the only things that can blur the noise and commotion caused by the outside world.

He paused to take a deep breath. 'It is, of course, standard procedure for my organization to investigate such matters with one of our own internal agents.' He paused again, composing himself. 'And we did. I did. But he was killed. In the middle of his investigation.'

My stomach churned, and the faint sniggering of Blind Eddie's voice echoed far in the background of my head. 'Are you sending me up there to die?' I snorted. 'Am I your bait to gain permission for some full-blown investigation? Two deaths can happen, but three is more than coincidence, right?'

I put the glass down and crossed to the door.

Nouir stood to his feet. 'I would never send a lamb for the slaughter, my agent or another. It's against my code of ethics.' He tugged the skin in between his fingers.

'But I am expendable?'

'Everyone I manage is expendable,' he said. 'Like it or not, that's part of being in the field.'

'You could've mentioned that upfront when you kept dangling that carrot in front me!'

'Why do you think your pay is so high? Did you expect this to be a cakewalk? For the amount you're being paid?'

I took my hand off the door and pulled my cigarette packet from my jacket. I left it open, motioning it towards him, but he raised his hand to decline.

'You mind if I do?'

He nodded, then spoke in a lower voice. 'Go ahead.'

I lit the cigarette and felt my nerves calm down a bit.

Nouir went to one the chairs and sat with his eyes wandering, likely caught in the sticky web of an old memory he couldn't quite untangle from. My guess is it wasn't a happy one. Whether he cared for me to know or not, I could read it on his poised face.

'I didn't intend for my agent to end up the way he did.' He left his mouth open to say more, but nothing came.

I exhaled a plume of smoke, letting it hang at the ceiling above my head.

'I sent him to investigate Miss Kage's situation.' He put his teeth on end when he spoke. 'I had no idea he'd be caught up in such an ordeal. If I knew, well, then I would've done it differently. You see, I sent him without any real suspicions of Senturion. My purpose in sending him was to clear my own paperwork more than anything.'

Nouir stopped then his eyes glazed over. 'But I got him killed,' he said. 'I got him killed due to my own negligence.' He stopped again, this time pinching his lips between his fingers. 'You see, he was more than an agent to me.'

A weight of silence dropped in the air after he said this. I couldn't watch him, so I eyed the holograms and blew some smoke through their red figures.

'I have hardly slept since he died.'

I eased back to my chair and sat facing him. I gulped the rest of my drink down and used the glass as an ashtray. He didn't seem to mind. Didn't even seem to be there anymore.

'So this agent, was your, your friend?'

His eyes caught mine. Softer now. Losing that incisive edge.

'This is personal?'

He wet his lips. 'No... and yes.'

I leaned further back in my seat.

'Senturion was originally a place of exile for political criminals or anyone else considered to stand in the Kaivus' way. The government banished these threatening figures to Senturion; from religious individuals to popular entertainers, underground crime lords, or anyone who gained any sort of following.'

My cigarette hissed as I put it in the empty drink glass.

Nouir regained his composure and then sipped his drink. 'I sought you out because no one knows who you are. Not even my own agency.'

I nodded to myself.

'And better you know very little about Kaivus, Senturion, or Eroth that not a soul will suspect you to be working at such a high level as this.' He looked at me dead center. 'I want you to find out why they killed her. Why they killed my agent.'

I cocked my head to the side, looking around the room at nothing in particular. 'Was there any contact with him during his time on Senturion?' I said.

'No. It's dangerous for our agents and us. No matter how clever or encrypted the form of communication might be.'

I nodded a bit. 'Why do you think they killed Miss Kage?'

He lifted his chin and squinted his eyes. 'I can't figure it,' he said. 'Tsuki came from a neutral planet. At first, we thought her death might be a message to her homeworld, but after sifting through it, we can't find any obvious link or what that message might be.'

'I need somewhere to start. Something to get onto the right track. What was the place your agent was killed? Where was he checking? The diplomat I can search myself.'

Nouir set his glass on a table and then straightened his back. 'I don't know where he was killed, but I know the city he was working in at the time and where he was found by an ocean troller.

'The city's name is Tosokh. Apart of the largest country on the planet and one of the select cities within the habitable zone. As for where he was searching, there's little I can tell you because we made sure to keep a safe distance from him. We never even received a distress signal.'

'Not much to go on here. A city, two deaths, and a raw feeling about it?'

He pursed his lips. 'It is more than a raw feeling,' he said. 'As you'll see.'

A large holographic photo arose, taking the place of the planets. It showed a woman dangling from a noose. The lighting was dim, but I could see her glassy eyes and a black shadow near her neck.

I moved closer to the photo. Then I pointed at the black spot near her neck. 'Can you enlarge this section?' The image zoomed, and I saw with more clarity that the black streak on her neck was her jugular vein.

My hand moved over my mouth.

'Do you still believe it's just a raw feeling, Mr. Sturgis?'

'The body?' I said.

'They never allowed us an autopsy. They sent us their own reports and these photos from the supposed scene.'

'Those veins are black?'

'You understand why I chose you?'

I started to rub my face, and then I laughed, but it didn't make me feel any better. Money is supposed to make you feel better, or so they say.

●   ●   ●   ●   ●

Parking my car across the street from my apartment left me feeling numb. Am I bitter? Do I make these sorts of decisions because I'm still mad at her ambitions or holding a grudge on Lemoshe's past death threats? Do I secretly want this town to burn into the wasteland I rummage through on a daily basis?

The pristine towers can be seen from the elevated train tracks near my place. It hangs in such contrast, how advanced with its air taxis and sleek buildings, compared to the hovel most of us live in order to support this city.

I told myself I wasn't bitter. Everyone needed money now and then, and to pass up such a large amount would be stupid. A ring of sirens awoke me from my meditations. Then a great billow of black smoke that emanated from my apartment complex caught my eye.

The fire engines stopped on the other side of my building and rushed in through the front entrance. I skirted around, then peered within, knowing the fire was coming from my flat. Feeling little need to stop and ask questions, I hurried myself to the nearest train station.

I passed a handful of local artists, busy painting the side of a brick building. They paused a second to watch me as I paused to gauge them. We didn't know each other, thankfully. So I kept walking.

An old rusted car sputtered around the corner, nearly clipping me in the process of crossing the street. They'd run the light and hurried along somewhere away from the sirens behind me. The car then stopped, twenty yards away, then began to back into reverse, as if they were going to come and apologize to me.

An uncomfortable ripple emanated in my chest, firing anxious waves up into my brain, making me jump a step faster to the train station. The car backfired like a rifle, and chugged its engines in my direction. I ducked myself into the station, nearly stepping over a homeless woman lying next to an exhaust vent, as the car zoomed by the entrance.

I told the lady sorry then plunged deeper into the station. The place was vacant, but I still paid my fare and hopped aboard the first line available.

There was an old man sitting across from me speaking to himself and drinking from his brown paper bag as the scenes changed outside the window, too quickly to be noticed.

There was a message waiting for me from Mae. I had a peek at it. *Reconsider. Don't go with Lemoshe. We need someone to do the leg work here. Reconsider the offer. Please?*

I deleted the message and put my wrist up to my lips. 'I'm not working for a snake like Lemoshe, and, honestly, I don't feel like being a pawn to your ambitions either. If you'd asked me as a friend, then maybe; but, Mae, I'm not stupid because that's never the case with you. There are only ambitions and people that can be used to acquire them.

'Also, I heard about Domiko's planned retirement from Reche. And I've no doubt her position would be happily given to whichever detective finds this Black Death's source first. So, why don't you handle the leg work yourself, if you need that title so badly. I'm going away for a while. I need a bit of a vacation.'

I closed my eyes down for the remainder of the ride. I woke up when we reached the central station. A large woman came through the trains, yelling at everyone to get out.

I pulled myself up and left the train. There was another message from her. *How's Phats and Blind Eddie, by the way? Have you seen them yet?*

Beneath it was a second message sent ten minutes after the first.
You've never left this town, Vince. Don't be smart.

I sank into the crowd of people, each going in their own direction, transiting to this train or that, like a busy hornet's nest ready to serve their faceless queen. I kept my head down and my hat over my eyebrows. There was my train hovering above the tracks. Its doors were open, ready to take me to the spaceport. I stepped inside and watched the doors closed me in.

THE ROAD TO
SENTURION

CHAPTER 8

The ship tore through the atmosphere, causing old childhood prayers to resurface and mumble out from my smeared face. Fire poured a steady stream behind us, fuming plenty of smoke back at the spaceport, as we soared like a tiny led bullet into the great sparkling universe.

Gravity calmed the further we drew away from Ceph. My chants slowly retreated into silly notions as they'd been in my brain. I thought about Mae while my guts twisted about my vertebrae, and eyes remained flat in their sockets.

It'll be good for her. She can do some legwork by herself.

We broke the dark void covering our planet, traveling out into the stars now with hopeless abandon. Things relaxed on the ship. The cylinder rocket began to produce its own gravitational field, and then in no time, a sign dinged above, and our restraints loosened their hold of us, passengers.

I got up fast from my seat and went into the lounge to have a drink. The bartender had a bottle of rye in his hands and several glasses at the ready. 'Double shot,' I said before I even reached the counter.

A few others joined in my race to the bar. The bartender was quick to serve their drinks, and the glasses he had lined up in a row now fit into a better context. One young lady vomited into her hands and onto the bar after gulping down her drink. The assistant bartender had a mop and bucket prepared. She shook her head while the bartender ignored the mess and moved over to my glass, holding the rye overtop it.

'Can you take another?'

I slipped a twenty-dollar note on the counter. 'I'll keep it down.'

Holding her hands over her mouth, the lady ran out of the bar to a nearby bathroom and slammed the door shut behind herself.

A slight pause lingered between myself and the barman.

Then pushing the bill back towards me, he said, 'We only accept Meta-planetary credits.' Then, he tapped his finger on the bar, presenting three different holographic logos before me. 'You can pay with any of these three accredited platforms.'

'Let me sort this out first, can you keep a tab for now?'

'Very well,' he said.

The bartender quickly filled my glass and then hurried to help the rest mopping up the vomit. My nerves soothed, and soon I was left alone at the counter sipping my drink all alone. The commotion settled around the spilled area, and the bar staff dispersed to their individual positions.

'There's always one,' mumbled the bar assistant as she shoved her cleaning supplies back into a cupboard.

Soon, a mixed crowd found their way up to the counter. One man, in particular, felt he must make a swaggering entrance into the lounge, wearing a large gold-encrusted cowboy hat, studded with rubies and sapphires, and donning a glitzed-up doll who pranced alongside him like a prized horse. It was hard to tell his wife's age, likely fifty, even though she wore a twenty-year-old's clothes.

'God damn,' he said. 'I'll never get used to being fired out the cannon like that.' The man had a platinum steer bolo tie holding his collar together and a flush red face, glowing even redder after each shout.

'Whiskey soda, my fine sir!'

His wife pat him on the shoulder, then glanced over at me. Her eyes were too aligned and too perfect to be natural, and her rural draw was as fake as her tits.

'You don't have to yell, darling. The man can hear you.' She put her back straight, letting her shirt stretch thin around her breast. 'Everyone can hear you.'

'Ahh hell.' He scratched his finger inside his ear, itching at a small transparent tube that must've been attached to his eardrum. 'I'm keeping it mild compared to what I'm really feeling. I'll never get used to being shot out of the cannon. Hell...' He paused to gaze around the bar, catching eyes with me.

I returned to my own business.

The cowboy drained his drink fast and smacked the glass onto the counter. 'Another one of these. And remember the whiskey this time, will you?' He crossed his arms and sat up straight, staring at me.

I glanced at him.

'How about you fella? What are you having?'

I finished my glass and slid it down towards the barman. 'Whatever he's pouring.'

The Cowboy laughed a strong bellow. His teeth were white, with dark gaps lining their cracks. 'That's what I like to hear.' He moved down one seat closer to me, his wife following. 'No sissy martinis for you?'

'What's he making?'

'Make it two sours then, my good man.'

The bartender politely turned to prepare the drinks while the Cowboy set his elbows on the counter to watch the process.

'That's what I like to see,' he said. 'A man who knows how to make a real goddam drink.' He flicked the brim of his hat up a notch and then spied about the lounge bar. 'People drinking nasty shit these days. Makes me want to puke.'

The assistant bartender's head shot up as he said this. Panic shown in her eyes.

Then the drinks came to us filled quite generously.

The old Cowboy lifted his glass up towards mine. We tapped them together and then drank.

His wife leaned past him to ask me a question. 'So, where you heading?'

'Senturion.'

'To see the lights?'

I nodded. 'Seems nice.'

The old Cowboy sat up and took another gulp. He smacked his tongue in his mouth. 'Yeah, we did that a few years back. Booked a caravan up at Mount Fadder and watched the skies light up something bright. A real nice time. Couldn't beat the experience.'

'Fauxvere,' his wife said fluently. 'Not Fadder.' Her eyes rolled.

'Whatever. We saw them. That's the point.'

'It's a man-made hill,' she said. 'But they have a nice lookout at the top. You have to reserve a campsite three months in advance, though, if you want to go.'

I nodded, taking a sip of my drink, then drew a cigarette from my inner coat pocket.

Smiling, the old Cowboy jutted his chin at the pack. 'Nice brand you got there.'

'Yeah?' I held the pack out towards him.

He shook his head, pulling out the same brand of cigarettes.

His wife leaned over him again. 'Oren works for Silver Mist.'

'Is that so?'

Oren gleamed with pride. 'For thirty years now.'

'And you're still going? I thought our type had shorter lifespans and trouble breathing after a while?'

His smile faded as he took a drag of his cigarette, looking unhappy about it. 'I go for a lung cleanse every month now. Burns like the devil, but...' He shrugged his shoulders.

I dropped some ash into the tray near me and put the cigarette in my lips. I turned to look at them both. 'Vacation?' I said.

Oren shook his head, leaning his elbows harder on the table and wrapping his fingers around the glass.

'Nope. I'm on business this time.'

'Is that so?'

He nodded. 'They're a hard nut to crack. I can't get any of their shops to carry our brand. They only want to use local cigarettes. Pansy stuff with scents and flavours and other nonsense.'

I tapped my cigarette along the edge of the tray. 'What about other brands, they having the same problem?'

'Across the board. You want to talk about a tight-ass planet.' He stopped to laugh. Then took a sip. Shaking his head afterwards. 'It's a great place to take a vacation, but don't get fooled into thinking they're good people up there. Never met such a group of backstabbers in my life. They'll smile to your face and say they want to do business, but when your foot hits that return ship, they've gone and changed their minds like you never even spoke with them.'

His wife rested her hand on his arm.

He pulled his arm away.

'You're going to Tosokh?' she said.

'That's right.'

'Do you have plans to go anywhere else, outside the city?'

I shook my head. 'No plans.'

Oren shifted on his stool. 'Probably best thing,' he said. 'It gets worse the further out of town you go. Shacks and shanties and what have you.' He snubbed out his cigarette. 'Word of advice. Stick to the touristy areas. No one's going to bother you there. Except for the hustlers.'

I moved my glass closer to myself. 'I thought it was a pretty safe place, no?'

He breathed a dry laugh. 'Yeah, right. They're so many cover-ups in that city. You'd think someone would've taken a look into it after a while.'

He pulled out another cigarette and lit it quick. 'Everyone conveniently commits suicide there, or gets into a boating accident, or drinks too much, and chokes to death on their own vomit.'

His wife sat up with her eyebrows arched. 'Honey?'

He shook his head, putting his hand up in protest. 'The guy needs to know. I'm not trying to be graphic. I'm telling him it like it is.'

She squinted with a feigned smile. 'It's a nice place to visit, though,' she said.

He sighed. 'Yeah. Nice. Until you start piecing it all together.' He lay the cigarette in the tray and started to dab his sweaty face with a handkerchief. 'I don't like the place one bit.' He then tapped his wrist, causing it to shine a blue glow. 'You take my information, and if you run into anything up there, give me a holler.'

I tapped my wrist, turning it blue, and then brought it towards his. When they got close enough, they exchanged contact information – mine, of course, were now fake thanks to Nouir.

Oren V. Velts.
Director of Sales
Silver Mists.

He was checking my holographic name card hovering over his wrist. 'Vincent H. Gavelman. Owner of Sturdy's Cars.' He stopped a moment. 'You know my uncle had a used car lot on Ceph some years back.' He put the hologram down and returned to his drink. 'You must be selling some fancy cars to afford a trip like this.'

I nodded with a faint smile.

CHAPTER 9

I went to do research in the ship's library. The books told me little, other than possible spots for a tourist to visit, or a glossy recounting of the planet's histories.

The library was a tiny nook in the ship, with a young pimple-faced kid at the counter reading a porno. He paid me no attention when I cleared my throat at his desk. He was engaged with his literature.

So I leaned up on the counter, tapping my fingers loud enough for him to notice.

The young man set the magazine down over his lap. 'Can I help you?'

I put a cigarette in my lips.

'You can't smoke that in here.'

I lit the cigarette and then went back to tapping on the desk.

'Where you from?'

'Senturion,' he said.

I already knew. He spoke like one and looked like one too.

'You can't smoke in here.'

'What made you take a job on this ship?' I said.

'Excuse me?'

'Would you say you enjoy living on Senturion?'

His face turned pale.

'I mean, if didn't, I could understand taking a job such as this,' I said. 'But if you loved the place - then it might be hard.'

'The pay is good,' he said. 'Compared to what's back on Tosokh.'

'Money's important,' I said. 'Real important.'

He didn't answer. But his face contorted even more in confusion.

'You ever heard of any tourist dying in Tosokh - on accident?'

His eyes widened. 'What? What do you mean?'

'I mean that.'

The magazine on his lap began to slid and then tumbled to the floor. He knelt down fast to gather it back in his hands and then hid it in a drawer near his legs.

'Can I help you find anything in the library?' he said.

'Nah, I've browsed it twice over and didn't find anything worth my time.'

'This is a no-smoking section...'

'Back to my question,' I said. 'Me being a tourist and what have you, I've got my concerns, Kaivus and Senturion are new planets for me. So, I'm more curious than anything about my personal safety?'

Reaching for a tour guide pamphlet on his desk, I snatched one up and opened it flat on the table. 'See, this here flamethrower park sounds scary to me,' I said, touching the picture, then reading from the brochure. 'A bunch of people igniting a patch of earth in flames, then waiting for bioluminescent insects to erupt out from the ground and to explode in the air... Sounds dangerous.'

His voice quivered as he spoke. 'I - I'm not sure.'

'You've never heard of anyone getting hurt?'

'There might've been some accidents, but I don't know.'

'How about in the last two months? You read the local papers, I'm sure. There must've been something that stood out, no?'

He licked his lips as his eyes went into a trance of thought. 'There was a man, out swimming in the ocean, last month, I think. The undertow got him.'

I nodded.

He opened his mouth, letting it hang a moment. 'Some troller found the body a few days later. Way out at sea.'

I dropped some ash on the floor. They were already dirty. What did it matter? 'Doesn't Senturion pride itself on its safety, though?'

The boy left his mouth open a second. 'But he went swimming early in the morning. No one was out there. It could happen anyplace!'

I paused. 'That's the thing, though, isn't it? These kind of accidents could happen anywhere.' I took another drag. 'You're from Tosokh?'

He blinked fast, growing nervous. 'The outskirts. But I went to school up in the city.'

I tapped my digits on his counter, leaving the cigarette in my lips. 'Fair enough. Maybe you can tell me some areas I should avoid then? If I don't want to get into any kind of trouble.'

He looked around, like he hoped there might be some adult there to help him with his answers. He blinked again, then picked at one of his pimples.

'Don't go swimming in the early morning, the sea serpents feed then in a cluster.'

Touching my watch, I rose a hologram from it, then began to jot notes from what he was telling me. 'Avoid sea serpents...' I said as I wrote. 'That's it?'

He swallowed hard. 'Maybe you shouldn't go near the southeastern part of the city,' he whispered.

Scratching my head, I pushed my hat out of the way and then furrowed my brows. 'That's vague,' I said. 'The entire southeastern part?' Then he lifted another brochure and lay a map of Tosokh before us.

Chewing his lip, he traced his finger from the city centre down to the edge of the map. 'There's a hotel near the coast here,' he said. 'Most locals know about it and do their best to avoid it.'

'Why's that?'

'We call it the Pink Flamingo, but it has another name.'

I jotted more notes on my holographic paper.

'The hotel never goes out of business even though no one seems to visit it. My dad says it's not exactly dangerous.' He paused. 'But, uhh, you should still find some other places to go. Too much commotion there.'

I dropped more ash on the floor. 'What's on the coast?'

He bobbed his head and then shifted his eyes. 'I'm not sure. But just - just keep away from that area.'

'Come on, kid. What's down there? More serpents?'

He looked as if he might cry. Then he glanced at my cigarette, eyes welling. 'I already told you, you can't smoke in here.'

I put the cigarette in my lip. 'Don't get all flushed, kid. I'm going. Take it easy.'

His lips were quivering.

'Thanks for your help, and see you around.'

•   •   •   •   •

There was a cramped room with a pathetic garden inside it, full of withered houseplants and a tiny window prickled with stars. I stepped in, walked around the plants, and gazed outside the window. At first, they all looked the same to me, blinking against a dark backdrop. But the longer I focused on one, the more its colors began to radiate.

The door opened behind me. I glanced over my shoulder. A chubby little girl stumbled in, holding a dried jerky stick in her plump hands.

'What are you doing in here?' she said, chewing on her snack.

'Is this a private room?'

The kid stared at me for some time, chewing like a goat and staring the whole time as if she'd never before seen another human.

'No one comes here except me.'

I turned my sights back out the window.

'I said no one comes here except me.'

I kept my back to her. 'That's nice, kid.'

She stomped her feet, drawing closer. 'Why are you here?'

I glanced over my shoulder at her.

Her snack was gone, but she continued chewing. 'Fine,' she said. 'You can stay. Five minutes. Then you're out.' She jabbed her thumb back towards the exit.

'Where are you headed to, kid?'

'I'm not telling you.'

'Fine.'

'You a pedophile?'

'No.'

'Where are you going then?' she said.

'Tosokh.'

She hummed to herself and then began ripping some of the plant's leaves. 'Where are you from?'

'Ceph.'

'Hmm.'

'What about you?'

'Same.'

The kid tore off a big leaf from one of the shrubs. She sat on the ground, ripping the leaf into small bits, then flicked them with her fingers up against the walls.

'My dad has to work in Tosokh. He doesn't like it.'

'Yeah?'

'They always mess things up. He says he has to ride their asses in order to keep the products moving. If he weren't there, the whole place would go to hell in a handbasket.'

'You seem well informed,' I said.

'It's not my dad's business. It's his boss' factory. They make handkerchiefs.' The girl pulled a bandana out of her pocket to show me. 'See?'

I nodded with a thin smile.

'But they keep messing things up. Sending crates full of shoddy work.' The kid stretched the bandana flush. It was an odd shape, misaligned from edge to edge. 'They're gonna get it this time.'

I reached out for the bandana.

She handed it to me. 'You keep that one. We've got plenty. Bunches of them that no one'll buy outside of Senturion.'

I slipped it into my pocket and searched my jacket for something to give her in return. Touched an old razor blade. A few loose bullets. Cigarettes. Lighter. And a pocket knife?

I brought out the knife and handed it to the girl.

She took it, twisted it a few times, and then quickly pulled the blade out to cut more leaves.

I went back to the window, putting a cigarette in my lips. I didn't light it. I just kept it there. 'Kid?'

'Huh?'

I turned back. 'Do you feel safe in Tosokh?'

She was busy cutting leaves. 'I don't know.'

'Do your parents let you go out alone?'

She shook her head, still cutting. 'They won't let me. Not where the factory is. We stay nearby, so dad is close to work.' She started flicking the tiny leaf bits with her fingers. 'There was a woman killed there the last time we went. Somebody wrapped her up in plastic and then choked her to death.'

I nodded. 'Anything else like that?'

She stopped flicking the leaves, sitting on her knees now. 'There was another lady killed. But they said she committed suicide. My dad told me it was a lie.'

'Really?'

She got up and cut another large leaf off the dying shrub. 'Yeah. She was a diplomat. Lived there for a long time. But she found out some secret, my dad says. And they killed her.'

I took the cigarette from my lips and slipped it behind my ear. 'Do you remember the lady's name?'

She squinted in thought. 'Susy, no, wait, Tsuki? Yeah. That's it. Tsuki.'

'What did your dad have to say about it?'

She raised her eyebrows. 'He said she should've kept her mouth shut about whatever she found. We all have an agreement working on

Tosokh. We keep quiet about things. Otherwise, we might lose our golden egg.'

I looked out the window again to think. Things were stitching up in my head. Might be uneven, but I still had enough thread to straighten it out.

'Hey. Your five minutes are up. What are you still doing here?'

I moved away from the window and pulled the lighter out of my jacket. I clicked it a few times on and off.

'You got any more stories?'

She shook her head. 'That's it.'

I went to the door. 'See you around.' I went outside, pulled the cigarette from my ear, straightened my hat, and lit my smoke.

CHAPTER 10

I woke up with a headache which, apparently, is common when you stay in a vacuum long enough. I slipped out of my bedroom cubicle and decided to take a stroll through the ship.

You have 13 new messages. Please be aware that each message costs 8 credits to open while aboard the ship.

I stopped outside a restaurant I hadn't been to yet. It was a narrow space with three foldable tables protruding out from the walls. The lights were dim, constantly buzzing, while black and brown moths crashed into the tubes every other second. There were ashtrays on the tables and conveniently placed suction vents in the walls beside the tables.

Sitting down at the back corner, I was met by a menu with frayed laminate peeling from its edges and a plastic table linen that felt used way past its use-by date.

An older man wearing a haggard ship uniform came over to my table. His gut reached out from his buttoned shirt, the last button missing, showing off an open triangle of hairy skin. He couldn't be bothered to smile, and the dark weights under his eyes were too heavy to lift anymore.

'What do you want?'

I scratched my chin with the back of my hand, then lifted the menu towards him. 'Set A with a cup of black coffee.'

The man took the menu from me and slapped it back down on the table. 'It stays there.'

I pulled a cigarette from my jacket and put it between my lips, holding the lighter there a second more. 'Hey, one more thing, keep those eggs over easy.'

The man turned away and went into the narrow kitchen in the wall. Dishes were clanking, and oil began to fry in an iron skillet.

I lit the cigarette and rubbed some sticky grease from my fingers.

As if appearing out of nowhere, a young man slipped into the restaurant, sitting at my table. His eyes were wide, and his bones thin. He smiled real big at me.

I flicked some ash off the end of my cigarette into the tray, then put it back in my lips.

He sat there smiling, not saying anything, just smiling.

I took another drag and let the smoke out at its own pace.

'Hello, sir. Good morning. Would you like to buy some souvenirs?'

I glanced to my right, looking for the server to see where the hell my coffee was. There was a standing coffee pot with a few mugs stacked beside it. I put the cigarette in my lips, stood up, and filled one of the mugs to the brim.

The wiry kid had a bag in his lap, which he started digging into. He pulled out a plastic toy and set it up on the table. Some kind of cheap robot, immovable at the joints, and welded by a quick one piece frame.

'Would you like to buy a souvenir?'

I sat back down at the table with my mug. 'I'm not buying any souvenirs.'

The kid had a slight twitch as he blinked his eyes rapidly. I think he was trying to smile, his lips were pulled back, but they didn't curve upwards. He then looked at me again, pushing the toy closer.

'No, sir. I wanted to see if you wanted to buy a souvenir. This is a magical robot. You'll see visions like him if you buy it.'

I shook my head and ashed my cigarette. I picked up the robot and turned it over a few times. It felt weighted inside. That's the prize in there. Crack open the cheap toy and find a bag full of white power.

I set it back down. 'You think it's smart to push these things on the ship?'

He seemed confused with his head cocked to the side.

'Where you from?' I said.

'Senturion.'

'Your boss flies you back and forth on these ships?'

He looked down at his bag. 'My aunt sent me,' he said. 'I don't have a boss.'

I breathed a dry laugh. 'That's rich.' I took another drag of my cigarette. 'You have any other guys working on this ship with you?'

He continued looking down with apprehension.

I picked the toy up again. 'How much for one of these?'

He lifted his eyebrows an inch. 'Seventy-five.'

I turned it over and set it down. 'Must be good stuff. At seventy-five.'

He then dug out a cheap plastic ball. There was an obvious weld going across its equator. 'We also have these. One-hundred-and-thirty'

I lifted it, feeling how heavy it was, then set it back. 'If I wanted to get something similar to this when I get to Senturion, how would I go about finding that?'

The guy blinked fast. 'There are souvenirs all over Tosokh.'

'Is that so?'

He nodded. 'Yes.'

'But is there one place in particular where I could get a lot of souvenirs, like say, where you go to fill your bag before you get on the ship?'

He started to bite his lip, shaking his head no.

Before I could ask him about the Black death, the server returned with my plate of food. He stopped when he saw the wiry guy sitting at my table.

'What have I told you about this?'

The kid quickly grabbed the toys and shoved them back into his bag.

'Jesus Christ. Can't you wait a whole fucking week until we get to Kaivus?'

The kid started to zip his bag as he stood up.

'I see you in here again peddling, and I'm talking with the authorities.'

The kid left the restaurant with the bag tucked under his arm.

The server let out a big sigh and dropped the plate on the table. 'Fucking hell.'

I snubbed out my cigarette and picked up my fork.

The man stood with his arms on his waist and a kitchen towel hanging over his shoulder. 'They're getting cocky these days. Sending these assholes up here.'

'Getting more common?' I said.

The man didn't look at me. 'Yeah, it's getting more common. There was none of this shit some five years ago. Now, everyone wants to sell you a magic souvenir.'

'How about Tosokh?'

The man shook his head. 'It's always been that way. Same as any other town.' He gritted his teeth and took hold of his towel, gripping it like a chicken's neck. 'I'm getting sick and tired of it on this ship.'

I broke apart the egg yolk with my fork. It bled a yellow mess onto my plate. I pushed some beans around, mixing the red kidneys with the coagulating yellow.

'Wait until someone overdoses,' I said. 'Then someone might really take note.'

He harrumphed. 'As if it hasn't already happened?'

I nodded, taking in the information.

Then, the man went to the small counter near the kitchen and wiped it with his dirty rag as he mumbled to himself. He kept wiping the same spot over and over again.

I sipped my coffee and sliced through the runny eggs.

•   •   •   •   •

There's little to do aboard a ship other than eat, sleep, and watch some mindless flicks. Pretty early on, in what should've been morning according to the clocks, I found myself back at the bar. No one else had the urge like myself. So I sat staring at the wall until a question arose.

'How long have you been working on this ship?'

Slowly blinking, the bartender turned his attention to me. 'This specific ship?'

'Or any ship.'

'Eight years.'

'What keeps you coming back?'

'Money.'

I snorted a faint laugh. 'That's it?'

'Bouncing between planets has its perks. I'm not chained to a daily grind on Kaivus, or worse Senturion; the poor bastards.' His face turned red at that last comment, and he quickly went to busy himself by checking the inventory.

I slid to the next stool and dragged my drink along for the ride. 'Is Kaivus really any better than Senutrion?'

'I'm only being cheeky,' he said. 'And how should I know? I spend most of my time on a ship in open space.'

'Where'd you grow up?'

'Kaivus.'

'And you've been to Senturion?'

He wanted to avoid the question, but I had him in my sights. He swallowed his breath before answering. 'That was years ago. Senturion is a unique place. Let's put it that way. At least Kaivus has two relatively progressive countries that persons not fitting the mold can flock to.'

Twirling my glass on the bar, I lowered my eyes and cracked my neck. 'Kaivus and Senturion are the same governance, though?'

'That's a tricky one,' he said, turning a slightly towards me. 'Have you studied up on our system before?'

'Never,' I said. 'My mother told me she saw a program about the lights about a month ago, and I thought to myself the hell with it, I might as well go see them before I get any older. Before that, I'd never heard a single thing about the system.'

His shoulders relaxed while he continued to examine me. He nodded his head then quit his inventory task.

'They used to be ruled by the same government but eventually broke away as independent planets after the fifty-year war. They still have open trade agreements and work closely with one another on certain aspects. But people born on Kaivus might take great offense if you ever mistook them to be from Senturion. Both consider themselves cut from a different cloth. Even if history says otherwise.'

'Fascinating.'

He hummed at me.

'You live in one of those progressive countries you were telling about?'

'I live on a ship and in hotel rooms.'

Silence crept into the conversation and sat down heavy between us. I focused on my drink, and he continued piddling around the bar.

'You know anything about these kids walking around the ship selling magical toys?' I said.

He froze then composed himself fast. 'No.'

'Weird, because this wiry fellow came and asked me to buy a magic toy for seventy-five credits.'

The bartender cleared his throat and looked at the table. 'If he's not careful, he might find himself off this ship sooner than the rest.' Then he went into the back without returning for a long time.

• • • • •

A loud scream awoke me one night. I shot up from my bed, slamming my head into the ceiling, and then rolled onto the floor, holding my cranium. Laying on the floor for a minute or two, saw me no avail from the tender welt or the throbbing pain atop my forehead.

After a cigarette and a mini-bottle of rum, I felt balanced enough to get off my ass and find out where that noise came from. Following my memory's sense of direction led me to a corner, where I saw three ship crew members gathered around a lady with glassy eyes and black veins running up her arms.

Keeping out of sight, I put my back along the corner and kept my ears pricked.

'Get her out before anyone else comes!' whispered a lady crew member. 'And go find whoever's selling this shit!'

I could hear the body being moved and a man grunting as he must've been lifting her. 'There's one of those refugees aboard the ship,' he said, in a strain. 'He's hiding in the ventilation ducts near the bridge.'

'I'll find him,' said the lady.

Then another woman cut in. 'No, wait, I'll go find him,' she said. 'You stay and help Bjorn - And find out who this guest is!'

Footsteps clattered on the floor, approaching me. I moved into the nearest intersection and cut my way through the area to find the bridge. As I ran down the halls, I felt myself turning circles, getting myself even more confused and lost.

And then I caught a drift of whispering voices nearby. I rushed to a small corridor and spotted the lady, carting along the young man that'd tried to sell me magical toys earlier.

'Are you kidding me?' she said. 'Are you selling this aboard the ship?'

'M-my aunt gave them to me to me.'

'Your aunt's a dumb cunt,' she said. 'Does she even realize her products are tainted?'

'I-I she told me...'

'Keep your voice down. And give me that bag!' She ripped it out of the young man's hand. 'How much of this mess have you sold? Huh?'

'Thirty.'

'Thirty!'

I crept behind them. Then she opened a door with her watch and slipped inside and out of sight. I tried to open the door, to no luck. It said ship crew access only.

'Damn.'

Turning and turning, I couldn't figure where they'd gone. I kept searching the corridors and peering and listening for any noise until I found myself at a dead end. I punched my fist against the wall then quickly soothed my knuckles with a rub.

'God damn it.'

I threw my back against the nearby wall and lit a cigarette. With my head craned upwards, I eyed the tube lights on the ceiling, and the tiny insects attracted to its glow. As I pushed myself off the wall, I heard a heavy door ram shut and a sharp whooshing sound hiss almost immediately. Sweeping the corner, following the source of the noise, brought me to a tight hallway, only wide enough for one person to pass at a time, that led to the airlocks.

Appearing from the corridor was the lady I'd tailed earlier. She unlocked a sliding glass door in the center of the hall, then carried on, unaware of myself standing in her way. She wore a sleek crew uniform, brim hat with a curly ponytail peeking out the back, and a sewn badge near her chest.

I cleared my throat before she bumped into me.

'The hell!' she said, jumping back. 'The hell are you doing here!'

'Did you hear that?' I said.

'This is off limits.' Her face skewed into a fierce glare when she saw my lit cigarette. 'Sir. You can't smoke here!'

I took a drag and let it out. 'Why does everyone keep on saying that?'

Tapping her finger at a glued sign on the wall, she straightened her posture, going militant. 'Are you blind?' The sign was a red circle with a slash in the center, swiping through a cigarette.

It was a bit faded and a little too small to be seen, obviously.

'Sir?'

'You're the boss.' I had a final drag then snubbed it out against the wall.

'Very well. Now can you please step aside so I may pass?'

'Did you hear that noise?'

'Is that any of your business?' she said, trying to squeeze past me. I moved to block her.

The anger returned to her face. 'Would you please step to the side to allow other passengers through?'

I lingered my eyes over her uniform, staring at the name sewn near the top of her chest. 'Sycamore?' I said. 'That your name?'

She scrunched her blue-painted lips and pushed a shoulder into the slight opening between me and the wall. There wasn't enough room to slink by, though.

'Sycamore,' I said. 'Is that right?'

She inhaled a deep breath. 'Sir, will you please step aside? I have an urgent matter to attend to.'

'Hold on a second,' I said. 'I really heard something strange just now. Right around this area.'

'Perhaps you heard another guest having a night terror. They're common on these voyages.'

'I never said anything about a scream.'

Her eyes and body went still. Then a paleness overtook her face.

I moved an inch further, closing her path. 'My dreams have been pleasant thus far,' I said. 'Meadows. Flowers. A nice waterfall trickling down the side of a cliff.'

Dread stared up at me behind her eyes.

'Was there a scream just now?'

'Please move aside.'

I filled the gap with my shoulder. 'What about you, what dreams are you having in deep space? Maybe you don't even have them anymore?'

'Sir?' she said. 'I'm needed elsewhere. Would you please?'

'No dreams then?'

'My dreams are private! And if you don't move out of my way, I'll alert the security.'

'Sure. No need to fuss. We're all friends here.'

I moved out of her way, allowing her to pass.

CHAPTER 11

You have 33 new messages. To view these messages aboard the ship, please click the accept button, and credits will be deducted accordingly.

I clicked accept on the first one.

Vince, what did I tell you? How many times have I said that you need to move out of that shitty place! I went by your house last night looking for you and found the fire brigade trying to save the apartment. Either you've pressed your luck one too many times and found one of your cigarettes burning the curtains or Blind Eddie and Phats came to pay you a visit. Can you please just tell me flat out if you're working for Lemoshe or not? Otherwise, I'm putting in a missing person report.

Mae.

Your account has been charged eight credits.

I clicked accept on the next.

Too bad about the apartment. You know if you change your mind, I'm willing to raise my offer by 300. Might help you find a cozy hotel in the meantime.

Lemoshe.

Your account has been charged eight credits.

I clicked accept.

You never told me your mom died? That's a shame, me and Eddie wanted to see if she could make us one of those famous blue snip pies of hers. Oh well. C'est la vie, right?

Philstine Faddius.

Your account has been charged eight credits.

I accepted the next.

Did you really go on vacation? Of all the times you chose to bounce. There's another victim if you were wondering. Black Death. I could really use a partner on this one. What do you say, for old time's sake?

Mae.

Your account has been charged eight credits.

Accept.

Where did you go? Mountains? I know you're not at the beach. I'm not worried, merely curious. I saw your car's still in the lot. Did you see the news where you are? Things are getting hot. Kind of like your flat. We caught up with Phats on a petty charge, but he said he hasn't seen you either. You think he's lying?

Mae.

Your account has been charged eight credits.

That was enough. I rubbed my face and sat up as far as I could in my tiny bed. The ceiling was so low that I had to crick my neck to the side. Sleep eluded me as it often did aboard the vessel, while boredom wrapped its arm over my shoulder, sticking close to my side.

I left the room and found the corridors quiet. As if nothing had happened the other night. No woman died in the halls, and no drug peddler found himself trapped in an airlock before it opened into space.

I walked by a control room. I don't know if it was the fuel station or what, but the walls were filled with gauges and glowing lights. In the center of the room were three large columns stacked neatly in a row, pulsing from yellow to a deep orange.

'What are you doing?' said a woman's voice behind me.

I didn't need to turn around to know it was her again.

'Can't sleep,' I said.

'Sir. This area is off limits.'

I glanced over my shoulder at her. 'Why are there so many places off limits here?'

Sycamore glared at me. 'Still hearing things?'

I shook my head, now turning my body to face her. 'Not since last night.'

'Ah.'

I cocked my head to the side. 'Well, I guess minds can play tricks on their owners.'

'Are you sure it doesn't own you?'

I shrugged. 'Either way. One of us heard something.'

Crossing her arms, I saw her nails painted silver with black stripes running down their centers. Her face was well sculpted too. Sharp along the jawline and yet soft near her cheekbones.

'Sycamore's a pretty name.'

She pursed her lips even more and avoided my eyes.

'Fitting for a lady like you.'

Her arms loosened from their cross. 'Why do I keep finding you in areas you're not supposed to be in?'

I raised the brim of my hat and licked my top teeth. 'Maybe you want to catch me?'

She laughed. 'Aren't you something? Now leave.'

'Or what? Put me in the airlock too?'

'I wouldn't put anyone in there.'

'But someone was in there, no?'

She withheld her thoughts even though her tongue was ready to lash and her eyes had already given me glimpse as to what she might say.

'Can I buy you a drink?' I said.

Taken aback, she uttered the beginnings of a reprimand then let out a sort of murmur that ended on an incomplete sentence.

I pivoted a little towards her.

She then peeked at her watch. 'Will you leave this area if I do? And stop smoking in the corridors?'

My head bobbed. It wasn't a nod or a shake, just a bob, there's no way I can answer a question like that.

She rubbed her eyes for a second. 'My shift ends in twenty minutes,' she whispered. 'I don't really drink, but if you want, you can join me in the game lounge later.'

'B-nineteen?'

'That's the one.' She then brushed a lazy wave of her hand. 'Now scram before you get me in trouble.'

'See you there.'

•   •   •   •   •

The game lounge was almost vacant, save for an older man at a virtual fishing game, asleep in his bucket seat, holding his rod and drooling a long strand from the corner of his mouth. I sat at a game of blackjack, losing more hands than I won when Sycamore entered and stood beside me.

'Follow me,' she said.

I stood up and followed her to a glass room filled with holographic stars and large planets inside.

She pressed a button and cleared the room in an instant. Then, she reached near the floor and tugged up a large burning sun. She positioned it into the center of the room and then fine tweaked its size.

'You need to stop picking at things you've no right to pry at.'

'I didn't realize these ships were so uptight.'

'They are,' she said. 'So, you'd be best to keep your mouth shut.'

I snorted.

Dragging a cluster of planets out of the thin air, she strung them before herself, marching around them, eliminating most with a clasp of her hand until she found the perfect one.

'You're from Ceph,' she said.

'That's right.'

'You're not going to Ceph,' she said. 'This ship lands on Kaivus, so don't act as if you're back home.'

She preoccupied herself by shifting the planet's color, then adding water or yellow deserts, before she walked it to the sun and set it in the glow giant's orbit. The planet went red if she was too close, then blue if she was too far.

'What do you do, Mr.?'

'Gavelman,' I said.

'Fine, Mr. Gavelman, what do you do on Ceph?'

'I own a used car shop.'

She placed the planet in the right zone. Then she stood back to examine her work. 'That sounds nice,' she said. 'Not as stressful as other occupations.'

'Everyone deals with stress in life.'

'Some more than others,' she said, pricking tiny star to life with her forefinger.

'You're from Kaivus?'

She ignored me for a time, walking about the room, igniting various stars in the empty space. 'Senturion originally,' she said.

I gave the room a try, picking up a small cluster of asteroids. 'What does that mean? Originally?'

'It means that I was born there and then moved to Kaivus while I was still young.'

My asteroids flew away from my hands, finding their own circuit in the universe. I glanced at her, still busy.

'Why'd you move?'

'Because I had to.'

'Troubles?'

Grabbing my asteroid cluster, she held them in her palm, then thinned them out. 'No, because the adults in my life were calling the shots.'

'Dad found a job there?'

'No, my father was dead at that point,' she said. 'And, soon enough, my mother found a boyfriend who begged us to move back to Kaivus with him. That man became my stepdad.' Releasing the asteroids, she paused in her thoughts. 'And then eventually my ex-stepdad, ten years later.'

I glanced sidelong at her. 'Did you go back to Senturion after that?'

'No.'

Catching a change in tone, my subconscious alerted me to be aware of the environment. A group of young men entered the game room and circled the sleeping old man; sniggering at him and moving his fishing rod out of his hands.

Sycamore made no notice of them as she immersed herself in the creation of this world.

'Would you ever go back to live on Senturion?'

'Never, I mean, it's nostalgic but... no.'

'Senturion isn't that great of a place?'

'Says who? There's nothing wrong with the planet. Don't get the wrong idea.'

'I heard there were a lot of shacks around the city of Tosokh.'

She opened her mouth then stopped. 'That's, well, yes, there are some. But that's not the reason I wouldn't go back to live there.'

'Then why not? It's home.'

Destroying a gaseous giant she'd been working on caused her to bar her teeth for a second, then start over on a new planet.

'Yes, it is my home,' she said. 'I get that. I just don't feel drawn to live there.'

'Too much going on in the city?'

'No.'

I raised my eyebrow. 'You know Ceph has a fairly pitiable country in the southern hemisphere that most people avoid,' I said. 'They're citizens live under an iron fist and yet have the highest rate of drug-related deaths.'

She winced as her hands trembled, while she painted her new gaseous planet.

'Can I smoke in here?'

'Yes, but please don't.'

I left her alone and went back to crafting an icy belt of meteors. 'You know something, I might've even met someone from that country aboard the ship,' I said. 'Although his accent wasn't from that area, he could've been from there. You see, he was trying to sell me these magical toys, which I'm sure you know...'

Snapping to attention, she cut my words short. 'Listen. You're a tourist going to see the lights on Senturion, correct?'

'Yeah.'

'And what did I tell you earlier? Don't come to another planet acting as if you're on your own.'

'I don't understand,' I said. 'I was telling you about this country.'

'No, you're not,' she said. 'Don't be daft.'

'I'm not.'

'You wouldn't understand Senturion.'

Taking a handful of meteors along, I walked beside her and released some around her planet. They began to circle the large body while some smashed into each other, creating a fine dust.

'Why don't you help me understand then? I'm listening.'

She marched her planet into the orbit of the bright sun.

'I'm waiting,' I said. 'What's this history?'

'We haven't always had it easy,' she whispered. 'On Senturion. There was a time when none of us thought about anything other than survival. Then we lost even more balance when Kaivus went to war and involved us in their fury.'

The group of young men were now pounding their fists on one of the carousel machines.

'It was tough,' she said. 'We had to rebuild everything we'd worked so hard for. Then there were complications with our second industrialization. Spills in our water supplies. Diseases spread from the lack of hygiene. And in the middle of it all, we had a very wealthy upper class that made up such a small percentage of our population and cared even less for the rest.'

One of the young men found a metal rod that he used to whack at the now broken carousel.

'So there's history there. We all know the struggles, but we don't talk about them. It's something woven into our blood. Cut one of us, any of us, and you'd find the same story stringing out like a tapestry.'

I saw the young men ripping a string of lights from the wall then edge towards the old man.

She was in a trance after creating a moon for the newest planet.

'If it weren't for the lights over the Senturion moon, then we'd never have made ourselves into what we are now. The filthy tourists. Making us whore out our planet to keep our citizens alive.'

'In a way, I'm helping to support that?'

She nodded with no smile. 'In a way, but we don't need it anymore. We have all the resources to make something more of ourselves. But the government doesn't encourage such ideas. The more educated we become, the more pressure there is on them to stop stealing our money and put it back into the people they're taking it from.'

Crashing outside, one of the young men got tangled in the string of lights before he could reach the old man.

'There's not much anyone outside the government can do about that kind of corruption,' I said. 'This is how wars start.'

She breathed a helpless laugh. 'You don't think I know that?' said in lower voice. 'We all do. It's not so simple, though. Any of it.'

The young men untangled their friend and rushed into our room. They started to destroy the tiny stars in the sky and misaligned the first planet Sycamore had arranged.

'You stupid pinhead!' said one of the boys, smacking another. 'You don't know a damn thing.'

Raising a middle finger, the smacked boy squared off with his friend.

'You want a real place, then we go to the one my buddies told me about,' he said. 'My gave me a map of locations, one building that's six floors of whores, real cheap too. That's the first notch I make on the list. Drain my balls dry until I can't fuck no more.'

The others laughed in agreement.

Sycamore sighed while she hid behind her planet.

'...get her to bend over like a...'

'See?' she whispered to me. 'There you are. Wouldn't you like to go back and live there? No matter how smart you are. How do you think outsiders will view you? Especially as a woman.'

'They're idiots,' I said. 'Their type is loathed on Ceph as well.'

'...choke her until she starts to...'

I turned to the men, clearing my throat and staring at them.

They turned their focus towards me, smiling like children with a foul secret. 'The heck do you want?'

I laughed to myself and walked towards them. 'You boys never smacked yourself down there or something? Never touched a woman's breast you didn't have to pay for?'

They narrowed their eyes at me.

'Keep it to yourselves then. The rest of us are gonna continue enjoying ourselves in our private conversations.'

One of them showed me two middle fingers. 'Fuck you, prick!'

I turned my back to him.

'Hey, pal, I said fuck you prick. Did you hear?'

Sycamore put her hand on my wrist. 'Leave them alone.'

I sniffed in a bit of air and reached to my side, taking hold of my gun. Swinging around, I leveled my eyes onto theirs, leaving the gun visible at my side.

They shut up real quick, their tails between their legs, keeping their stupid yaps shut.

'We're trying to talk here,' I said. 'Now, I don't mind a nice squeeze the same as the next. But keep it down. And get your nasty fingers off our work.'

They mumbled to themselves and slowly left the room.

Sycamore gazed down at her wrist for the time.

I put the gun back in my jacket and watched them exit the game lounge.

She finished decorating the planet. 'I should really get some rest.'

'They won't be back.'

'It's not that,' she said. 'Everyone's leaving the ship tomorrow. It's a busy day for the staff.'

'Thanks for chatting.'

'No problem,' she said, lingering her departure.

'How about we exchange contacts?'

Thinking it over a moment, she pursed her lips then nodded.

I reached my wrist towards hers, and then a blue light fluttered between us. She smiled, and I did the same.

'Remember what I said,' she told me. 'You're not on Ceph once we land.'

I nodded to her. 'I will.'

CHAPTER 12

I stopped in at the narrow restaurant for breakfast, a couple of hours before we landed. I had a smoke and ate some eggs. The coffee was black, and the server mad.

When I got up to pay, I lingered near the counter, taking a toothpick from an old plastic dispenser. I dug it in-between my teeth, causing one of them to bleed a warm salty liquid that tingled underneath my tongue.

The server gave me a look, his belly peeking out beneath his tattered uniform, as I stood picking my teeth next to the counter. He started to scratch the last remnants of his hairline–so far back now, it was tough to differentiate where his forehead ended and his scalp began.

I bit down on the toothpick, leaving it in my mouth as I spoke. 'You remember that kid we saw in here last time. Anxious guy. Selling toys and the like?'

The man dropped his hand from his head. 'Yeah, what about him?'

I started to twist the plastic contraption that held the toothpicks inside. Another one fell down into a kind of trough, waiting for its owner to pick it up.

'You haven't seen him back here, have you?'

The man closed his mouth and lowered his head, still looking me in the eye. 'I haven't seen him.' He paused as if there was more to say.

I took another toothpick and put it in my pocket, and started twirling the contraption for another. 'I haven't seen him either. What would they usually do with a guy like that on one of these ships, say if someone reported him?'

The man blinked his eyes and stepped back to cross his arms. 'Put him in confinement. Then give him over to whichever planet'll take him.'

I took a third toothpick, dropping it into my side pocket with the other. 'Confinement.' I twirled the circular piece for a fourth. 'Now that I think about it, that kid didn't seem all that right upstairs. One too many knocks on the head or one too many stings in the arm'll do that to you.'

The man glanced at the toothpicks. He watched me put the fourth one into my pocket, and wind it for a fifth. 'Senturion boys. What do you expect?' A vein began to pulse on the side of his neck.

I dropped the fifth into my pocket. 'That's another thing,' I said. 'What's he doing on a ship leaving Ceph?'

The man reached out, stopping me from taking a sixth toothpick. He dragged the plastic contraption off the counter and put it on a table behind himself.

'You go see your lights and enjoy yourself. Spend as much as you can, and don't you worry about Senturion; they'll treat you fine. Just keep to the bright areas and don't buy any of those toys.'

'The drugs aren't clean there?'

He laughed. 'That's one way of putting it.' He pulled a dishrag off his shoulder and rubbed the counter. But there were no stains on its surface. 'I feel bad for these refugees. I do. But he can't be stupid in the process. No matter how strapped he is.'

He stopped rubbing at the imaginary stain and clenched the rag in his hands. He made a slight grunt as he blew air past his rigid teeth.

'You think he missed the stop on Ceph?'

The man shrugged.

'And what do you think will happen to him now?'

He didn't want to look me in the eye, so he only looked a second and then distracted himself with the rag in his other hand. The man started to wipe the same spot again. The paint was either coming off or shining like it did when it was first put there.

'I didn't rat him out. I don't condone what he does in here. But I'm not a snitch. Not on kids like him.'

There was a red lightbulb on the side of the wall that started to pulse. I stared at it for a moment. The old man did the same.

'You'd better head back to your cubicle for checkout,' he said. 'We'll be on Kaivus soon enough.'

•　　　•　　　•　　　•　　　•

The ship rumbled like a car going down the highway with a flat tire and then evened out with a massive slam. I'd assumed we'd landed. I lay back in my tiny cubicle, staring at the ceiling above me for some time before anything was announced.

Soon, the doors opened, and everyone began filing outside and down towards the various immigration counters. I stood there at the desk feeling annoyed, waiting for the thin lady to clear me.

'Vacation?' she said.

'That's right.'

She contorted her lips as she looked at her holographic screen, tapping some items here and there. 'You're carrying a firearm with you?'

'Yes.'

She kept tapping. 'Have you ever been convicted of any form of crime?'

'No.'

She went back to her tapping. She was intent on it. Glued to the screen like a pianist to her sheet music. She stopped to take a breath from her frantic tap.

'Now, will you be visiting Senturion at any point on your trip?'

'That's the plan. Do any tourists actually come all the way to Kaivus without seeing the lights?'

She leaned back with a strange smile. 'You'd be surprised.'

'I'm sure.'

'Well, you're all clear. You can stay on the planet for ninety days, and if you plan on staying longer, you'll need to extend your visa.' She lifted a hologram towards me. 'The best way to contact the office is through this number. It'll automatically appear on your watch when you walk out of the booth.'

I stood quietly, waiting for the booth doors to open. They opened, and I went out into Kaivus' spaceport. The walls were white and grey, with a few moldy stains running down their sides. The floors had fine dust on them that caused my feet to slide every fourth or fifth step.

I was approached by a group of men and women, each offering the same thing. To taxi me around the city, showing me the best places to go, taking me to where all the tourist traps were. Some of them had company logos stitched into their shirts. Others wore commonplace jackets, making them seem like ordinary citizens.

A middle-aged man with a lot of pep shoved a city map into my chest. 'Where are you going? I can take you there cheap. Only thirty credits.'

I pushed the map out of my chest and moved past the man.

He jumped alongside me, still trying to barter. 'Okay, twenty-eight. And I'll even take you to a famous diner to eat. Best roasted meats along the mountain ridge. Cooked for forty-eight hours in a smoke pit, dug out near the hot springs. Come on, pal. You can't get anything better than that.'

I kept walking towards the doors. The winds were cold outside, bitter as they scratched my nose and clawed their icy fingernails at my neck.

'Hey, tiger. You're gonna get ripped off by everyone around here. They'll charge you some forty for what I'm offering. And they don't even know the good places to go. You'll get canned pork thrown over some hot coals. You want that, or you want the real traditional Kaivus roast?'

I pulled my collar up around my neck and threw a cigarette in my lips. The winds were blowing hard enough to keep me from lighting up. I turned my back to them, making a cavern with my chest, and finally got a flame to shine.

The peppy guy was still standing there. He started to lift his thick eyebrows up at me. He moved closer as if there was some secret we both shared.

'I'm after a different experience,' I said. 'Something to rip open my mind.'

A wicked smile creased on his face. 'I hear you.'

'I wanna try this Black Death.'

Almost as quick as the smile came, his face hardened, and he took a step back. 'Never heard of it,' he said.

'You know everything here, though?'

'Maybe you should find another taxi,' he said, moving further away. 'One of them over there.' And then he scuttled on to another small knit group of tourists.

The winds were blowing even more now. I turned my focus to the city ahead of me. It was pristine with a sleek coat of mirrors in cement frames. The roads were clean. Too clean for my taste. There was plenty of ground traffic running by the curb, and enough congestion from the hovercrafts, buzzing like bees between their city comb. But it left an awkward coil ready to fire inside me.

CHAPTER 13

I stood near my hotel's window for most of the night, watching the rain wash over the dark city and create sluices down the wavy pane before me. A bright neon sign flashed opposite my building, smearing radiant light along the wet glassy asphalt in pulsing winks. They bounced off my eye and tempted me like a curious bug drawn in by a buzzing lantern encased in mesh.

Checking my watch, I had banked on a dozen or so new messages, but all I found were old clients asking me to carry out some form a vengeance on their behalf and a lone message of defeat from Mae.

Putting my wrist down, I spotted the largest cat I'd ever seen in a city, dashing along the pavement, trying to avoid the wet rain. It had grey fur with sharp yellow eyes that shined like headlights on a country road. If I knew more about wildlife, I might've given it a fancy name like a bobcat or lynx. I didn't, though. I just kept smoking as I watched it pass by the neon signs and the cars parked along the walk.

There was a loud knock down the hall from my door. Some drunken creature pounded at the walls screaming for the door to open. It went on for some time before I heard him stumbling back down the hall. He spoke even louder as he descended the stairs, or maybe it was the echo that made it seem that way.

I returned to the window, pulling the curtains a sliver to watch the neon streets below. The rain was faint to a hanging mist now, and a car was parked firmly across the street. It'd been there for most of the night. Two, maybe three, black figures sat inside the dark interior, lighting their cigars to remind (me?) - or someone of their presence.

I moved away from the window, glancing down at my wrist for the time. There was a new message there.

Hey, Vince. I just got off the ship to roam the city for a while. I don't know if I'll sleep tonight, might save me some credits on a hotel. Anyway, you let me know if you need a tour guide or whatever. Sycamore.

The car was still outside when I slid the curtain back an inch. They weren't going to move for a while. So I went to the door, checking the locks, and sat at the back of the bed with my gun in my hand.

The room felt tight around me. The bright signs outside outlined my curtains in a deep red and trickled a nice line across the wall. I moved down lower into the bed. The springs creaked as they drooped to the floor.

I woke up to the sound of a siren weaving through the city. I sat up with my gun still in hand. I thought for a moment about turning on the dim lamp in the corner of my room. But I didn't. I already knew the walls used to be white and that the carpet once had a nice color without any stains.

•   •   •   •   •

From my window, the morning looked a grey blot while flakes of dirty sleet pelted against the glass. My mini coffee maker exploded into a plume of black steam after I tried to whip up a batch this morning with no luck.

The city below began to produce signs of life. There were a few commuters with narrow umbrellas covering their heads. Everyone wore dark colous—Navy blue, dark grey, grey, black, and one man with brown trousers. The sight gave me hope to find a diner in the area.

So, I backed away from the window, picked up my hat, and fixed it on my head. When I went outside and tried to lock up, I realized the bolts weren't perfectly aligned with the hole in the doorframe. I stood outside fighting with my keys to keep the sad room safe. A thin, older man walked past me in a red bathrobe, speaking to himself about the money he'd lost.

The lock and I finally came to an agreement, and I went down the uneven stairs into the lobby. There was a sleepy woman sitting at the counter with her arm up on the table, keeping hold of her chin like some pedestal, while a fuzzy holo-screen played on her desk.

I approached her counter.

She sighed, pausing her film. 'Yes?'

'Any good diners nearby here?'

She was too lazy to roll her eyes, so they merely drifted to the side. 'There's a place down the street. That way.' She clicked her head towards the right of the building.

I nodded, moving away from the desk, and went outside into the icy cold rain. I found the diner fast. It had a cheap name painted on the glass windows and thick curtains at the sides.

The door only opened halfway as it caught part of the pale green carpet, ripping into it further with each customer that entered. I slid through and glanced at the booths inside. I went to one in the corner that had a steady hanging light over it and scanned the room.

There was an older couple eating in one of the booths four rows away from mine. The man was trying his best to keep the soup from trembling from his spoon, as his hand never seemed to stop quivering. He brought his face lower to the bowl, shortening the distance between sips.

I studied the menu, looking at the pen marks scratched through certain items and scrawled writing above others. There was a fat mom and pop near the kitchen in the midst of a heated argument–they were throwing their hands in the air and pointing in different directions as they shouted at one another. Then a thin man came out of the kitchen with his head down and a small notepad in his hands.

His hair was cut a straight line around his head, and his shirt was tucked taut into his high-waisted trousers. He stood next to my table, trying to look at me, but it seemed difficult for him to manage. His speech was breathy, with labor behind each word.

'Hello, sir. Can I take your order?'

I set the menu down and licked my upper lip. 'Eggs. Toast. Coffee. And you got any sausage patties?'

He focused intently on writing my order down, smiling as if he couldn't choose any other expression. Then he rushed over to my menu, grabbing it quickly out of my hands. He flipped through it like he were late for dinner and stopped on the second page.

'Set C has eggs, toast, coffee, and sausage. It is cheaper.'

I slowly looked at the menu. 'Fine, kid.'

He shot back up and wrote something down with his pen. He fixed his hair a few times, still with a painful smile.

'Hey, what kind of eggs are these?'

'Scrambled.'

'I mean the animal.'

He took some time to examine the room. Not sure of his answer. 'These are yellow eggs.'

I put a cigarette in my lips and opened my lighter. 'Never mind, champ. Can you get me that coffee first?'

He bowed a little and then rushed back to the kitchen, keeping his eyes focused on the ground.

I lit my cigarette and waited for the coffee. It came within no time in a dense off-white mug. It tasted of beans that might've been swept up from a factory's floor after all the good ones had already been packaged and sold.

The sleet continued to fall outside, pelting soft nicks at the window. I let my cigarette hang in the corner of my mouth as I pulled up my watch and put it under my chin.

'Getting some breakfast now. I'll send you my location if you want to join me.' I lowered my wrist and sent the message to Sycamore.

A hot plate of food came to the table, and the young kid with a bowl cut ran back into the kitchen just as fast. The older couple were getting up to leave as I broke into my food. I had no clue what animal the eggs came from. They had an earthy taste, wild, and quite chewy. I washed some of it down with the bitter coffee and took another inhale of my cigarette.

There was a message coming through. I tapped my wrist. *I'm close to where you are. I'm having breakfast now too. I'll let you know when I'm there. Sycamore.*

The doors opened at the entrance, and two police officers entered, allowing the cold, damp winds to rush inside. The officers wiped their black vinyl jackets and dripped water all over the carpet. They were both young. Sharp jawlines with clean-shaven faces. The taller of the two had his nose in the air, and a malicious grin spread evenly across his lips.

I pushed the eggs about and sliced them into the sausage patties with my fork.

The tall officer clicked the small bell on the counter, smirking at his partner.

The restaurant owner leaned out from the kitchen, wearing a red apron and a sneer that he quickly swabbed off his face.

'Yes?'

Taken aback, the smaller officer bunched up his face at the owner. 'Excuse me, what did you just say to me?'

'Sir, officers,' said the owner.

'What kind of place is this? You have two hungry officers standing here for over a minute now. Let's go. Find us a booth before we buy you a one-way ticket to Senturion!' The small officer then snapped his finger in the air.

Without missing a beat, the owner held his hand out as if serving in a fancy restaurant towards the dining area.

'This way.'

He moved them fast towards a booth with the strongest lightbulb above it. He wiped the table with a dishrag in an unsettled manner. His grey sweats were hanging off his backside, showing a slight crack from his hind corners.

The smaller officer slid into the booth, snatching the menu from the owner, then began searching it over. Pushing the owner out of his way, the second officer sat himself on the other side of the booth, grabbing a menu on the way.

'Bring us some coffee and not the day-old crud; I'm talking a fresh brew.'

The old man nodded. 'Yes, sir. One moment.' He wobbled back towards the kitchen, knocking his waist on the corner of a table but carrying on without tending to his side. His wife was leaning through the door, watching the officers. He pushed her inside, along with himself, whispering in a dull roar.

The officers scanned their menus for some time. The old man rushed back out, carrying two clean mugs in his fists.

'Freshly blended beans imported from Eros-two,' he said. 'I keep a special bag in the back for a gentleman such as yourselves.'

Slapping his menu on the table, the smaller officer caused the old man to flinch. Both men sniggered while licking their teeth.

'Where's your boy today?'

Lips trembling and sweat gathering at his forehead, the old man shuffled his words about. 'He's out for the day.'

'Hmm. All right, pops. How about you get me four eggs overeasy, two red croquettes with cheese, and a stack of buttered cakes to go with 'em. How's that?'

The old man took the menu into his withered hands, shaking his head. 'That's fine. Whatever you like, officer.'

The tall officer shoved his menu towards the old man as he spoke. 'Get me the same except substitute one of the croquettes for a few sausage links. With some tree syrup to dip them in.'

The old man swallowed hard as he bowed to them out of reflex. He then backed away and hobbled into the kitchen.

The room went quiet. Except for the sleet tapping at the window, louder now that silence took captive the mood. I stubbed out my cigarette and sipped the last bits from my mug. The old lady came from out of the kitchen with two large plates of food. She set them down for the officers and flashed them a nervous smile.

The taller man clicked his head to the side, motioning for her leave, and sighed his annoyance to his partner. She bowed out and turned away without hesitation.

I finished my food, took a good look at the officers, and slid out from the booth. They paid me little attention as they consumed their food like the pigs they were. I hit the bell on the counter to grab the old man's attention and took a toothpick from a small cup on the counter.

The old man wiped his forehead and stared at me in confusion for a moment. His wife peered out of the kitchen and whispered a hiss at him.

'Hold on,' he said to her. 'One thing at a time.'

I picked my teeth and smiled at the old lady, who darted back into the kitchen.

Wiping his brow several times, the old man seemed lost as he shifted his eyes about the restaurant.

I cleared my throat.

'All right,' he said. 'Uhh, you, uhh..."I had set C,' I said.

He snapped out of his trance and pulled a triangular piece from under the counter. 'That's right. Let me fix this real fast.' He tapped on it a few times and then got the bill to show.

I sent him the credits with a tip and then turned away towards the door. I could hear the officers moaning about their coffee mugs not being full as I left.

•   •   •   •   •

The sleet was quick to remind me of itself, tossing frozen beads upon my cheeks. I put up my collar and started back towards the hotel.

'Vince? Vince?'

I back into the awning hanging from my hotel and searched the mist for her voice.

She had a clear umbrella covering her body and a pair of goulashes that ran up to her knees. She lifted the umbrella from over herself as she reached the awning.

'I thought we were meeting at the diner?' She closed the umbrella and shook the water from it.

'I needed some fresh air.'

She wound a strap around her umbrella while she spoke. 'And how do you find the air on this planet?'

I gazed across the street at the unlit neon signs and the dark streaks trailing down the building's surface.

'Fine, I guess. Is it always this cold?'

She glanced over her shoulder at the falling sleet. 'You came during the worst season. Wait until the buildings freeze over.'

'No wonder the tickets were so cheap.'

A gust of wind howled along the streets, casting a spray of rain and sleet upward at a sharp angle. The water began to spray underneath the awning, getting my feet wet and soaking my legs.

Sycamore stepped out of its torrent and moved closer to the hotel entrance.

I sidestepped to join her. 'I can see why you appreciate the ship.'

The winds changed their directions, casting more beads of rain and sleet under the awning.

'You get used to living indoors or underground. The ship's not that different.'

'I can imagine.'

She leaned her back against the wall, looking out at the rain. 'When are you going to Senturion?' she said.

'I was hoping to go today. You know how to get there?'

She nodded. 'You have to take the gravitational transport.'

'Yeah, I heard.'

'There's a station up near the spaceport. I can take you later?'

'How long do the ships run?'

'The last one leaves at six.'

I glanced at my wrist. It was only ten-thirty. 'You want to show me the city before I go?'

'What would you want to see?'

'Whatever you can show me.'

She looked down and then up at me with her hands together. 'There's a folk art house ten minutes away. We could go check that out?'

I nodded for some time. 'Is it full of tourists?'

She laughed. 'No, it doesn't appeal to them.'

I cleared my throat and eyed the sleet dropping from the grey skies. 'I'll ring us a cab then?'

'Let's take the train.' She pointed her umbrella past the diner. 'There's an entrance over there if you don't mind getting wet?'

I glanced at my legs, lifting my foot, and turning them to the side.

She rested her hand on my upper arm. 'Or we can try to share my umbrella?'

I fixed my jacket around my neck even more. 'I'll be fine. I don't think the two of us will fit.'

'We could try?'

'Okay.'

She threw the umbrella over us and held to my arm, guiding me to the station entrance. Even as we descended underground and pushed through the turnstiles, she kept hold of my arm, not releasing until we reached the platform.

We sat on a vacant bench waiting for the train to emerge from the tunnel ahead. Then a pack of rodents raced across the floor, stopping when they noticed us. I swished my hand at them. But they didn't move; their beady eyes fixed upon us without a trace of fear.

'You won't scare them,' she said. 'They're not bothered by humans anymore.'

They stirred discomfort in me, the way they watched. With their animal gazes and thick hay-like whiskers twitching at their cheeks.

Feeling smug, I took out my lighter and ignited a flame, expecting them to scurry. They remained still while the orange flame reflected off their dark eyes.

'Cretins.'

'I'm telling you they're not scared. Especially not the grey ones.'

I closed my lighter and shifted on the bench. One of the bigger rats titled its head to keep an eye on me.

'Is there anything they're scared of?' I said, reaching for my gun.

'Not really.'

Sighing a bitter pant, I relaxed my fingers off the pistol's handle. Part of me wanted to stand up, throwing my hands in the air to chase them off, but a premonition stopped me. Then a reel played in my mind. A vision of myself rolling on the floor, swiping at these gnawing vermin, latching to me like a pack of rabid dogs.

I rubbed my jugular.

'Don't let them bother you,' she said. 'They'll move on, eventually.'

We were locked in an unmarked contest. My eyes met theirs, neither of us breaking our gazes. The vision of blood spewing on the platform rose like a wisp of smoke in my brain.

'Where did you hear about the lights?' she said.

Sweat rolled down my temples. Memories of the past tightened binds at the tubes in my heart.

She lay her hand on my arm. 'Vince?'

'From a client,' I said. 'I heard about them from a client.'

Her head titled, reminding me of the big grey rat in the pack.

I'm not a fan of dogs. Not a fan of any wild animal large enough to inflict a fatal blow.

'Oh,' she said. 'What did she say?'

'I can't remember the details, but kept talking about the place over and over every time she visited. She wouldn't shut up, you know.' I paused, still eyeing them. 'So I thought if this lady ever buys a damn car, then I'll go to Senturion and give it a try.'

She glanced at the rats as she crossed her leg atop the other. 'I'm surprised you came so far. You don't strike me as the well-traveled type. No offense.'

I thought about shooting the big one. He was really getting on my nerves. *What are the laws about shooting guns in the subway? Probably don't need that kind of attention on myself. Not over a fucking pest.*

I looked slowly away from them to her and then back to them, as if they might jump in that short amount of time. They hadn't. They were statues there. Waiting for me to die or crumble to the verge of death for when they could take the ultimate advantage.

'Are you really here for the lights?' she said. 'Or are you searching for something else?'

The last word carried a bite.

'Why do you ask?'

'Because you don't fit the type,' she said. 'And if I were a different person, then I'd keep a fairly watchful eye on you.'

The rats began to move. The big one paused a few times to glance back at me, before they disappeared down near the tracks.

I opened my lighter, lit it, then clicked it shut. I did this for a while without thinking.

The train broke through the tunnels and stopped in a screech at the platform. We both stood and went aboard in a vacant cabin. Then, before we could sit, the train sped onward into the darkness.

'My brother still lives on Senturion,' she said. 'At least, I think he does.'

'Have you thought to visit him?'

'Of course,' she snapped. 'Have I ever thought to visit him?'

'Never mind I asked.'

She was quiet for a moment, scanning the train, I presumed. The cart bumped us up and down as we passed over an intersecting track. She turned her back to me a little. Then the train stopped, and the doors raked open.

'This is our stop,' she said.

And we both climbed off in silence.

We stood outside the train as the doors shut and whipped out of sight with a quick breeze. There were no rats at this station. At least none we could see.

She pointed up the cement stairs at the end of the platform.

'That way.'

We walked up the grey steps and clicked our credit pieces on the old turnstiles, and went through an underground passageway that connected to the station. We passed by a line of makeshift shops, where people logged on tarps or foldable chairs, selling plenty of knickknacks and homemade foods.

'Umbrellas, only five credits.'

'Need a pair of Goulashes?'

'Herbal remedy to keep you warm this season.'

And then, of course, those too defeated to even raise their heads and say anything to potential customers passing along.

Sycamore pointed towards an intersection with a narrow staircase climbing upwards.

'This way.'

We went up the tight passage, moving our backs against the wall as others came squeezing down it. The rain had stopped outside, but the grey had yet to pass.

Then, without warning, she took hold of my arm and dragged me the rest of the way to the art house. It was in a standard building, a grey slab of concrete and green glass windows in its face. I paid for both of our admissions and went inside.

There were lights hanging from exposed wires in the ceiling and wallpaper peeling away from the corners. The floors were like that of a factory's, with thin wooden pieces at the sides that had nails sticking out of them where they used to hold carpeting down.

The first installation was a large stone sculpture of a crescent moon, with a smaller crescent near the top right and then an even smaller one near its midsection. I rubbed my forefinger along the rough stones and then read the artist's profile.

Satovis G. Halliam. 219-283 KSC.

Satovis was born on Kaivus in Nikktte City's lower district to parents Geriumn L. Halliam and Ella T. Halliam. Little is known about his childhood, and even less is known about his parents. Satovis spent the majority of his life working the factory lines at Quill Press, a manufacture of car seats, now defunct.

Satovis was never married and has no known descendants. It is said that Satovis began sculpting this piece titled 'Crescent Light' when he was laid off from work, due to a malignant form of lung cancer.

I backed away from the bio and looked at the crescent moons again. Sycamore was quietly waiting behind me.

I turned towards her, looking into her eyes.

She nodded a little and then moved to the open door frame that led to the next room. The walls were filled with paintings and the floors with tall clay urns.

I went down the line of paintings, gazing at each for some time. They weren't happy pictures. Every one of them depicted something dark. Giant prison-like cities with animals eating dead children in the streets or blacked out humans laying skewered on the sharp ends of a crescent moon.

I pulled a cigarette from my jacket and lit it, taking in a deep inhale.

'Too much?' she said.

I rubbed my eyebrow with the cigarette in my fingers. 'No. I wouldn't say that.'

'You think this would appeal to tourists?'

I didn't answer. I went back to the wall and looked at one of the few bright-colored paintings in the room. I examined it for some time and then realized it was the lights over the Senturion moon. But everyone watching had holes in their heads where their eyes should be, as they gazed upon the phenomena.

CHAPTER 14

We walked back to the train station, and she offered to show me where the gravitational transport stations were in the spaceport. We stopped in at a small restaurant overlooking the station, watching the transport ships rocket into the air without the use of standard fuels. It was great, what they'd done. Figuring out how to make use of the gravitational force between the satellites to power their ships.

I lit a cigarette and asked the waitress to refill my mug. Sycamore was quiet ever since we left the arthouse. Maybe her tight-lipped syndrome started when we hopped on the train. Who knows? I couldn't pinpoint it at the moment.

I took a sip of coffee and dropped some ash in the tray. 'Do you have any messages you'd like me to pass to your brother up there?'

Picking at her lip, she didn't quite catch what I'd said right away, then quickly, I saw a peak of horror in her eyes that she quickly poised before I read into them any further.

'No. No, I don't.'

'You want to join me then? I'll pay your fare?'

She wrapped her fingers around her mug and then lifted it up slowly under her lips. She kept it there as she thought to herself.

I checked the time on my wrist. *3:56.*

'Part of me wants to go,' she whispered. 'Deep down. But the way things work...'

I nodded. 'Go on.'

She still had the mug under her lips as she peaked around the diner at all the patrons eating. She opened her mouth to say something but then hesitated.

I turned over my shoulder to make a quick glance at the place. There were two kids with tattoos and piercings necking at the back table and a well-dressed couple that kept checking their wrists for the time while gazing at the transport ships rising into the sky. I turned back to face Sycamore.

Her eyes bore into mine. 'Sometimes, that's all I can think about. Going back.' She paused to wet her lips. 'I've asked about him and tried to make contact, but that's not so smart.' A shiver trembled in her bones. 'It's the wrong thing to do.'

I left a cigarette in my lips and started to rub at a stain on the table's surface. 'And why is that?'

She took notice of her mug and lowered it down to the table. 'Do you think it's better to know the truth no matter how painful it is, or to live the rest of your life blissfully unaware?'

I took my time to give her a response. This was something I had to contend with almost every day of my life. Getting information for people who want to feel extreme pain, saying it's for closure, convincing themselves that it's what they need. But I know when I take on a case, that's rarely the truth. They want to try and imagine the exact details of their loved one's painful death. To live it and breathe it as if it'll absolve the situation. Absolve their guilt and grief.

I exhaled a plume of smoke and set the cigarette down in the tray to rest for a while. 'That's the question, isn't it? I wish I could tell you which it is, but I honestly don't know.'

'Sure. Sure.'

I rubbed my thumb around the rim of my mug, then looked at another ship coming in for a landing. I leaned forward on my elbows as I spoke to her.

'And for you?' I said.

'I've never found out. So you should know my answer.'

The waitress came over to the table and lingered with a coffee pot in her hand. She looked at us a few times back and forth.

'Either of you want dessert?'

'Bring us something with chocolate,' I said.

'Are you kidding me? We can't grow that stuff here. You think we're paying for imports either?'

I raised my eyebrow and stared at the lady. She glared back at me with a hand now on her hip.

I continued to eye her. 'Then bring us something else.'

She frowned. 'We have glutinous cakes and snail-lip custard.'

I turned to get Sycamore's confirmation.

She nodded. 'We'll take the custard.'

'Two?'

'Yes,' I said, putting my coffee mug at the edge of the table.

She glanced at my mug and then back at me as if she wasn't going to fill it up. After some time, she poured more and then went behind the bar into the kitchen.

'Snail-lip?'

She wiped her damp eyes. 'It's a type of fruit. Like a date mixed with the cream of an ancient durian. Of course, they call it snail's lip because it has a spiral on top of it, similar to an acorn, but much bigger.'

I nodded, picking up my cigarette to take a final drag.

The lady returned with two cold bowls of custard. She let mine drop on the table with a sharp clank and set Sycamore's down a little more gently.

I didn't mind. I know how this situation must appear to her, so I picked up my spoon and broke into the firm custard.

'I thought about hiring someone to find him,' she whispered. 'But I can't bring myself to do it. To know what really happened or screw anything for him or myself.'

It was a bitter type of custard. I don't know if the fruit was unripe or if the lady gave it to me from a neglected fridge.

'What do you expect happened to him?'

She stopped her spoon mid-air and closed her eyes. 'Let's talk about something else? Okay?'

'Fine.'

We ate more of our custard and listened to another ship rip into the sky.

'What are the other big cities like on Kaivus?' I said.

She turned her head a bit. 'Not that different,' she said. 'This is one of the few habitable regions. Everything else above and below is arctic. The only other countries are along the equator but living in similar conditions.'

The conversation went flat again. I cleared the rest of my custard and pushed the bowl aside. She ate a few spoonfuls behind me. The time had come. I needed to go.

We finished our drinks, and I paid the bill. She walked with me over to the gravitational port.

'I hope you enjoy yourself,' she said.

'Yeah.'

'I'll be back on the ship by the time you leave.'

I nodded.

'Thanks for the meal.'

'No problem.' We lingered a second more. Then she waved bye. I turned then turned back, touching my lip with my index finger. 'Can you answer me one more question?'

Her eyebrows slanted into a furl. 'What question?'

'Do people ever get shipped from Kaivus over to Senturion without their consent?'

She chewed on her lip then stepped nearer to speak in a lower voice. 'You know that's a weird question,' she said. 'Especially from a car salesman. What makes you ask such a thing?'

I picked at the lobe of my ear. 'Something I heard in the diner at breakfast this morning. An officer threatened to send an old man up to Senturion - I wasn't sure if it was a lingering threat people carried from the past or if their words had any real meaning.'

She lowered her voice even more. 'You never hear of any protests on Kaivus, do you?'

'I'm not that well informed.'

'Have you ever heard of the one-eighty-eight march?'

'Can't say I have.'

'There's one law that's never been overturned between Kaivus and Senturion, even after they both declared themselves independent planets. Can you guess what that code of law is?'

'Extradition?'

She nodded her chin downward. 'No matter what happens between Kaivus and Senturion, we're still sibling planets and carry on the ritual of scratching one another's back. Any citizen on this planet can be detained without any due cause and sent on the next ship to Senturion without the slightest repercussion or intergalactic protection to themselves. When I say I enjoy living on the ship, I mean that I enjoy living on a ship.'

•　　　•　　　•　　　•　　　•

The station was more of a ferry service between the two celestial bodies than anything else. They told me there was another ferry station up on Senturion that went between it and its moon Eroth, but those were under strict watch, and no tourists were allowed near the area.

Other than that, the insides of the terminals were quite nice and clean. A very different atmosphere compared to the hotel I bunked in for the night.

The walls were lined with posters, all too happy to gush the story behind the gravitational transports and the scientist who brought them from imagination into physical creations. Telluria, the lady who'd invented them, had her face plastered on every inch of the station; and on a closer inspection, I realized that every statue within the terminal was in her image as well.

It was their prized achievement as a society. I get it. Built out of necessity during the war. They needed a cheap way of trading cargo between Kaivus and Senturion. Good for her and the rest that profited such an advancement in space travel.

I sat in the terminal waiting to board the ship, twiddling my thumbs and poked my head up whenever the crew made any movement that might signal our time to board.

When the announcement was called throughout the station that our ship was ready, everyone shot from their seats and piled into a long line.

The ship was nearly full when the doors shut. A screen appeared at the front of my cabin, showing me an animated diagram of what was about to happen next. If we should experience any problem in deep space, other than being screwed, we were supposed to remain in our gravitational seats and wait to die.

Then a red light flickered over the screen. *Prepare for take off.*

But there was no way to prepare for such a wild ride.

SENTURION

CHAPTER 15

The screen over my head showed me a small green ship following a blue line to Senturion, and in the bottom right corner, there was a timer clocking down the duration still remaining in the trip.

We began to break into the atmosphere when I heard a loud battering hit the ship, as if some kids were outside throwing heaps of gravel at the hull.

'We're sorry about the noise,' said the head Engineer. 'We are currently headed through a field of orbital rubbish. No need to be concerned. We'll pass through it soon and land in no time.'

The debris lasted for longer than I expected. I felt uncomfortable listening to them hammer against the ship, some with huge thuds that seemed to change our direction. Then, in an instant, it faded like a summer's storm.

The ride went calm for the rest of the flight. That is right before we hit down. I'm sure these crafts were a great invention, but if they had a suggestion box, I would've gladly told them to focus on landing the damn thing with a bit more grace.

The Engineer spoke over the intercom, but I don't know what he said. I was still thumbing through all the mental promises I'd yet to fulfill in my life and the people that might come to spit on my grave if I was so fortunate to have one. Then my restraints unfastened themselves, and my seat lowered me to the ground.

I stood up and joined the queue forming in the aisle. The line moved slowly as everyone trickled out into the station. It was a smaller station with the same amount of posters covering the walls. And with every step I took, I felt grit catching underneath my shoes.

The narrow hall started to widen into a large opening where more cabbies waited to give us fresh landers a tour around Senturion. I put my hat down over my eyebrows and tried to slip through the crowds undisturbed. There was a small flow of traffic bustling outside the station, but I was able to cross the four-lane highway without getting hit.

The weather was still cold, but at least the skies were clear. It marked the first time I'd seen the sun since leaving Ceph. I pulled a cigarette from my jacket and then my lighter. I stared into the city as I brought the lighter underneath the cigarette.

'Senturion,' I whispered to myself. The smoke drifted around me in a white fog.

I took another strong drag and let it creep between my teeth. There was something almost invisible hanging in the sky, an inch above the city. It was a yellowish moon above. I'd almost missed it too.

A dark van pulled up to the curb where I was standing. The passenger window rolled down, and a man leaned across the seats, trying to take a good look at me.

'Hey?'

I took another drag of my smoke and stepped aside to have an unobstructed view of the city.

The van went in reverse, blocking that sight from me. 'Hey? You here to see the lights?'

I glanced at the man with my cigarette hanging in my lips. 'You going to turn them on or something?'

The man cocked his head to the side with a click of his tongue. 'What? I'm trying to ask you a question here. Do you realize the type of hook-up I've got? Prime view and other perks no one else can manage.'

'How about a bag of Black Death?'

His eyes nearly popped from his head. 'I can't even understand your dialect,' he said. 'The what? You're strange, man. Real out there.'

'I've heard two out of three die when they take it,' I said. 'But for those that return from the trip are never the same afterwards.'

'Huh? You speaking the universal tongue?'

'I can understand you.'

'Whatever, you aren't interesting!' He leaned back into his seat and clicked his gears with a nasty grumble. 'Your loss, sucker!'

I stood there smoking as he struggled to get his clutch out of its grind. It sounded like a power saw trying to cut through a lead pipe. The van then jerked into a stall.

'Shit,' he said. 'Son of a bitch.'

The van started to rumble as he cranked it back up. The engine purred for a moment and then cut out again. The man hit the dashboard with the flat of his hand. He then glanced at me as I stood there smoking.

'Sprat! The hell are you still doing? This ain't no show.'

I looked down at my cigarette and flicked some ash off it. 'I'm feeling entertained.'

'You ain't from here. You don't know. Why don't you go smoke your fag somewhere else? Dumb louse.'

I inhaled and let the smoke out slowly.

The van started, and the gears cinched into the right place. The van wheezed ahead with a few clamors and then rolled into a steady pace.

I finished my cigarette and threw the butt onto the street. A few more cars passed by and stopped to offer me a VIP location to watch the lights. I declined.

I walked down the streets up into the city, where a tunnel of wind surged from east to west. I stood up against one of the taller buildings where the wind couldn't reach me and checked my messages.

I told some officers to keep an eye out for you in certain locations. The city dump, the snake river, and down in the canyon. So if you think I'm searching in all the wrong places, then let me know.

Mae.

I lifted my wrist and thought it might be time to send her a message.

'I don't enjoy swimming or hiking down any canyons,' I said. 'I do visit the dump pretty often, though, but you won't find me there for a while. Like I told you before. I'm on vacation.'

•   •   •   •   •

By the time I found the train, the sun had already dipped behind the horizon. I walked atop the standing platform and waited for the next ground line to reach. A group of two scrawny individuals see-sawed the bar of an old handcart along the rails, then slowed their pace as they crawled into the station.

'No train for the next eight hours,' the young teen called to me.

His friend at the other end of the cart wiped his nose on a ragged shirt. I glanced between the two young teens, their faces covered in soot, and the one cleaning his nose had a lame right hand.

'How am I going to reach my hotel by tonight then?'

The first teen dug into his pocket and showed me his credit piece. 'We'll give you a ride for fifteen credits.'

Shooting his head up, the second boy was shocked at his friend's bargaining.

'Is that the going rate?' I said.

His expression all but told me they were lying.

'I'm going to a pink hotel along the southeastern coast.'

Taking in this information, the boys huddled amongst themselves, whispering, then turned back and nodded.

'Twenty-five then.'

I gazed along the train tracks. 'You're sure no other train is coming?'

They shook their heads.

'Twenty-five to get me there, then a possible ten each if I arrive safely.'

Both teens hopped off the hand-cart and patted down the center section, fixing a sackcloth, then presented me my seat. I climbed aboard, and they quickly pumped the see-saw that powered us along the tracks.

The ride was smooth, and the two young men let me off a kilometer from the last station. They told me they needed to keep moving before anyone saw them. I transferred the agreed credits and told them farewell.

Stepping out from a patch of tall grass, I emerged at the outskirts of a small coastal town. Mist crept over the beach and filtered into the streets. A car swished past me, then skidded at the next intersection, disappearing from sight.

I clamped a cigarette in my teeth as I heard a dog barking a couple of blocks away. Crossing the street, I pushed myself into a narrow alleyway then paused when I heard someone following behind.

There was a man emerging from the shadows, walking in a springy manner as if he were bouncing off each leg to the next. I rotated to see what he wanted.

'The dogs run up the hill at night,' he said like his mouth were filled with cotton. 'Especially if a shadow chases them.'

I cocked my head a little. 'Is that so?'

He came closer towards me into the faint streetlamp shining above. He wore a loose green coat with a pair of grey baggy pants that were frayed at their ends. His hair was peppered grey and black and pointed into a sharp widow's peak at his forehead. His eyes couldn't stay focused on one place at a time, they kept wiggling back and forth in his sockets.

'Dogs don't like the dark. They go up the hill if they see a shadow nipping at their heels.' He smiled and then started to laugh.

I creased a fake smile as I lit my cigarette.

'There was a big dog in the road yesterday,' he said with a swollen tongue. 'A car hit her. Then left. There was blood, and white milk spilled onto the asphalt. I couldn't see it very well without my glasses.'

'What are you saying to me exactly?'

'That she was dead.'

'Right.'

He laughed again. 'Then a man came by and told me to leave. He said you go back to where you came from and don't go walking the streets no more. I went home after that. Back to the cafe. Where I usually stay.'

I let the smoke run out my nostrils. 'It sounds like you should be getting back to that cafe. Someone might be looking for you.'

'People say that all the time,' said Dogman, his eyes flickering. 'I shouldn't go out. I might embarrass myself or get lost. But I have to find my black dog.'

'You mean Black Death?' I whispered.

'No! My dog!'

I nodded and then peered down the alleyway at a large pack of rodents shuffling through the rubbish bins.

I turned back to him. 'A real dog?'

'My dog.'

'Then, perhaps, you should return to this cafe of yours.'

'People tell me that I'm going to Shaded Oaks real soon. Everyone tells me that.'

'You know, I heard a dog over in that direction there.'

He followed my pointing finger. 'My dog?'

'A dog.'

Then Dogman shoved past me and lumbered out of the alleyway and into the dense fog.

'Good luck,' I whispered, then carried on my way to the shoreline.

The city was awfully quiet for a coastal town. There wasn't enough light to see the waters clearly, but I could hear them, and I thought I might've seen white foam crashing upon the shore.

It smelt like dead fish and rotted kelp. The night felt calm enough. I couldn't understand the hype or why people kept whispering to me about Senturion. Even the sections I'd been told to stay out of seemed, to me, nothing more than a quiet beach. A quiet beach with a quiet pink hotel up ahead. One with a nice ocean view that I'd be a fool not to check in for the night.

What with the neon green sign telling me they had vacancies and even more that smoking was allowed.

CHAPTER 16

A large flathead man sat at the receptionist's counter listening to an old turn dial radio. He had his thick hands wrapped around it, like he couldn't decide whether to hug it or crush it to pieces.

I walked into the room across the yellow floors to the desk. The man turned the volume down, focusing on the radio and not looking at me. I tapped a little bell resting on top of the counter.

Flathead glanced up at me, mumbling to himself, and pulled out a dead cigar from under his desk. He lit the black end of it with a match and said, 'What?'

'You have a room?'

The man kept looking at the radio, listening to the voices speaking through it as the cigar filled the room with smoke.

'Ehh.'

'We got a tourist bag that needs to be claimed,' said the radio. 'See if you can get the squirrel up here to tinker some glasses...'

The man caught sight of me peering over the counter at the radio. He turned it down even lower. 'You've seen the place, it ain't so full of tourists. The beach is covered in jagged rocks, and the water looks like an old sewage dump. You sure you don't want to stay further up north?'

'You got a room or what?'

Flathead rolled his eyes and went under the counter, throwing a drawer open and shuffling through a bunch of keys. He slapped one on the table with a plastic keyring tag.

'Seventy-five for a night.'

I laughed. 'Seventy-five.'

'Where was it I saw that?' said the radio. 'Two balls in the park and thirteen windows on the door. You grasping what I'm saying?'

Raising his eyebrows into his flat head, he grew interested in the radio's chatter and turned the volume a touch higher.

'Seventy-five?' I said.

'Give me sixty. Or get bent!'

I gave him my credit piece. He tapped it real fast and then tossed it to me without looking up from his radio.

'Now leave,' he said.

I tapped my fingers on the counter, watching him.

'It's a big bag,' said the radio. 'We're talking loaded with tickets and what have you. You might need an ox to plow the field but...'

He shot a mean glance at me. 'Can I help you, bud?'

'What radio station is this?'

'You have your room. Why don't you go check it out?'

I lingered at his desk.

'You know how much those things cost these days?' said the radio. 'I've already seen the Hound over there sniffing the bag. Someone ought to wake up the squirrel and tell him to get his wiry ass...'

Calmly, Flathead lowered the volume and put the cigar in his teeth. He slowly rolled his chair back, reaching into an open door behind himself, dragging out a thick led pipe. His tiny eyes scanned me over as he stood to his feet.

'How about I walk you to your room,' he said. 'That way, the two of us can take a gander at your sink pipe to make sure it's not leaking, and nobody has any tumbles on the slick floors tonight? What do you say?'

The voices paused over the radio. There was a static hum like rain that filled the void. Rushing to his radio, he jiggled the dials until he cleared the white noise.

'There's a ghost on the line,' said the radio. 'Everything's happening too quick. Keep it low and don't go flashing anything fancy now.'

Opening another drawer, he lugged out a type of microphone and then began to mumble into it. 'The horse isn't nibbling, is he?' he said. 'We've cranked several syringes, and if I'm not mistaken, hasn't a black carrot or two have landed in the vicinity?'

Then he pushed the microphone away in disgust.

'You care to back those words in gold...' said the radio.

Snarling at me as he turned, he lifted the pipe from his side again. 'Aren't you busy checking out that room of yours?'

I picked up my key from the counter and rubbed the plastic tag with my thumb. 'Breakfast is when?'

He curled his fist tighter about the pipe. 'We don't serve breakfast.'

I gave a faint smile and then a face of disgust as I moved away and to the stairs. When I paced the second-story walkway, facing the beach, I caught a glimpse of two flashlights moving up and down along the beach.

I couldn't make out the figures holding the lights–it was too murky from the fog, but I could tell by their pace that they were in a hurry. The two figures stopped near the water, shining their lights at the jagged rocks piercing above the foaming surf, then clicked them off and simply vanished.

Seeing nothing more, I unlocked my room and sat on a small chair near the window. Then, a moment later, another three lights appeared and walked the same trail as the others, stopping at the ocean, scanning the black waters. And then, after a fruitless search, the lights rushed off the beach, and out of sight.

I leaned into my seat, cut on a seashell lamp, and pat my jacket for my cigarette pack.

Waking from a drowsy nap, I decided the best thing to do now that this noose was already fastened at my neck was to trek out of the crummy motel and start to hammer away before the executioner cranked the platform out from under my feet.

The main lobby was empty. No one sat at the receptionist desk or lingered outside for a cigarette break. Flathead had left with no trace of where he'd gone. I walked across the carpeted floor, avoiding the wooden boards that wanted to creak, and reached the receptionist's counter. Leaning over the edge, I saw the radio and slithered my hand down towards it to switch on the dial.

'Wasn't our boys. Everyone's paid their dues tonight. We'll chat with our neighbors in the morning. But for now, I'm hoping the squirrel can find the bride before we're cut...'

The lobby door started to open. I turned off the radio and leaned my elbow up on the counter, keeping both hands clear in sight.

It was Flathead, carrying a flashlight at his side and wiping grains of sand off his legs. He snarled at me as he approached the desk. When he sat himself down, he forgot to regard me and went about his business.

'Any places to get a drink at this time of night?'

Raising an eyebrow, he glanced at me. 'I'm sorry, but who are you?'

'Hotel guest.'

'No-no-no, I said, who are you?'

'A tourist.'

'What kind of tourist?'

'Seeing the lights.'

'What are you doing here?'

'Looking for a place to drink.'

He closed his mouth and growled in his throat. Then he closed his eyes and reopened them slowly.

'You picked a bad night to go out.'

I spied over the desk at his radio a moment, eyeing the needle and taking note of its frequency, and then pushed off the counter.

'I guess there's always something open in town. I'll find it myself.'

His attention lay elsewhere as he murmured to himself, quite unaware of my presence anymore. I moved away from the counter and exited the hotel lobby.

CHAPTER 17

A blanket of fog greeted me outside the hotel while a blot of shaded lights gleamed within the humble town ahead. I hurried across the street and shirked down a tight alleyway. A pack of rodents scattered as I stepped through the passage. They weren't the fearless kind, but they weren't the small ones either.

My feet brought me onto the main strip and showed me the various shops, now vacant with barred windows or metal curtains, to keep them safe throughout the night. Marching alone on the strip had me wondering if this were a big joke. If, somehow, I'd died and been sent to a ghost town where I'm expected to wander for all eternity.

But the thought was tepid and passed out of my head once I rounded the corner of another alleyway. Cramped shops were wedged inside the narrow space, with one red neon sign painting the brick walls and cobble path underfoot.

The humming sign pointed an arrow downward at a dugout set of stairs; leading deeper into a violet-lit venue. There were beads hanging in the stairwell, like a veil you had to pass through before reaching your unholy bride.

I looked back up at the neon sign. *Drinks. Girls. Bets.*

Leaning aside, I gazed at another staircase bathed in fluorescent lights that led down to a separate shop. I glanced in at the faded sign on the wall above the staircase: *Pawn Broker.*

I scratched my chin, feeling the stubble that needed to be shaved, and then eyed both stairs for a second. Pawn broker or the usual dens I frequent?

The fluorescent lights were buzzing as loud as the neon signs. Change is the keyword here. In a sense taking this case was already the change in motion. That's what some psychobabble prick might tell me. That I've started the journey, and now I'm married to that decision.

So, instead of visiting the nightclub first, I decided to check out the pawnshop. Inside the dug-out basement sat a middle-aged man behind a protective glass window; with the most expensive items behind him and presumably a sawed-off shotgun underneath his counter.

The man wore a pair of black spectacles held by a loose chain at the back of his neck. His eyes were splotched with red and yellow patches, likely due to a surgical procedure or a chemical in the wrong doctor's office.

'Tourist?'

I pointed a finger at him. 'You're sharp.'

'Who are you?'

'Vincent.'

'No, I mean *who* are you?' The obvious emphasis on who.

'A tourist.'

He leaned back from the glass window and fixed his brown vest and then raked at his white hair with a thin black comb.

'You're in the wrong neighborhood. The lights don't shine so brightly down here. Let me call you a cab. I know a lady, been friends for years, you can trust her.'

'No thanks.'

His face turned dark.

I glanced up into his glass enclosure and scanned the necklaces dangling from hooks behind him. After a nice look, I turned my back to him and went into the shop, searching the cluttered shelves for a radio. There was a bin full of them, all different shapes and sizes.

Then I heard a door click in the room and next a solid lock bolting the outside door. Footsteps crept through the tiled floors until they reached me. The man watched me with his spotted eyes through his black-rimmed specs.

'What are you looking for? Guns?'

I took my hands off the bin filled with radios and opened my jacket enough to let him see my holster.

He eyed it. 'I don't sell any drugs,' he said. 'So if that's what you're after, maybe have a look elsewhere.'

I went back to the bin and picked up one of the radios. It didn't have any dials on it, just flat buttons along the sides that pointed left or right.

'How much for the radio?'

The man drew in a sharp breath and let it back out. He took the radio from my hands and nudged me to the side. He started to dig in the bin until he pulled out a thick portable radio.

'What clan are you in?' he said, turning towards me. 'I've heard about foreign runners before. Never this close, though.'

I shook my head. 'No clan.'

He reached out, handing me the radio.

It had silver knobs on it, similar to the one I saw back at the hotel.

'You can only get preset frequencies with the flat buttoned radios,' he said. 'If you want a specific frequency to tune into, you'll have to scroll yourself with these dials.'

I turned the circular dial. A static whine came out of the speaker.

'I won't ask what you're scanning for, but I can imagine you already know.'

I clicked the radio off.

'Thirty-seven,' he said.

'Twenty?'

He licked his lip and lowered his head, still eyeing me. 'Thirty-five.'

'Twenty?'

'You want the only dial radio in town or not? Thirty-three. Final offer.'

'Twenty?'

The man laughed as if this were a game for him. 'I break even at thirty.'

'Twenty-five?'

He squinted at me for a moment and then turned to one of the shelves near us. He picked up an electric watch, flicking it in the air near his head.

'Thirty, and I'll throw in this one.'

I took the watch from him and looked it over. 'I don't need a watch.'

The man snatched it back. 'Fine. Give me twenty-nine.'

I nodded. 'All right.'

He rolled his eyes. 'Twenty-nine.'

●   ●   ●   ●   ●

I left the shop with my new hand radio tucked into my jacket and decided to stop in at the joint next door. I went down under the neon sign, through the hanging beads, and tapped on a black door at the end. There was a violet light shining over it, attracting all sorts of insects to the place.

The door sliced open a crack. A dark figure stood behind it.

'You selling any strong drinks in there?'

The door shut, and several bolts rattled on the other end. Then it opened fully to a dim room clouded in smoke.

I stepped inside.

The bouncer stopped me with his arm before going any further. He pat my side, lifted out my gun, dropped the magazine, loaded a bullet from the barrel, and then handed it back to me.

'Tourist?'

I put the gun away and fixed my jacket. 'In a way.'

He cocked his shaved head at the bar.

I went over and sat on one of the stools.

The barman was leaning against the back mirror with his arms crossed and his eyes up on a pornographic film playing on the opposite wall. He had a strong pair of shoulders, a thick set of arms, and a long ponytail covering the back of his neck.

I glanced at the film playing on the wall behind me. There were two women rolling around on a naked bed. They must've been having a good time with all their moans and screams of yeses and ohs.

I turned back to the barman. 'You have a whiskey?'

He didn't take his eyes from the film as he spoke to me.

'We got a Bortzmin.'

'Put it on the rocks.'

The barman uncrossed his arms and went to the liquor and poured me a glass. He dropped it on the bar and then went back to his corner. The girls were moaning even more now.

I turned on my stool, rubbing the top of my glass as I glanced around the venue. There was a dolled-up lady at the bar sitting three stools down. She caught eyes with me, although her eyes were moving in her head slowly drifting, and her arm spazzed out from her side without her own consent.

I went back to my drink and felt her moving closer. I could see the porno in the bar's backdrop mirror–the girls were having fun with their toys. I then felt a hand touch my upper arm softly.

'Eighty'll get you whatever you want,' she whispered.

The barman shifted, glancing at her, then me, and then back to his film.

'If only you knew what I wanted,' I said.

The girls were wailing in passion behind us.

'I have a friend if that's what you're after?' she said. 'She could join us?'

I gave a dark laugh.

She did her best to look at me, but her eyes kept moving in her head, and her arm kept twitching at her side.

'One too many jabs of the needle, sweetheart?' I said.

Her arm and head jerked aside.

I turned even more, trying to put my back towards her.

Her hand found its way onto my lap, reaching for the most tender part of me. 'Please,' she said. 'Sixty is fine. I have a kid back home with a fever.'

I took a sip of my drink. 'Is that what you tell everyone?'

She opened her mouth as if she were out of breath.

'I'm not knocking you if that's how you make a living. Just know that story isn't gonna work on me.'

Her hand was now moving off my leg.

'It wasn't my choice to have her,' she said, with a touch of acid. 'He took me when I was drunk. Without my permission!'

The barman squinted his eyes as he watched the film with even more interest. I caught another glimpse of the ladies in the mirror. Still twisting and moaning.

'What's your name?' I said.

She seemed as if she wasn't going to answer at first. I raised an eyebrow at her.

'Ju,' she said.

'And were you born on Senturion?'

She hesitated, lost in the abrupt change of conversation.

'Yes? Why else would I be here?'

I pulled the last cigarette from my jacket and lit it. 'You know this place pretty well then?'

She put her hand back on my lap. 'Why, what do you want?'

'Not sure, really, but I'd be interested in a chat.'

She reached closer, gracing my erection with the tip of her fingers.

'I'll tell you whatever you want.'

I let some smoke fall out of my nose, drained my glass, and slapped it down onto the bar. 'You want to bounce then?'

She twitched as she linked arms with me. 'Lead the way.'

The barman made notice of us, uncrossing his arms. 'Where are you staying at, chief?'

'On the shore. Nice pink hotel. I've forgotten the name, but it's full of roaches and cigarette butts.'

He spied over my shoulder and nodded to someone else.

The bouncer clamped his large hand on the back of my neck and spoke in a deep baritone voice. 'You'd better leave the man a good tip. Finder's fee, you know.'

I breathed a laugh, taking out my credit piece. I tapped it a few times and added an extra heap of credits for the barman.

'Happy?'

The bouncer let go of my shoulder. Ju continued to twitch as we walked over to the door. The bouncer handed me my bullets then opened the door, bathing us in a violet light.

As soon as our feet were out the door, it slammed loud behind us.

I jumped a quiver.

She pat my arm softly. 'Ready?'

●   ●   ●   ●   ●

Flathead was asleep at the receptionist's counter when we came back. His eyes slit open as we passed by him, and he grumbled something incoherent.

I lead her to my room, turned on the seashell lights, and pushed the covers back to give her a place to sit. She started to remove the straps from her black dress.

I went to the side of the bed, grabbing an ashtray from the nightstand.

Her arm twitched as she tried to fix her straight black hair over her shoulders. She then scooted to give me some room to join her on the bed, but I'd gone to the other side to sit on the chair.

She sat upon her knees atop the bed, her nipples pointing in the cold air, as she waited for me. She then pulled her dress out from under her legs, sitting almost bare save for her orange lace underwear.

Putting a cigar in my teeth, I flicked my lighter on, bringing the flame to life.

'You don't have to take that off,' I said.

I couldn't tell if she shook her head or shuddered. I drew the flame higher up to the end of my cigar, letting it engulf the brown leaves until they were evenly red. She sat quietly at the edge of the bed, her hands gentle on her lap.

I clicked my lighter shut.

'Senturion... Nice place?'

She blinked a rapid eyelid flutter. 'Yes.'

'Doesn't seem that way. Not really.'

She shivered, and her arm jerked out at her side.

I bit down on my cigar, put the lighter away, and dragged out the radio from my jacket. It was a rectangular box with one crosshatch speaker in the center. I clicked the circular dial near the top with my thumb and flipped through the frequencies, back and forth.

'What stations do you like?' I said.

'Anything is fine.'

'Yeah, but if you wanted to find out more about this town, listen in to what others are saying. Which would you choose?'

She pinned her bottom lip in her teeth.

'I don't know.'

I kept scrolling the dial, whirling through the static, and then stopped near the frequency I'd noted in the lobby earlier. It was blank. Only white static poured out from the speaker.

'You're from Ceph?'

I nodded.

'Do you have any more of those cigarettes?'

I shook my head. 'Fresh out.'

She gave a small laugh. 'That's too bad.'

I switched off the radio. 'Why is that?'

She tried to focus on me with her eyes drifting in her sockets. 'They're the best. Everyone loves them, but no one can sell them here. Not with all the restrictions in place.'

I took another cigar from my jacket and handed it towards her.

'I don't like cigars.'

I put it away.

'There was an expat who let me try one, two years ago? He said he always fills his bags full of cigarette packs when he visits home. He even gave me an extras stick before he kicked me out of his room.'

The light was growing pink outside the window. The sun would be up soon.

'So what are these restrictions about?'

She moved her hair back over her ear as she spoke. 'It's all about money. They don't appreciate foreign products on either planet. If we take in too many imports, we'll lose our circulating cash.'

'That's not how it works,' I said.

'Then I don't know.'

I dropped some ash in the tray that sat on my lap. 'How much is a pack of smokes up here?'

She blinked a rapid flutter and twitched her arm.

'Ten credits?'

I laughed. 'That's blatant robbery. They want to control the market; that's what they're really after. A pack on Ceph is no more than four credits, not even the premium brands.'

'They taste better too.'

I bobbed my head. 'They sell them on other planets just as cheap. Maybe a credit or so more. Naizerine doughs them out for six credits, three for the shitty brands.'

She tried to keep her hands in her lap, but they kept moving.

I sighed with a billow of smoke. 'How long have you lived in this area?'

She blinked fast again. 'Eleven - no - twelve years?'

The lights outside were turning blue and grey.

'You ever hear anything about a diplomat doing herself in?'

She opened her mouth a little and left it like that.

'Hanging from the rafters of her home?'

Her cheeks squinted underneath her eyes as they wandered in her skull. 'Miss Kage,' she whispered.

'Is that her name?'

She leaned further on the edge, trying to keep her voice down as she spoke. 'That's her last name. First name was Tsuki. I knew of her. I even touched her jacket at one of the rallies.'

I shifted in the inflexible metal chair. 'Rally for what?'

'For women's rights.'

'You were there?'

'I loved her,' she said. 'So many of us loved her. She spoke her mind and...'

I waved my fingers a bit, asking her to continue.

She shook her head. 'I should go.'

I took the cigar out of my lips and kept it in-between my fingers. 'I won't harm you.'

'It's getting light out.'

'You guys are really spooked up here?'

She started to lift her dress from the floor, placing it on the bed beside her legs. She paused, touching the straps with a sigh.

'I have a daughter to think about.'

I moved to the edge of my chair. 'She'll be fine. Don't worry about her.'

She crumpled her dress with both hands. 'Miss Kage didn't kill herself,' she whispered. 'I know she didn't.'

The lights were burning pink along the curtains, and the waves were crashing heavily on the shore.

'Does it have to do with the Black Death?'

Her eyes caught mine a second.

'Ju?'

'No,' she said, lowering her head.

'The local gangs?'

'I doubt it.'

'The government?'

She didn't respond.

The lights were getting brighter and starting to hurt my eyes. I stood up, looked out the window, and down at the beach. There were lumps of seaweed thrown onto the shore alongside gnarled sticks and giant rusted pipelines running into the ocean.

I set my cigar in the ashtray and pivoted towards her. 'You think Miss Kage found something important? Something your government might not like?'

She didn't answer as she held her dress limp in her hands.

'Do you know what Black Death is?'

Her lips were sealed.

This is useless, I thought. *You're not getting anywhere this way.*

Feeling tired, I closed the curtains, walked around the side of the bed, and sat at the back of it, resting my head on the filthy walls. She turned around to look at me for a few seconds, then put her dress down and crawled up to my side.

You're getting cheap, Vince, I thought. *To think you're going to pry apart a giant situation like this with some tough words and a tipsy head?*

I slid down the bed and let my head fall onto one of the coarse pillows. This wasn't going anywhere. And I hadn't much experience with any sort of time zone lag, but I felt unbearably tired at that moment.

Lifting my credit piece, I transferred her more than she'd asked for and let my eyes close down.

'You can get back to your daughter if you want,' I said.

She moved closer towards me, lowering her head on my chest, and reached her arm up near my shoulder to keep hold of me.

My eyes had grown too heavy to keep open any longer, and my mind was spinning on the same stupid loop that I couldn't get any sort of break from. So I shut my eyes and felt everything fade away.

CHAPTER 18

There was someone talking in my room as I awoke. I leaned up against the bed's headrest and pulled my gun out of its holster, aiming it straight ahead. The room was dark. The curtains were drawn, and my lady friend had gone.

'…another dead body found last night. Right now, the police are keeping things tight, making sure no one finds out about it. We'll take a break here and listen to a record from The Metal Water Trio as we get more information on the murder…'

A song began to play in my room. There was an invisible drummer tapping his muted cymbal as a raspy saxophone echoed off the walls. I turned on the lamp near my bed and saw the radio on the chair, left switched on, playing music.

I knew I'd turned it off last night. There was only static coming from it then.

I threw my bare feet out over the bed and paused, remembering that I'd left my shoes on last night, socks too. She must've removed them for me.

The floor was cold against my naked feet as I stood. I picked my neatly folded socks, worked them over my ankles, and dragged myself into the bathroom. I turned on the hot water to splash my face. When I looked up, I saw myself in the mirror and thought, *I have to shave. Before this turns into something else.*

I opened the mirror, took out a thin razor, and tore it from its plastic sheath. The water was beginning to steam in the basin. I left the blade under the hot vapor for a moment and then dragged it across my jawline. My stubble didn't care to leave my face, but with enough force and hot water, they eventually vacated the premise.

I saw a dirty towel lying on the floor and thought better of it. I cut off the water and went outside, wiping my face clean with my shirt and jacket hanging on the door handle. The song was drawing to a close when I picked up my shoes from the ground.

'That one goes out to the poor soul floating along the coast last night, whoever he or she was. We're still trying to find out more information about this case to make sure you the people know what's going on in your own homes...'

I threw my shoes over my feet and then slipped my jacket up on my shoulders. I stretched my neck to the side, feeling all the tension and bad sleep wound up in my tight muscles.

'The longest-running underground station, yet to be caught, yet to be ratted out, that's right you've found us. Now, try and catch us if you can.'

A record started to play as his words faded.

I picked up the radio, turned off the volume, and then went to the door and patted my jacket. Everything was in there. She hadn't taken a dime. Nice girl.

I put the radio inside my pocket and stepped out into the hall. There was no point in locking the door, so I continued on down into the lobby and stopped at the receptionist's desk, waiting for Flathead to come by.

After a while, I heard someone stumble in from the back of the lobby. I turned my head to the side, watching a small stout man with a thick mustache, walk towards the desk. He was much smaller than me, but a full body wider than myself. He looked mad as if it were a permanent fixture upon his face, and every second or two, he'd tug at his mustache.

The guy went behind the counter, pulled out a stepladder, and climbed eye level to me. He twisted his mustache ends, still angry but now staring me down.

'Yes?'

I then reached into my jacket, taking hold of my room key, and took it out, holding it up in the air.

'Can you put me down for another night?'

The guy glanced up at the key, squinting one eye. 'That'll be fifty.'

'Do I get clean towels?'

He hissed with a mean growl and then brought up a bill for me to pay.

'Asshole,' he said.

I tapped my credit piece inside my jacket and then walked out of the lobby. There were cars passing through the street but nothing to cause a jam. The air was filled with salt and the smell of fish spending too much time out of water.

I continued walking along the cracked sidewalk, gazing at the jagged ocean to my side where a pack of seagulls gathered to squawk up and down as if they'd found a giant meal to peck from.

Up ahead of me lay a long boardwalk that reached out into the sea. An event was happening atop the wooden dock, complete with a ferris wheel near the middle, a carousel at the entrance, and a mass of tents spread throughout. I took a cigar from my jacket, put in my teeth, and gave it a light.

There were no clowns along the boardwalk. Not too many kids either.

I pushed by the entrance and passed a squeaking carousel, where a man leaned against the guardrails and trying to wave me down.

'Got a basic spin here,' he said as I walked by. 'A light spin. Nothing big like the ferris wheel.'

I lingered a second longer.

The man looked over his shoulder and slid along the guardrails, edging closer to me. His eyes were red with dark bags underneath them.

'What are you looking to score?' he whispered.

I took the cigar out of my teeth and looked at the orange end hidden under a stack of grey.

'I'd kill for a pack of Silver Mist right now.'

The man rubbed his hands together and then picked a wide gap in his front teeth with his thumbnail.

'I haven't heard of that strand,' he said. 'You get it on Kaivus?'

'It's a cigarette brand from Ceph.'

The man laughed real quick. 'Oh, right, that's right.'

'Can you help me out?'

'You'd think those things were illegal the way they act about them.' He leaned off the guardrail and tapped the bar with the flat of his hand. 'There's a new fellow, from Ceph as well, intent on selling them to the public.'

He dropped his lips in the corner of his mouth, not like he was sad, but more of a way of thinking. He looked down the boardwalk towards the ocean.

'We set him up a tent over there. But he hasn't shown yet.' He pinched the skin near his throat and began tugging at it. 'I wonder what happened to that cowboy.'

I felt my cigar beginning to char, so I chucked it into the sea, over the boardwalk, and cocked my head to the side.

'Did you say Cowboy?'

'Yup,' he said. 'Decked in a glittery hat and wearing a pair of golden spurs.'

'He hasn't arrived yet?'

'Nope.'

'Has he sold his cigarettes before?'

'He's passed them out,' he said. 'But if I'm correct, then this is the first tent he's rented on the boardwalk.'

'Interesting.'

He rubbed his hands in his coat pockets. 'You want to take a ride?' Then he grew distracted, fixing his eyes at the street. 'Is that your car?'

I glanced over my shoulder at a black sedan waiting near the entrance. There was someone in it, smoking, with a friend in the passenger side.

'No,' I said. 'Do you normally have such nice cars visiting here?'

The man flicked the tip of his nose with his thumb like he had a dull scratch. His eyes were on the car as he spoke.

'Sometimes, but not so often. The big guys don't usually come to the boardwalk. It's small-time vendors here. Who knows, maybe they're lost?'

I turned my back even more to the car, slipping my hand into my jacket's outer pocket. 'You happen to know anything about radios? I've got ten credits ready to transfer if you do.'

The man licked the gap in his teeth. 'Fifteen.'

I tapped the credit piece in my jacket. 'Done.'

He looked at the car again as he leaned up against the railing.

'All right. Shoot.'

'There's an underground station here. You know anything about it?'

He shrugged with a nasal laugh. 'Shit. I thought you were going to ask me something real.'

'Go on.'

He eyed the sedan and then glanced at the palm of his hand. 'Everyone knows that station,' he said. 'No one knows where it is or who runs it, but we all tune in. How else are we going to get the real news on this place?'

'What do you mean?'

He made a clicking noise with his tongue. 'Come on. Don't be stupid. You think this is a nice place to live? That the government's going to keep us in the loop or something?'

I heard a car engine starting near the entrance. I glanced over my shoulder, catching the black sedan's tail lights whipping out sight.

The man licked his teeth as he watched the car leave.

'I guess your friend had to go.'

I nodded at him. 'I'll catch up with them later.'

The man hit the guardrail with his wrist a couple of times. 'I'm surprised you found their station. How long have you been here?'

'Landed last night.'

'They keep changing frequencies every time they get blocked. But I guess if you have enough time to scan, you can find it.'

There were people browsing along the boardwalk, all dressed in suits, but not the clean business kind.

'So this underground station - do they talk in code?'

The man was now watching the suited men perusing the boardwalk up ahead. He straightened his posture a bit and kept his eyes on them.

'Not like the other channels.'

One of the suited men stopped by a vendor's stall, picking something up from it and showing it to the others behind him.

'What other channels?'

'Private ones,' said the man. 'Used to communicate between different groups. You get it?'

I nodded. 'Yeah.'

The man clicked his tongue off his teeth again. 'Listen, you gonna buy anything or what? I can't be chatting without closing any deals.'

'I'm hunting the Black Death if you're selling?'

'Woah,' he said. 'Woah. That's a death sentence, you know?'

'Can you point me in the right direction then?'

He shook his head. 'No,' he said. 'I told you I have a basic spin here. Shit.'

'Thanks anyway.' And I started to walk away.

'Yeah. You tell your friends if they're looking for anything to come find me.'

My attention was drawing towards the small knit group of suited men. They seemed to know every stall owner by name. I kept acting interested as I moved closer without catching their eye. My back was to the group while I listen in on their conversation. Something about a new package arriving at their warehouse later on. If only they'd give me a specific location.

Then they all went quiet.

I turned enough to see their faces. The leader was a thin man who was squinting his eye towards the entrance. A vein crept along the side of his head while the tough guys behind him started to laugh.

'I guess he's looking for a fix,' said one of the tough guys.

'Shut up,' said the thin man. 'And get him out here. It's mid-day, for Christ's sake!'

I turned my sights to where they were looking. I saw a man hobbling along the boardwalk, shaking his elbows like he was always losing his balance. There was something familiar about the guy.

The thin man sighed. 'Somebody get on the radio now and do something about him.'

'Yes, sir.'

I knew the man. His eyes were familiar. They kept moving in their sockets, back and forth, like they couldn't sit still. Then it hit me–it was the same man I'd met outside the train station; Dogman.

One of the tough guys raced to Dogman, pinching the back of his neck and shoving him along the boardwalk. Another guy jumped inside a small vendor's tent, dragging a transmitter out his jacket, and began to speak into it. The first guy brought Dogman into the stall, where the second guy was speaking into the radio.

That's what you get with these kind of places. Junkies who've taken too many drags, killing their system and showing everyone the effects. It's never difficult to find a narc's den. There's always someone him leading you right to the source.

The thin-suited man looked near the entranceway and then over his shoulder as the tough guys kept Dogman inside the tent, radioing to their fellow men to get rid of him, I assume.

I started to walk back towards the entrance, passing by the carousel, when a car pulled up near the curb and dropped two big men out onto the boardwalk. The cronies walked smoothly up to the tent, disappearing for twenty seconds, then both came back out, lugging Dogman by the armpits out to the car and tossing him into the backseat.

I heard him saying something about a dog again that he ran away from his house.

Then the car sped off into the town. I stood outside listening to the waves crash and the seagulls yap.

CHAPTER 19

I made a call to Oren, the cowboy I'd met on the ship, but found my details blocked from making any connection. *Strange,* I thought. *But then most people don't say what they mean.*

Whether I cared to or not, I found myself watching the ocean and a line of troller boats heading towards an unseen port further down the shore. I grinned to myself, happy to have another lead, and then wondering why I hadn't thought to search out the trollers earlier?

The skies remained grey above me while the winds blew new grains of sand onto the asphalt around my feet. The walk was lonely. There were two cars that passed by in a slow trickle, but other than that, it was just me and the seagulls.

I decided to turn on the radio in my pocket and listened to some jazz and information the government didn't want its citizens to hear.

'That's right, we're only a week away from the lights going off up above us,' said the host. 'Am I the only local who's so damn tired of this shit? I hope to god I'm not. I mean, who cares anymore? Honestly, when we've got tourists bobbing in our surf, face-down in the waters, do these things really matter anymore?'

So far, so good, I thought. *Now, if you could so kindly tell me where you're located so, we could have a nice chat? A proper interview, maybe?*

'Poor guy wasn't alone,' said the host. 'He had his wife up here with him. We found that bit out a few minutes ago. The police don't want you to know that, though. But we do.'

Then the clouds broke apart overhead. Random spots opened, revealing an orange sky and an outline of pink clouds.

'Apparently, his wife is on the run. The authorities can't seem to find her. She was last spotted leaving their hotel, right before her husband's body was found. I personally hope she's with one of our listeners out there. And that you're keeping her safe, whoever you might be. Give her a warm cup of tea for me and make sure you have a dry shoulder for her to cry on.

'And lady, if you're listening - know you're not alone. I've got my team looking for you. We'll take care of you. Don't you worry about a thing. We'll get you back to Ceph or wherever you came from, without the faintest inkling from any sort of authority. This may be a bad memory fermenting right now, but know that-'

The radio turned into static. I waited for some time as I walked, letting the static roll, hoping that it might come back. My hopes were misguided, though, as the station never returned. Eventually, I killed the sound and came to the same conclusion various other listeners most likely drew to; that their frequency had been jammed.

The skies were growing purple as the clouds retained a splash of red on their underbellies. A car drove by, coasting down the road, and then stopped a good fifteen meters ahead of me.

I put my head down and kept walking, letting the smoke from my cigar drift out behind me.

The car put its gears into reverse and glided backwards, engine whining all the way towards me. It stopped, and I kept walking. The window rolled down as the vehicle matched alongside me.

'It's not safe out here at night,' said a woman's voice.

I shrugged and continued on.

'You're not from here.'

'That's true.'

'Where are you going? Let me give you a ride.'

I paused, taking my cigar out of my teeth, and stepped closer to her vehicle.

She hit the brakes and measured me over.

Her hair was red. Who knows if it's natural or not, but it complimented her black lips and her bright green eyes. She leaned a little more towards the window, stretching her tight dress along her curves.

'Where are you headed?' she said.

I stepped closer, putting my hand on the roof of her car, drawing nearer to the window. I took my time looking her over, all the way down to the tips of her stockings.

'The better question is, where are you heading?'

She didn't smile, and she didn't frown, but her eyes were set so confidently in themselves. She looked up at me with those emerald greens and almost raised a well-poised eyebrow, but she didn't. She didn't have to. Her aura said everything for her.

'I recently found out that I own a house right down this road,' she said. 'It was my late husband's. Before he passed.'

She started to drag her forefinger along the curve of the steering wheel—subconsciously, I presumed.

'Now I know where his mistress lived all this time.' She straightened her lips and took a breath through her nose. 'I thought about letting her stay, but then I realized that I don't have to be polite any longer. If he forgot to add that in his will then - fair game.'

The lights were growing dimmer the longer I stood there. The clouds were disappearing, and the stars were beginning to take form.

'Anyway, I thought to stop when I passed by you, as no one walks these streets at night, especially not tourists.'

'That's nice of you.'

She pursed her lips and then peered out her front windshield. 'Are you going to Nerium Island? If so, I can give you a ride. That's where I'm headed.'

Leveling my gaze down the road, I focused on a small boat port in the distance. I wanted a cigarette. Not just any ole kind, either. Then, after a brief thought, I opened the passenger's side door and flopped inside the car.

'You see that port up there?'

She followed my finger then turned her eyes back at me with repulsion. 'You're not going there?'

I nodded. 'That's where I'm headed.'

'You don't want to go there. It's full of common workers. What are you after, a tour?'

I closed the door shut, and the lights went out above us.

'Yeah. That's exactly what I'm after.'

She sat quietly for a time and then lifted a small handbag from her side. She opened the bag and pulled out a metal case filled with rustic brown cigarettes. Slipping one out, she put it between her black lips and then held it towards me.

'I'm not a fan of Senturion smokes.'

'They're not.'

My suspicion rose higher, but I still took one, ready to affirm my bias that they were terrible.

'Where'd you get them then?'

'Aoldii,' she said.

'Aoldii?' I snorted. 'That's a pretty long way off.'

She clicked a black lighter under her cigarette, then cranked down her window and let out a gentle plume of smoke from the corner of her mouth.

'I was there on holiday. I needed to get away for a while. Clear my head before I came back to deal with everything.'

Deal with everything. Meaning deal with the generous heap of assets she'd inherited from her late husband? Tough life.

I lit my cigarette as well.

'Fair enough,' I said.

After stowing her lighter away, she pulled her tight dress down an inch more before returning her hand to the gear. Then, without any pause, she shifted into drive, taking us out of our stagnation.

'You won't find any tour guides at that port. If you want, I'll take you to a better one on the island. There are some private charters there you can hire.'

I inhaled on my cigarette. It was a mild one. Plenty of flavor, like a spiced rum, but it was missing the kick of my old cheap ones from Ceph.

'This isn't a good area to be in at night,' she continued. 'It's chocked full of gangs and drug addicts. I don't know if you've heard the news, but a tourist was found dead in this area late last night.'

'I heard.'

'And you still go about walking these parts at night?'

'Seemed fine to me.'

Sighing a cloud of smoke, she shook her head a little.

The lights were dim outside the port, and the moon was clipped to a sliver in the black skies above.

My mind wandered to Ju. I thought to give her a call or send a message to see if she'd meet me again this evening.

The car began to slow down as we approached. We halted a couple of meters away, the headlights cut off, and the engine died. The lady took a last drag of her cigarette and then dropped it outside her window.

I smoked mine down to the filter and then flicked it past the curb. It fell in a patch of dune grass, slowly fading from orange to grey.

'Well, here you are,' she said. Her eyes were fixed outside the windshield at a yellow light, hanging over the port's entrance. 'Having second thoughts?'

I clicked the door open, letting one foot hang outside. 'You know anywhere to get foreign smokes on this planet?'

She kept her eyes out the window, not answering. Then she looked down at her handbag, unsnapping it, and reached over a metal pack of cigarettes, handing them to me.

'Take them,' she said. 'I brought several boxes home.'

I took the cigarettes. 'You sure?'

She almost smiled. 'Take them. You won't find them sold anywhere else out here.'

I put them inside my jacket next to the portable radio.

She set her hand on the wheel, staring at the faint yellow light shining in the dark, with a curl in her lip.

'Are you going to be awhile in there?'

I slid out of the car and shut the door behind me, then leaned back through the window.

'Who knows?'

Taking out a new pack, she opened it and lit another cigarette.

'Do you have to go into the port?' she said, smoke touching at her face. 'This area is dangerous. Especially at night.'

'I'll keep that in mind.'

'Why don't I wait out here for you? In case they don't want to let you go or...'

I pat the car with the flat of my hand. 'No need to wait. I'm a big boy.'

She gave a small pitiful laugh.

'You've got things to do. Don't wait up for me.'

'I'm a widowed trophy,' she said. 'I never had things to do. And now I have even less.' She took a gentle puff of her light brown cigarette and let it out, just as soft. 'Don't I deserve a bit of excitement too? I'll wait outside and flash my lights when you return.'

I stood up, looking at the ship port. There were a few trollers pulling in from the dark waters with little green lights blinking off the ends of their ships.

'Fine, it's your choice,' I said as I moved away from her car.

It felt nice walking again. Listening to the grains of sand, crunching under my heels and tasting the nick of salt in the air.

When I reached the port's entrance, I stopped to take out my radio. I turned up the volume but only heard static from the underground station. I started to move the dial, listening for anyone talking, especially anyone out in those trollers.

Nothing returned to me other than a government talk radio station. Turning down the volume, I hesitated, grinding my front teeth in a quandary; then slipped it into my jacket beside my new pack of cigarettes.

The old wooden port creaked louder as the trollers approached the docks. I made out the glimmers of conversation while a group of people chatted to each other, their voices dull, muted, and echoing into faint whispers.

I snaked my way to the topmost platform, near a metal railing, where I watched the workers talk in a loose semi-circle. Two men were busy winding ropes, while another kicked his boot at a post, and a fourth shucked a hardened creature's shell with his knife.

'Takes five weeks time,' said the man, shucking. 'But you don't get the confirmation until they send you a stamp. The triangular one is a note that things are pending, and the square means they'll pick them up the next day.'

'Gaia be damned,' said a man, curling his rope. 'The next day?'

'I'm telling you what he told me.'

Spotting a rusted bench at my side, I crept to it, sat down, and continued to watch the group. A fog horn bellowed out in the dark waters, causing the men to freeze a second, then pick up their pace.

The man, shucking, plopped the creature back in the water and concealed his blade. 'I'll see you loons in the morning,' he said. 'I'm out.'

After him, the man kicking the post left, followed by the fellow wrapping his rope. Only one worker remained. And he spied after his group before he returned to his troller and dug something out from the boat. Hiding it in his shirt, the man broke into a jog, heading for the port's exit.

Lighting a fresh cigarette, I waited on the bench until he ambled upwards in my direction.

I coughed loudly when he stood before me.

The man snapped around, gazing in the dark, then caught focus of my cigarette. His face was puffy and splotched with dark patches, while his springy white hair peaked underneath his troller's cap.

'Who are you?' he whispered.

I flicked ash from my cigarette. 'Just a tourist.'

He didn't take his hand away from his shirt, where I saw him put the hidden item earlier.

'What do you want?'

'What's in your shirt?'

'Nothing.'

'Ah.'

'Tourists aren't allowed in here,' he said. 'You'd better scram and do it fast.'

'But I can't, you see?'

'And why is that?'

I shrugged. 'I've got an obsession for boats,' I said. 'Trollers. Fishing boats. Military vessels. Any and everything that sits on the water. People tell me I'm neurotic, but when we live in a world full of addictions and consumerist propaganda, then who are they to talk?'

The man cracked his neck and moved his feet back an inch. 'You've got the wrong port,' he said. 'There's a better place on down the road. Nerium Island. Where the rich folks go.'

The docks continued to whine up against the wooden post as a second fleet of trollers approached the docks.

I jutted my chin towards his boat over the railing.

'Is that your troller?'

'What of it?'

'Have you been working on it for a long time?'

He relaxed his hand at his side. 'Eight seasons now.'

'I bet you've dug up some interesting things in that time. Maybe some gold. Heaps of trash. And possibly floating bodies tangled in fishing nets?'

He pushed his hand behind his back, further concealing whatever he was holding.

'What kind of talk are we having here?'

I put my hand inside my jacket and pulled out my credit piece. Tapping it, I popped a holographic number for him to see.

He gazed at the glowing number, his eyes deep in concentration like he didn't fully understand what was going on. Then his eyebrows raised.

'Make that zero a five.'

I tapped the piece, adding five credits, still showing it to him.

'Add another, and I'll keep it quiet.'

I bobbed my head, tapping it again.

He nodded.

And I transferred the credits.

'So?'

He looked over my shoulder and then back over his. 'Yeah, I've found a body before. A couple years back.'

I moved a little to the side. 'Anything recent?'

'No. But my nephew found one not too long ago.'

'Yeah?'

'Yeah.'

'Did your nephew know who he or she was?'

The man cleared his throat. 'Not personally.'

'But he recognized them?'

'Nah, he didn't know him,' he said, scratching the back of his head underneath his cap. 'I have my guesses about the guy. But I don't really know who he was, and neither did my nephew.'

'I assume your nephew got a nice reward for finding this fella?'

'Not even close,' he whispered. 'Between you and men, that was one hell of a situation for him. Let's put it this way; it was an unlucky and unfortunate thing that he found that body. Yeah?'

'And why is that?'

The boatman turned his head to the side. Without noticing, he let the item peer into sight. He was holding a brown bag, but I still couldn't figure what it was.

'Who knows?' he said.

'I thought we had a deal?'

Hissing through his teeth, he turned back to look at me.

'Who put you up to this?'

'No one.'

'Bull shit.'

'What are you scared of?'

'That I'm going to be snatched in the night and thrown into a dark room with a spotlight in my eyes, just like my nephew.'

I rubbed my chin with my thumb. 'So, after he found that body, they picked him up and asked him a series of tough questions?'

'That's one way of putting it.'

I kept quiet for a while as he mulled over the thoughts in his head.

'It was pretty recent,' he said. 'Maybe a month ago?'

'Is this a common practice?'

'No,' he said. 'That's what's so odd. Plenty of trollers have found bodies before, but none of them were grilled the way they did my nephew.'

'I'm curious here,' I said.

'I only know this because he spilled his guts one evening when we were both piss drunk. He broke down and cried, like a baby, sobbing in the streets while I puked in a dustbin nearby. I had to drag him to the beach and toss him in the water before he'd shut up. Then I blacked out and woke up the next morning still wet and smelling of saltwater in my bathroom. Of course, we've never spoken of it again. Just continued about our lives, a little more hollow and a lot quieter.'

'Did he tell you about the person he found?'

The man laughed. 'He didn't have to tell me. I knew. The private radio stations were each discussing the same thing. Who this guy might be and the conspiracy behind his death. He wasn't your average foreigner coming to see the lights. He was something more than that. Even now, I still wonder, but if you listened to the radio at that time, they'd have you believe he was some sort of spy out in these parts searching for well, take your pick.'

I rubbed under my chin with the back of my fingers. 'What about a Miss Tsuki Kage? You ever heard of her?'

His eyes widened. 'Hold on. That's a whole deal in itself. And something I'm not going to talk about with no tourist. Sorry.'

I raised my hand to keep him from leaving. 'Fine. Then let me ask you something else. Did the radio stations ever make a link between this man's death and that of Miss Kage's?'

The man furrowed his brow. 'No. I never heard anything like that.'

I stood there, looking down at my shoes a moment. I heard something odd in the air. A sound I couldn't put my finger on right away.

Then the man burst into a wheezing fit. He pulled his hand into a fist before his mouth as he lurched into a curl. I thought about giving him a pat on the back, but he seemed to manage. He stood back up, his eyes flushed with wetness, still trying not to cough.

'So why do you think that guy had to take a swim the way he did?'

The man held his fist over his mouth, trying to contain his breath. He shook his head a few times. 'Found something he wasn't supposed to.'

'And where do you think he was looking?'

The man laughed and coughed at the same time. 'Anywhere,' he said. 'It's all over the place if your eyes are sharp enough.'

'Miss Kage knew?'

The man waved his hand in the air as if he couldn't say anymore. 'She was a smart lady with a good heart, which is bad in this kind of place.'

I kept hearing that noise. It wasn't the docks. It wasn't an animal either.

The boatman glanced at his wrist for a moment and back up to me. 'You got any more questions? The next troller's coming in soon. Might not be good for them to see you here.'

I bit some chap from my lips and leaned to the side of him where I saw another boat trolling along towards the port. I nodded at the man.

'I'll see you around then.'

He repressed his cough inside his throat, waving his hand, like he was shooing me off and saying goodbye.

I went, flicked my cigarette into the dark, and headed for the exit. I stopped right before I reached the dim light over the entrance and touched at my jacket, hearing voices coming out from it.

There was a mixture of static covering what someone was saying. I pulled out my radio and put it to my ear in an attempt to decipher it.

'Tell the rooster... hiding out... if you can... take from... when they... mist brand...'

I took a step further out underneath the dim yellow light and kept listening to the hazy station. The static grew louder, blurring out the words, eventually muting them all together.

Swirling the dial carefully, I tried to hone in on the frequency these voices were using. They must've switched channels or found another means of communication because my search was utterly fruitless. I wish I knew what they were saying. I wish I had some context for those fragmented words.

The car flashed its beams twice in my eyes, letting me know its location in the darkness. I bit my lower lip, glanced at the radio once more, and then decided to turn it off.

CHAPTER 20

Lingering between the car and the port, a thread of hope weaved its needle wire through my ribs, keeping me planted in denial that sooner or later I'd have to slip back into that car and deal with the ex-housewife I couldn't seem to shake.

Then again, socialites rub elbows amongst important folks and carry encyclopedias full of gossip. Plus, there was nothing more to see out there, so I shuffled my feet towards the car and sat inside.

'Fun?' she said.

I wiped my jacket. 'You might be right. They're not that friendly in there after all.'

'See? I told you.'

I cocked my head to the side, making a clicking noise with my tongue.

She smiled a faint crease, flashing a glimpse of her porcelain whites at me; while her emerald green eyes beamed in a ray of moonlight.

'So, where to next?' She opened her pack of cigarettes to me. 'Do you have to book a boat tonight, or can this wait until morning?'

I slipped one out and gave it a light.

'It might have to wait,' I said.

'That's a shame. But if you want, my place is vacant; you can come over for a drink?'

I watched her black lips glisten in the moonlight.

'What drinks you got?' I said.

Her eyes narrowed on me. 'My husband was a collector of Terran brands,' she said. 'There's some amber scotch in there, with a few rustic bottles of bourbon to keep it company. I never touch the stuff and probably never will.'

I glanced down at her black nylons tucked inside her sleek pair of heels. I took another drag of my cigarette and let it out through my nose.

'I have to get back to my hotel later on,' I said. 'I have a meeting later.'

'With another girl?'

'You can drop me now at the curb if you have second thoughts,' I said. 'There'll be no hard feelings on my part.'

She tapped her fingernail on the dash then tightened her lips into a knit.

'I enjoy a nice walk anyhow.'

Quickly, she cranked the car and twisted on the headlights. Then she slapped her empty hand onto the shifter and rammed it into first. My head jerked back as we peeled out. And when I made a sidelong glance at her, I saw her face had contorted into a grimace.

'So what brought you to Senturion?' she said. 'The lights?'

'Like a moth.'

'Says everyone.'

The roads were dark ahead, void of any street lamps or houses to light the way. A single car whooshed past us and, soon, its red taillights vanished far behind.

She held a cigarette near her face as she drove one-handed. 'What's your name?' she said.

'Vince. And you?'

She put her hand back to the shifter and thrust it into a higher gear. The car sped faster down a very narrow and winding road. I started to grip a handle on the passenger door. We quickly changed directions, twisting up a sharp hill, then curling right back down it, shoving me into the corner as she straightened the car out onto a flat road and rose the gear.

'Midori,' she said.

I loosened my grip from the handle near my door and went about fixing my hat.

'Midori?'

'Yes,' she said, taking a drag of her cigarette.

'That's fitting.'

'You're from Ceph?'

I nodded. 'Nice guess.'

She took one last inhale on her cigarette then slipped it outside her window, closing it up after that.

'It isn't hard to tell with your accent.' She made a smooth glance at me and then gazed back out the windshield. 'Same with your clothes. They scream out of town.'

The car forked onto a two-lane stretch that weaved along the shore, then began to lift off the ground, onto a small bridge over the water.

'You born here?' I said.

She lifted her chin a little. 'Kaivus.'

'Close enough.'

'I'm not so sure about that.'

The car started to rise over the bridge's peak and then soon climbed down toward the gated island at the other end.

'You can see the port on your right,' she said. 'There's a cove where they moor their boats. Most are privately owned, but one or two give tours, I'm certain. I've seen them taking people out before.'

I eyed the well-lit port hugging the small island. There wasn't much to see of it at the time of night, though. A few lights in the dark was all.

The car broke onto the island and stopped outside a large gated wall where a security officer came along to check our vehicle. The man walked close to the car, peered inside, and caught sight of Midori. Without any hesitation, he opened the gates and bowed respectfully to the car.

She drove through the gates and floated on towards a row of symmetrical houses, each stacked neatly in the uniform grid. We weaved through the suburban maze and slipped up a white driveway and into a large garage.

She turned off the car and stepped outside. There was one light shining above and other cars wrapped under special tarps in the wide garage. She strut to a pair of brick steps, unlocked the door and turned back, waiting for me at the top.

I followed behind her.

We walked through a long hall that expanded into a giant kitchen, connected with an even wider living area and a sunroom attached at its side. She turned on the lights in the sunroom, and then a bright chandelier in the tall kitchen.

'Why don't you go sit in the sunroom while I make some drinks?'

I nodded, kept my hands in my jacket, and slowly went into the adjacent room. It was filled with brown leather couches and armchairs, all facing the glass walls overlooking the ocean. I placed myself on a leather couch, pat it a few times, and then slumped myself further into it.

Midori came in with two crystal glasses full of amber liquid. She handed one to me and sat down on the same couch. 'Cheers,' she said as she lifted her glass. 'To trying new things.'

'To new things.'

We drank them neat. I was surprised by the taste. It was like a vat of crisp autumn leaves, scented with a hint of spice and left to ferment in a barrel made out of the same oak tree they fell from.

She held her glass up near her lips as she looked at me. 'What do you think?'

I tipped the glass and studied the drink.

'It's nice.'

She bit her lip with a wry grin as she watched me.

I swirled the liquid around the glass and then set it down on the table beside me.

She looked in my direction, right where I'd set the glass down. 'There're some cigarettes inside that cabinet if you like. Ignore the thin ones, though. I don't know which whore of his left them in there.'

I knelt from the couch next to the little cabinet. Opening the middle drawer showed me a vast collection of cigarette packs from all over the universe. A good many I'd never seen or even heard of before.

I opened the bottom drawer and saw even more underneath. And then my eyes widened when I saw a pack of Silver Mist. I picked it up and unwrapped the plastic from the top. They smelt great. The scent of comfort, familiarity, and home.

She smiled at me. 'Of course, you'd go for those.'

I shook one out and gripped it in my curled lips. It lit fast and hit straight into my temples.

'My husband hated those,' she said. 'That's why they're in the bottom drawer. You can take them along if you want.'

I pocketed them at my side and inhaled another wisp. 'Poor guy doesn't know good taste when it's staring him right in the face.'

She lifted her drink an inch higher. 'You don't say?'

I looked at her as she crossed her legs, letting her dress ride higher up her thighs. I pulled the cigarette down from my mouth.

'Not in everything, I guess.'

She raised her eyebrow. 'You guess?'

I sat back down, closer to her, gazing into her green eyes. She set her drink on the cabinet beside her and inched closer to me. I took hold of her waist, bringing her lips onto mine.

She pulled her lips back and eyed the cigarette in my fingers. She took it from me and set it in an ashtray beside her glass. I tried to guide her back together, but she didn't follow.

She stayed in place, looking beautiful for as long as she pleased. Then, when she was ready, she reached her hands slowly inside my jacket, touching my gun in its holster.

'I thought I felt something in there.'

I laughed dryly, feeling bothered.

She unfastened the holster and took the gun out from my side. I thought to stop her but decided against it. She brought the gun closer to herself, turned it over in her hands to examine it.

'Now, what is a man like you doing with one of these?' she said.

I reached out to take it back from her and slipped it into the holster. My face must've been black and my ears growing red.

'I like to feel safe,' I finally said.

She lay one of her hands on my leg, rubbing soft circles with her fingernail.

'Safe from what exactly? Must be in a hot line of work.'

I stood from the couch and picked my cigarette out of the ashtray. 'It's not just about the work.' She was teasing me. I could tell. The woman wanted a toy to play with. Nothing good ever came from this kind of mind games.

She blinked at me softly. 'If it's not involved in your work, then what?'

'The benefit is knowing you have one,' I said. 'Try carrying a gun around for a week. See if you don't feel better each time you're alone at night.'

She raised her glass and sipped it while staring at me. I turned to my side and picked up my drink, downing it in two quick hits.

'I didn't bring you here to lead you on,' she said. 'Why don't you come sit back down?'

I shook my head as I looked out the window, smoking my cigarette. 'You're fine,' I said. 'I need to get back to my hotel anyhow.'

Harrumphing, she slapped her drink down onto the cabinet and groaned loud enough for me to hear. I touched the windows, feeling the cold night behind that thin glass barrier. Her reflection showed in the window, and she crossed her arms and legs, tapping one foot in the air.

I refused to turn back and look at her.

'You want me to drive you?' she said. 'To your other woman?'

'I told you not to wait for me at the docks.'

She rolled her eyes.

'I can get a cab from here. Or walk.'

Silence rang heavy in the room. Eventually, she sighed and stomped her feet, and waltzed up behind me. Her arms were still crossed. I turned to look at her.

She stared back at me and slowly relaxed her face and rolled her eyes once more.

'And what am I supposed to do tonight?' she said. 'Sleep alone in this mistress's houses?'

'You can borrow my gun?'

She scowled at me, then picked up both glasses and rushed them to the kitchen. I trailed slowly behind and appeared in the doorway. She poured some water into the drinks and refused to make eye contact with me.

'Fine,' she said. 'I'll take you home. I guess I need some company before the night gets lonely anyhow.'

CHAPTER 21

We drove over the bridge and along the winding roads back to the pink hotel. She stopped outside the lobby and asked to see me again. I told her I'd see her around and shut the car door behind me.

She raced off, and I went inside. The short receptionist paced the lobby floors as I entered. He stopped abruptly and twisted his mustache with a sour glare in his eye. Behind the desk sat Flathead, listening to his radio and giving me a similar leer.

They both watched me as if I might draw my gun and brighten up the joint all of a sudden. After a brief staring contest, I started walking through the lobby, they were watching me and I was watching them until I reached the stairs and broke from their sights.

'Weirdos,' I mumbled.

When I emerged from the staircase, I heard a door shut hard nearby my room. There were people whispering, and a woman's voice mixed into the batch that soon petered off into silence.

Pausing outside my door, I waited to listen for anything more, then shrugged and entered my room. I stepped in, took off my jacket, and threw it on the chair.

'You leave your door unlocked?' said Ju, sitting on my bed.

I clicked on the portable radio and swiped through the static channels as I kneeled down next to the chair; trying my best to find the right station.

'They've been jammed,' she said. 'You won't get a clear signal until tomorrow.'

I left the radio on the chair, buzzing like a snowstorm. Ju's arm twitched, and her eyes fluttered into a rapid blink.

'You fell asleep last night.'

I rubbed my forehead. 'I was pretty tired.'

She twitched her neck to the side. 'What do you-'

'Shhh,' I interrupted.

Her arm jerked to her side. 'What?'

I stood up slowly from the floor. Using my thumb, I unlatched my holster and slipped my fingers over the gun's handle.

'Vince?'

'You hear that?'

She shook her head with a twitch. 'It's just static?'

'Not the radio. Outside. In the hall.'

'I can't hear anything.'

I slipped over towards the door and set my ear upon it. I could hear a struggle outside.

'The dog went up the hill.'

'We already heard, pal.'

'It's a big dog with big furry-'

'Shh! Keep it down.'

'Come back with him.'

'Shut up!'

I cracked the door open a sliver. There were two big guys shoving Dogman into a vacant room and shutting it behind themselves.

Ju sat up on her knees atop the bed. 'Vince?'

I kept my eye out that sliver for some time and then shut the door back and turned on the seashell lights. They were dull in their withered yellow glow.

'Is everything all right?'

I focused on the radio for a moment, listening to the static hum, and then went to the edge of the bed to sit down.

She crawled closer to me, touching my back with her hands.

'I can help you relax?'

'I don't need to relax right now. I need to figure something out.'

She kept rubbing my back, slowly working her hands around my waist.

I took hold of her hands and moved them off me as I stood. I went over to my jacket and pulled out the pack of Silver Mist, and put one between my lips.

She watched me from the bed.

I left the pack open and stepped closer to her, offering her one. She slipped one out and glanced up at me, waiting for a light.

I sparked a flame and drew it near her. Her head twitched a bit, but she kept it steady enough to light the cigarette.

She took a deep hit and sighed out on the release. 'I thought you were fresh out of these?'

I closed the pack and threw it onto the bed. 'Some broad gave them to me earlier tonight.'

Ju picked up the pack and rubbed her thumb on its surface. 'A dangerous brand to smoke right now.'

I exhaled and went over toward the window, dragging the curtains back enough to see outside. The beach seemed calm, save for the fierce waves smashing into the rocks. There were even stars out in the sky and a scraped-out moon drawing light across the ocean.

'Yeah, but aren't they all dangerous for that matter?'

She then blinked an uncontrolled flutter. 'I don't mean cancer. I mean the brand. They're pretty dicey right now.'

I turned around, raising an eyebrow at her.

She blinked again. 'I left the radio station on for you this morning. Didn't you hear?'

'Hear what exactly?'

'There was a foreigner killed.'

'I heard that.'

'Do you know who he worked for?'

I shook my head.

She lifted the pack of Silver Mists. 'This brand.'

I dragged on my smoke and let it exit out my nose.

'He was found in the ocean last night. His wife's on the run. No one can find her, though.'

I pulled the curtains shut and went to the door, cracking it open again. The hall rang quiet with a fluorescent light humming above. I shut the door back and licked my lips.

She turned the cigarette pack over, still examining it.

'Who gave these to you?'

I stared at the wall, thinking to myself.

'Best be careful, she might be connected to the brand somehow.'

I went along the back wall near the bed and pressed my ear up against its surface. The room next door was quiet. I moved my ear slowly off the wall and had another drag of smoke. The static radio poured in behind me, faint words arose, then faded back into white noise.

Ju sat looking at the radio as well.

'They're changing locations,' she said.

I rubbed my eyebrow. 'I'm going for a walk,' I said. 'You want to join me?'

She put the cigarette pack down on the bed as her arm twitched.

'I shouldn't be out tonight. It's not smart. And neither should you. Being a foreigner and all.'

I flicked some ash onto the floor and went over to the bed, picking up my cigarettes.

She grabbed my wrist and tried to pull me down with her.

'Stay here,' she whispered. 'Please? I'll make you feel better. I promise.'

I smiled at her and then slowly took my arm out of her grasp. 'I'm sure you would, but I have things to do tonight.'

'Please don't go. Not tonight.'

I went over to the radio and slipped it inside my jacket.

'Why did you ask me over then? I need to be working right now. I have a daughter to feed.'

I stood still for a moment, biting some chap from the corner of my lips.

'I'll give you something for meeting me,' I said. 'Even more if you want to show me around?'

She lowered her head. 'I can't. Not tonight.'

I shrugged with a nasal sigh.

She didn't bring her head back up.

I pulled my jacket around myself and transferred some credits to her account. I went to the door and cracked it open. She looked pitiful sitting on the bed behind me. Hesitating, I pulled the extra metal case of cigarettes Midori had given me out of my jacket and contemplated them.

She gazed up at me from the bed.

I reached the case towards her.

'You want these? I don't like that brand much anyhow.'

She took them with apprehension, squinting at the nice metal case. 'These are real expensive, though?'

I cocked my head to the side. 'No matter.'

She blinked a rapid flutter and jerked her elbow to the side. 'Thank you.' She cradled the metal case in her chest.

I opened the door all the way. 'I'll give you a call later.'

She nodded her head. 'That'd be nice.'

I stepped out into the hall and shut the door behind me. The fluorescent light buzzed amidst the silence. I went to the door next to mine and placed my ear up against it. All was quiet, so I went to the next.

It was quiet too.

Then I heard a door handle jiggle at the end of the hall, and two big guys exited with pinstriped suits over their broad shoulders and hats tight over their big heads. They shut the door back as if there might be a bomb attached at the other end and then stepped away, glancing quickly at me.

They kept their faces straight as they looked at each other out of the corner of their eyes. One of them swallowed and then relaxed his stance.

'Nice night out,' he said.

I took a last hit of my cigarette and then twisted its end until the embers fell to the ground.

'Yeah,' I said. 'Everything's real clear out there.'

They stared at me, picking their back teeth with their tongues.

I moved away from the door, putting my hands inside my pockets, and turned out towards the stairwell. I went up to the third floor and waited there for a while. After some time, I headed back down, peered through the second floor, and saw the tough guys were gone.

I made my way to the door they'd exited, putting my ear up against it.

'...Dog went up the hill... Big fluffy ears... Dad's out to find... One day soon... with a big black coat...'

I turned the handle, but it was locked.

Then a set of deep voices echoed through the stairwell and across the hall. I rushed to the other end where the janitor's closet was and squeezed inside it, finding myself cuddling a mop and smelling some noxious chemicals.

The tough guys went to the door in silence, opening it and closing it back again.

I pushed the janitor's closet open and slipped down the hall towards the stairs. I went out of the lobby past Flathead, who sat listening to his radio. I made a detour towards his desk and leaned up against it, glancing at the frequency on his dial.

'Any good places to eat at this time?' I said.

The man wrinkled his forehead and squinted his eyes.

'This isn't the best area for tourists, you know?' His cigar was in an ashtray beside his large hands, wafting with little concern.

I rubbed my eyebrow, taking another glimpse at the frequency.

'Yeah, but some guys like to avoid all the cheap touristy stuff. Get a real feel for the place.'

Flathead picked up his cigar and filled his cheeks full of smoke. He stared blankly at the lobby's entrance for a moment.

'There's an old diner up the road. Cross the street and make a right at the third alleyway. Small joint, down in the basement. Mom and pop. Don't make a fuss, or I will, got it?'

'Thanks.'

He set his cigar back in the tray and focused on his radio, waiting for me to leave.

I did him a favor and left. As I walked out the door, I noticed a car sitting along the curb some distance away with two people inside it watching the hotel intently. Crossing the street, I avoided their gazes, and passed into the third alleyway. There were plenty of old shop signs hanging on the wall, but only one basement grate open at this time, with stairs leading to a dim restaurant.

I went down the stairs, past the broken lights, and into the cramped diner. I sat at a table covered by an exotic tablecloth. I'd never seen such patterns before in my life.

No one else was inside. I was the only guy looking for a meal at this hour. No one rushed to take my order either. So I took the radio out of my jacket and turned the dials to the frequency I saw earlier.

'Line is compromised. We'll move the feather before the hawks get any closer.'

'Take the bullet to the sign then.'

'What about the sift?'

I turned the volume down a notch when I saw an older lady approaching my table. She dragged herself over towards me, her mouth hanging open a sliver. She neared the table and started to scratch her curly grey hair.

'You want something to drink?'

'Coffee?'

'Synthetic okay?'

'Fine.'

'You looked over the menu?'

I pulled up the tattered black menu and opened it. A flickering hologram appeared. I flipped through the unstable pages. Everything seemed foreign to me. Thankfully, there were pictures, so I jabbed my finger at random to one of them.

'I'll have this one.'

The lady looked down at the menu. 'Plov?'

'That's the one.'

She didn't smile at me as she walked back towards the kitchen.

By the time I had a chance to turn the volume up, it had already gone to static. I could hear some commotion in the back kitchen – someone yelling, and metal pots hitting the floor.

Sliding the ashtray over to myself, I thought of that old Cowboy I met on the ship. I then slapped the pack of Silver Mist on the table. I imagined him floating face down on the shores outside. It had to be Oren they got, I was sure he was the only guy working for Silver Mist here.

There was more commotion in the kitchen. Then a young girl peeped out from the door and stared at me behind a thick pair of magnified specs. Tears streamed down her face as she inched further out from the kitchen.

I noticed her shirt had slight tears near her shoulders. And several dug-out blisters on her skin. Then just as quickly as she came in sight, she was yanked back into the kitchen, her two pigtails being the last thing to whip out of view.

I hummed to myself and took a drag of my cigarette.

After some time, the old lady returned, carrying a hot mug of coffee. She set it down on the tablecloth and blew through her nose before she spoke.

'Food is almost done.'

I tipped some ash into the tray. 'Was that your daughter?'

The old woman laughed without any heart.

'My granddaughter,' she said. 'I'm not producing any children at this age. Can you imagine?' She looked around. 'It's ridiculous!'

'You never know.'

She glared at me for a moment. 'What is your business here?'

I took a sip of coffee. 'Just a tourist.'

'Well, keep it that way. Don't try to be funny with the locals. Okay?'

I held the mug under my chin. 'Wasn't trying to be.'

She pursed her lips and then stormed off into the kitchen.

Pretty young to be a grandma, I thought. *Then again a bit too old to be a mom.*

Turning the dial on my radio, I was in search of something pleasant to listen to while I waited for the food.

'Hope to enhance your earnings by ten percent this coming year...'

'Give her that special kind of rub...'

'Shaded Oaks when your options have run out, and there's nothing else to do but...'

'Just a few more days until we get to see those lights over...'

I turned it off.

The old lady threw the kitchen door open, carrying a plate of food in my direction. She set it down on the table before me with furrowed brows.

I stubbed my cigarette in the ashtray.

'You hear about that tourist found on the shore?' I said quickly.

She paused with shock, her hand over her chest, unsure of how to answer.

'Come on. You live close enough to the beach.'

'I don't know anything about it. He was probably hanging around places he shouldn't have been.'

'He worked for a cigarette company. Silver Mist. You ever tried them?'

She crossed her arms and glared at me. 'I don't smoke.'

Her granddaughter peered out from the kitchen again, grinning at us. The lady turned around and shouted at her.

'Get back in there! Unless you want me to boot your ass outdoors for the night?'

The girl stood in the doorway, leaning out a little further, giggling.

'Oh! I think I hear them coming now,' she said. 'Going to take you away. Is that what you want?'

The girl slipped back inside the kitchen.

I moved the rice around on my plate.

The old lady growled to herself as she pinched the bridge of her nose. 'They never listen.'

A grin worked across my face.

She caught my smirk.

When I glanced up at her, she had a mean scowl on her face and dishrag, having its imaginary neck wrung in her meaty hands.

'What's the joke here?' she said. 'Because I seem to have missed the punchline.'

I put my hand over my mouth and wiped away my smile.

She showed me a glimpse of her teeth.

'Well, go on!' she said. 'I'm dying to hear it!'

Pushing my chair back, I lifted my chin and straightened my back.

Her eyes bore down into me.

Then, I finally met her gaze.

'There's nothing funny,' I said. 'Not in a laughing matter, but it's what the body does after bouts of extreme stress when a solution finally starts to rise.'

'What problem?'

'I wish I could tell you.'

She curled her upper lip at me and harrumphed as she turned back towards the kitchen. 'Stupid ass foreigners. Problems my foot.' Then she shoved off out of sight.

I rubbed my face for some time, then saw my meal, and thought better than to leave it untouched. God knows I needed my strength.

CHAPTER 22

After the meal, I headed back towards the hotel, as nowhere else was open. Nearly rounding the corner, I caught sight of three different cars; one was the same as I'd spotted before I left, while the other two were police cruisers.

I remained in the dark alleyway cautioning myself.

Then at the side of the hotel, I saw two cronies rush out of the hotel, lugging Dogman at their sides, swiftly chucking him into the back of their car. Without missing a beat, they then opened the two front doors, jumped in, and closed them at the same time. The car cranked fast and sped off even faster down the road.

I leaned up against the alleyway, waiting for the other vehicles to move. But their owners didn't show for a while, so I thought the coast was clear. When I shifted, another set of folks came out of the hotel. Officers of the law. Dressed in black uniforms with sharp hats on their heads and guns at their sides.

They lingered outside their cruisers, shouting back and forth to one another. I inched closer on the wall, staying in the dark but getting nearer to the road.

'Shady Oaks,' said one of them. 'But we'll see. They can only run for so long.'

The other officer near his vehicle hung in the open door, tapping his hands on the roof. 'You going back to the station then?'

'You want to check the lounge down the road? I know he'll be there.'

'It's up to you.'

The officer rubbed his chin and then shut his own door. 'I'll ride with you then. Easier to surprise them this way.'

They both got into one car and hit the accelerator.

I watched the vehicle disappear around the same corner as the other. I moved out of the alley and went into the hotel. Flathead chewed on his cigar like a dog grinding a bone in his maw. I had a question for him, but at the chance of getting my hand snapped at, I kept it to myself.

Off I continued through the lobby, climbing the stairs, and reached my landing; when I heard a door slam shut. I stood in the center of the hall for a while when a strange thing happened. The same door opened to a crack and a small eye stared at me from inside.

Stepping closer caused the door to shut again. I then inched closer, softly tapping my knuckle on the door. It opened a sliver.

'Vince?' a voice whispered.

'Yeah. Ju?'

'No.'

The door opened wide, and then I felt a strong hand grasp my coat and pull me in. The door slammed behind us, and a woman threw her body into mine in a tearful hug.

'Thank god,' she said. 'I need a familiar face right now.'

I had no clue who she was. I tried to pry her off me to have a look, but she wouldn't budge.

'I don't know what to do right now,' she said. 'I really don't know, Vince. I thought I saw you through the window earlier tonight when you came near my door.'

Her voice sounded familiar. 'Mrs. Velts?'

She sniffed and then buried her eyes even further into my chest. 'They killed him. I know it. They killed him when he went to talk with those boys. And when bought that tent space on the boardwalk!'

'What boys?'

'The local companies!'

I pulled her back and then sat her down atop the bulky heater on the side of the wall. Her hair lay in tangles on her head, distracting from her pale face, now void of the gobs of glitter and make-up I'd seen her wearing on the ship.

'What company?'

She sniffed, choked for words. I turned on the seashell lights. Only one of them worked in the room.

She sat on the large heater, her platinum hair frizzed like she hadn't seen a shower in days. Her eyes were swollen into red puffs, and her clothes were too big and dark.

I took a cigarette out of my jacket and offered her one.

'Get those things away from me,' she whispered.

I put one in my lip and lit its end. I tossed my lighter into my pocket and took the radio out of my jacket.

'What are you doing?' she said.

I turned on the radio and let the static pour.

'Seeing if I can get some information.'

She stared at me with blotches in her eyes. The orange ember of my cigarette reflected off her eyes, glistening in the forming tears.

'You're not a car salesman, are you?' she said.

'Sturdy cars is my bread and butter.'

She touched her lips. 'Oh, god, please don't tell me you're working for them.'

I shook my head. 'Not working for anyone, I'm on vacation.'

Her lips began to tremble behind her fingers.

'How'd you end up here in this place, Barbra?'

'Oren,' she said. 'It was all him. We'd always had an emergency plan if anything ever went wrong and well...'

I pulled a chair out from the side of the room and sat it down next to her.

'You had a plan?'

'In case anything ever happened. He made connections with some locals. They're the ones who brought me here. As a safe house. They wouldn't let me see where we were going. They had a blindfold over my eyes the whole time, and I thought they might take advantage of me.'

I exhaled a plume of smoke. 'You didn't go to the authorities?'

She shook her grim face. 'God no!'

I rubbed my eyebrow with my cigarette in-between my fingers.

'Oren told me never to trust them. No matter what happened - to stay away at all costs.'

'They're looking for you,' I said. 'The police were just here at the hotel.'

'I know,' she whispered. 'I saw.'

'Funny they picked this hotel. Of all places.'

She paused for a moment then rubbed her hands along the metal heater.

'But those officers weren't looking for me,' she said. 'At least, not yet. They were after someone else. Someone with a dog?'

I sat up in my chair. 'How do you know?'

She pointed towards the window. 'I heard them moving him in the hall. He was talking about a dog, and they said the authorities were after him. They wanted to take him to some oaks place. But they didn't find him. Least I don't think so.'

'Did they come in here?'

She nodded. 'I hid in the wall. Behind the cabinet there. The men in suits told me to keep quiet if anyone came.'

I glanced over her shoulder at the cabinet fixed in the corner of the wall. The doors were wide open, and a few of the hangers were on the ground, scattered along the base.

A single tear rolled down her cheek.

I reached out for an overturned waste bin to flick my ash inside it. She pursed her shaking lips and held the warm tears inside her eyes.

'Did he tell you anything before it happened?' I said. 'A message or something?'

She shook her head. 'No, The only thing he told me was to go find the salamander.'

I raised my eyebrow.

She curved her lips in a mix of pout and smile. 'It was our code for emergency. Go find the salamander.' Her face began to scrunch after she said that.

I nodded and pulled some air through my teeth. 'Do you know what he was going to do that day?'

She bobbed her head and wiped her eyes again.

'Something about a factory,' she said. 'He was meeting some people to discuss their cigarette factories. His company wanted to partner with them, to get a foot in the door I assume.'

'Did he tell you where the factories were?'

She paused, biting her lip. I took a drag of my smoke and let it out the corners of my mouth.

'Most of the government ones are up on the moon. The rest down here are mostly run by a small group of elites. Every one of them is a local, of course.'

'Was he planning a trip up there to the factories?'

She laughed hard, causing a tear to rush out of her eye.

'No one is allowed up there. Authorized personnel only. Get the picture?' She paused, putting her hand over her mouth. 'I'm sorry - I didn't mean-'

'It's nothing.'

'I just meant...'

I tapped some ash into the bin on the floor.

She didn't say anything more.

The room went quiet for some time. I could hear the waves crashing outside our window. I stubbed my cigarette out as a police siren roused through the night and slowly died in the distance.

'They'll be moving me again soon,' she whispered. 'You should go.'

I nodded, stood up from the chair, and put my radio back in my jacket.

'I don't want you to get involved with any of this mess,' she said. 'As much as I like your company. It's not right of me, bringing others into my business.'

I went to the door and clicked the handle to the side. 'Keep your head down for the next bit.' I opened it with a creak. 'And you're not home free until your feet are back on Ceph. Don't be foolish, you hear?'

She nodded, her eyes full of tears.

I slipped outside and shut the door back behind me.

The ocean rang loud outside, and the salty breeze began to nip at my face. I put my collar up around my neck, went down the stairs through the lobby, passed by Flathead, and legged it into a dark alley across the street where I collected my thoughts while keeping my gaze at the pink hotel.

•   •   •   •   •

Nothing stirred at that time, so I called a taxi service and waited for them to arrive.

The car approached with its headlights burning through the shadows and halted near the curb where I stood. The lights went off, and the engine died.

I slipped out from the alley and over towards the passenger side. I opened the door, sat inside, and closed it back. A small picture of himself was pasted on the dash with the name: Serik, written on it.

The driver was a middle-aged man with a thick face and a couple of scars running down and across it. He wore a dark blue toboggan on his head, covering the full extent of a gash that was peeking out from underneath the cap. His hands were gnarled around every joint, like they'd been burnt off, leaving clean, shiny patches of skin.

'Where to?'

'I'm waiting on someone else,' I said.

'I can't be sitting around all night.'

'Start the meter then.'

The guy leaned forward and clicked the meter in his dash. He sat back and glanced at me from the corner of the dark car.

'Where you from?'

'Ceph.'

'Seeing the lights?'

'Isn't everyone.'

He pursed his lips and let out a big exhale through his nose. I put a cigarette in my mouth and offered him one. He took it.

We both lit our smokes and brought the windows down an inch.

'You mind tailing a car for me?' I said.

He turned his cigarette in his fingers to examine the hot coals at its end.

'Spouse or something?'

I laughed. 'An old friend.'

He licked his lips and took another drag of his cigarette. He slowly nodded his head as he exhaled a billow of smoke.

'All right. I'll do it. Gotta pay a little extra, though.'

'Fine.'

'It's no cop, is it?'

'No.'

He then peered outside his window towards the hotel. 'Your friend stays here?'

'Yeah, I'm just waiting for them to move.'

He hummed to himself as he watched outside his window.

CHAPTER 23

The fog began to creep out from the ocean and up into the quiet streets. The only streetlight outside was covered in a light mist, expanding its rays into a yellow cone along the walk. My clothes started to feel cold and damp, and everything smelt of tiny rotted fish.

I saw a group leaving the hotel. They'd done a nice job making the dame look like a man. Probably shaved that head of hers and put a sleek cap over it. Serik watched them as well.

They slipped into a long sedan and closed the doors as the engines came alive. The lights burnt ahead of their car as they pulled out from the curb.

'That's them,' I said. 'You know how to keep a safe distance?'

The driver grunted. 'Calm down.'

I sat back and let it ride.

He turned on the engine and listened to it purr.

We moved away from the pavement and kept the lights soft as we followed the blurry red trail ahead of us. The car made a smooth turn at the intersection, drifting through the town with ease. We weaved for miles, right left, left right, until we reached a dark factory surrounded by abandoned houses and broken street lamps.

Serik stopped several meters away, cutting off the lights and killing the engine. He sat back, watching the men pile out of the vehicle, taking the disguised woman with them. They walked like black shadows stretched across the road – dark, towering, with an illusion of stature.

The factory door slid open, and a thin old man stuck his head out of the crack, looked them over with a cigarette in his lips, and then waved his hand over his shoulder, letting them inside. When they all disappeared, the old man peered outside, glanced down the streets, and then backed in and shut the door.

I took another cigarette out and offered the driver one. We lit them at the same time and clicked our lighters shut in accord.

'You knew where they were going,' I whispered.

The man curled his calloused fingers, keeping his cigarette between his top knuckles. He stared at the factory for some time before he cleared his throat.

'You'd better have a good reason to go in there. Personally, I'd stay away and let bygones be bygones.'

I pulled the door handle down and creaked the door open an inch.

'Thanks for the ride.'

'I'd offer you one back.' He laughed. 'But I don't know if that's going to happen.'

I stepped my foot out onto the asphalt and exhaled a draft of smoke. The man grabbed my arm and held it firm. He pointed at the factory with his other thick finger.

'There's a ladder climbing up the side of the building,' he said. 'A few windows at the top you can look in from. But I wouldn't go knocking at the front door.'

I nodded and removed my arm from his grasp. 'Thanks,' I said and stepped out, closed the door shut, and walked along the dark street.

The sidewalks had ragweeds rising out of the cracks with shattered bits of glass and broken hubcaps spread around them. A faint siren played in the distance, and a handful of stars poked through the sky above.

A gust of wind pushed lonesome blades of tall grass against the brick walls, scrapping them like a match on the side of a box. I paused near the entrance of the factory, finished my smoke, and flicked it to the ground before I continued down the street to the side of the building.

It wasn't hard to find the fire exit, all rusted up, with a patch of tangled weeds growing along its bars. I tested the ladder, trying to see if I could pull it down or if one of the rungs might snap off, but they didn't.

I climbed all the way to the top with some effort, where a long, murky glass, like a white frost, showed me the interior of the factory. There was a solitary light hanging in the middle of the warehouse, swaying back and forth, casting a dim glow upon the dark floors.

Pushing the glass to the side rang out a nasty screech. I paused to look down, watching for any movement other than the swaying light. I continued to slide the window further, letting it creak as little as I could manage, and when it was open far enough, I slipped inside onto a metal staircase within the building.

Everything was dark and smelled of used motor oil and accumulated mildew. I reached to my side, unlatched my gun, and held it in my hand. There was a faint sound that echoed in the factory, like a mistaken whisper spoken a notch too loud.

I held my gun at my waist and crept down the first step with care. A large bug scurried along the railing, disappearing at the bend. I went down further, crouching all the way, with my eyes scanning beneath me. When I reached the next landing, I stepped out and pressed my back against the wall.

There were doors lining the walk and one at the end with a faint light shining through its cracks. I glanced over my shoulder, down the other end, and then continued on towards the outlined door. My steps were quiet, and my figure shrouded in the dark. I stopped outside the door and pressed my ear against it to listen.

'The black dog went up the hill,' said Dogman. 'Dad went to find him but couldn't. That's why he hasn't come back. That's what my mum says.'

'God. Would you shut up about the dog? Seriously, give it a rest.'

The door handle started to jiggle. I moved to the side and slid myself into a corner of the wall. The door wrenched open, pouring light into the hall. A tough guy strut out onto the walkway, then turned back to speak with another man inside the room.

The door stayed open as they spoke to one another. I couldn't make out their faces, but they had to be the same guys I saw at the hotel.

'How do you get this fella to shut up?'

The man in the room laughed.

'I'm tempted to ship him off to Shady Oaks myself if I hear any more about that damn dog.'

The tough guy pivoted as he flicked some ash from his cigar.

'You laughing?'

The other guy cleared his throat. 'No.'

'Fucking hell.'

'Ah, let it go.'

'Fucking hell,' growled the man.

'They'll be here soon anyhow.'

'Thank god.'

The two men went quiet, and I saw their orange cigarette embers burning in the dark. I held firmly onto my gun at my side as I watched them. A man shouted from the ground floor below. I couldn't make out what he said, but it sounded like someone's name.

I shifted in the corner, burrowing deeper into the crevice.

'Go check it,' whispered one of the men.

The tough guy started walking down the dark hall as the second guy shut himself back inside the room.

I waited for ten seconds before I started to follow my new friend. I could hear him tromping down the old rusty staircase, his big feet clanking heavy on the steps. I slipped to the railing, peered down to the next landing, and then descended behind him.

He was getting further and further away from me as he rounded the next set of stairs.

I hurried quietly to the next flight and paused to make sure I was alone. Everything was dark. No lights shining under any doors. Or any shadows nearing. I then toed down the next flight and checked the area, spotting the outline of a door instantly.

Rushing to the door, I set my ear upon it and then reached for the handle. There was no one talking inside. Only grating silence. I started to turn the handle when I felt two hands grab my shoulders.

'Wrong door, fella.'

I laughed as I started to slip my gun upward. 'Everyone makes mistakes, no?'

Then I felt another set of hands grabbing my wrist, clamping down on my hand until my bones popped at the joints.

'Easy, pal.'

'Drop it.'

A swift twist released the gun from my hand. I listened to it clatter on the floor. Then a bright smack plowed across the back of my head. Everything went dark before I crashed into the metal walkway below.

CHAPTER 24

I woke up with my face covered in wet sand and a headache ripping open the back of my skull. The ocean waves crashed near my feet as I lay in the darkness, hearing slams of the roaring surf behind me.

After what seemed an eternity of pain and wallowing, I pushed myself up and sat on my knees. I touched the back of my head. There was a nice egg swelling and splotches of dried blood matting my hair. I growled, then started to brush the grains of sand off my face and looked around for my hat. It was close enough, so I reached over and picked it up.

'Fuck me.'

I closed my eyes and rubbed them ferociously, trying to regain my sights. My head was off its axis. Spinning at a wobble I couldn't quite straighten. I opened my eyes again and saw my breath steaming white from my mouth.

The waves kept crashing, intent on their one obnoxious job.

'Oh, shut the fuck up.'

I slowly rose to my feet and started patting my chest and pockets to see what they'd taken. I found no gun. No lighter. No more smokes. No radio either.

I saw the main road ahead and the boardwalk to my left. I shuffled my feet and kicked into something hard. Bending down, I swept the sand off the cold metal gun and returned it to my jacket. I then spotted my radio nearby, pouring out static, half-buried in the grainy sand.

Walking towards the road, I caught a wink from my lighter as the moon reflected off its surface; and then saw the glisten of my cigarettes from their plastic wrap. I went about collecting all my things and lit a smoke while I sat on the curb. It didn't make the headache go away. Nor the swelling ease. But it gave me a sense of balance again.

A car passed by on the black road up ahead. It swept by without paying me any attention.

The waves swelled along the shore. Another car hissed by. I then felt a faint spray of saltwater hit the back of my neck. I climbed to my feet again and found a broken lamppost to lean my aching body upon.

Another car drifted by, stopping some distance ahead. After a second or two, its rear lights shifted into white as the vehicle reversed towards me.

'Fuck me,' I said.

I recognized the machine. I'd taken a ride in it earlier in the night.

The window rolled down. 'You're up early,' she said. 'Out for a morning jog?'

I exhaled a bit of smoke and blinked a few times.

'Is this your favorite road to cruise along or something?'

A light snapped on inside the car. Midori's green eyes beamed in its glow.

'I couldn't sleep,' she said. 'They say the moon can have that effect on you. Depending on its alignment with Kavius and whether it's full or not.' She inhaled on her cigarette and let out a gentle plume. 'I don't know exactly how it works, but that's what I've been told.'

I rubbed the back of my head, feeling the tender welt. 'Yeah?'

She eyed me from inside the car, keeping her cigarette in her fingers right underneath her lips.

'Of course. Everyone knows that up here.'

'And I thought I was the only insomniac tonight.'

She almost smiled, but her face was too poised to allow it. I stood along the sidewalk, finishing my cigarette as the winds began to pick up.

'You need a ride?'

I gazed into the skies and about the building tops. The night was losing its dark power. Soon, the skies would be turning from violet to light blue with pink clouds dangling across the horizon.

'I've given up on sleeping tonight,' she said. 'Maybe it's the house I'm not used to yet. Not like his tramp anyhow.'

I tossed my cigarette into the sands and brushed my coat, dropping more grains from it.

'I could use some coffee.'

She broke from her blank stare out the window.

'I know a place,' she said, then paused a moment with her cigarette between her fingers. 'Might not be your style, though.'

I kneaded the back of my neck with my knuckles. 'I'll take it if they make it strong.'

She smiled at me. 'Okay.'

I went around the front of the car, bathing myself in light as I went to the passenger side. The door opened with a whinge and a burst of warm air. I slipped in and closed it back.

'Maybe you're getting a feel for the moon as well.'

'Yeah. That, or something else.'

She put the car in gear and nudged the pedal slowly into a glide. The skies were growing lighter. The stars were fading, and the moon went pale. Midori took another drag of her cigarette and let it out like a soft whistle.

We turned down a narrow alleyway that had just enough space for one car to go through at a time. She then turned onto another cramped street with a row of parking meters lining the walk and a lone car parked in one of the spots.

We continued on towards a wider street, heading west for some time, and then turned into a weave of tightly laid buildings. There were more cars in this area, nice ones too, all packed in any free space they could find.

Midori turned into a car park and waited for a thin film barrier to dissolve before we could go inside. It vanished, and we rode high into the risers, taking a spot near the lifts on the ninth floor.

She turned off the engine and sat in the car for a moment longer, staring out at the red lines streaking across the horizon right under the light blue skies. She took a final drag of her cigarette and tossed it out the window.

'You might like this area,' she said. 'It's a place of convergence - an estuary of sorts - where all the tides meet in one.'

I finished my smoke and tossed it out the window too.

She left the keys at a quarter turn in the ignition, leaving the electric power on while the engine was off. She turned on the radio to a soft jazz station, lulling us into a trance as the sun climbed higher and higher into the sky. The clouds were glowing orange and the horizon bright red.

'How do you think a place like this exists?' she whispered.

I stared at the horizon without answering her question.

'Kaivus revolves around the sun right there,' she said, nodding at the bright orb. 'And then we revolve around Kaivus. But then, on top of that, we have our own little satellite revolving around us.' She squinted as she chewed her upper lip.

'Life happens,' I said. 'Even that's a mystery in itself.'

She slowly moved her eyes from outside the windshield over to me. She smiled her violet lips around her white teeth.

'Best not to get caught up in questions that don't have a definite answer.'

'Then what questions are you asking then? Are you sure they have a definite answer?'

I clicked my door open and slid my foot outside. 'There's only one way to find out.'

She clicked her door open too.

I stepped outside and shut mine.

She stood up from the other side, looking over the car roof at me. 'It's only a few more days now until the lights ignite,' she said. 'Then I guess you'll be heading back home?'

'That all depends on if I like the place or not.'

'And?'

I didn't respond.

She shut her door fully and waited for me to join her near the boot. I did. She took my arm, linking it with hers, and then led me to the elevator lift.

•   •   •   •   •

The restaurant was filled with antique wooden booths, polished to a gleam, and lit with handmade yellow lights hanging above them. Discomfort wiggled in my stomach the instant I stepped inside.

There were a couple of different groups nestled in the posh cafe. Some young adults with coffee in their hands and heads bowed low as if they had weights in their skulls from a heavy night of drinking or cramming for exams. Another group in the corner consisted of well-dressed businessmen or, more likely, Politicians, chatting over their plates, their guts bulging over their tightly wound belts, and red and blue bow-ties wound at their flabby necks.

Midori slipped us into a booth along the side of the wall and sat across from me with a faint smile.

A tall waiter with neatly tied dreadlocks came over to our table. He flashed a pleasant smile.

'Can I start you two with anything to drink this morning?'

'Coffee,' I said.

'Which flavor would you prefer?'

'Coffee flavor.'

Closing his eyes half-notch, he stopped himself from rolling them and politely slid the menu towards me, pointing to the various selection of beans they were willing to grind into a brew.

I pointed to the first one.

'Alphane claw?' he said.

I elbowed the menu to the side of the table. 'As long as it's strong.'

Midori raised a finger in the air. 'I'll have the same.'

The man jotted down our order and then nodded his head before leaving.

Midori opened her little handbag and slipped out a metal case of cigarettes. She laid them on the table between us and raised an eyebrow at me.

I shook my head, taking the Silver Mist out of my jacket.

She glanced at the metal case, slipped a thin brown cigarette out, and put it in her dark lips.

Striking a flame, I reached it first across the table, to which she leaned into it, lighting her cigarette. As she leaned back, she covered herself in a veil of smoke, and I went about lighting my own.

'The lights,' she said, taking the cigarette in her fingers. 'Everyone wants to see those lights.'

'Who wouldn't?'

She left the tip of her cigarette in the ashtray, her lips barely open, waiting for the right moment to talk.

'Vincent H. Gavelman,' she said. 'What a fascinating name.'

I cleared my throat.

'From Ceph,' she said, raising her eyebrows a bit. 'The promised land. The golden frontier.'

I grunted. 'The land of dust and canyons.'

'No,' she said. 'I've seen it before. There are some beautiful landscapes there. And not an inch too far from your own tiny star. It's a perfect recipe for nice weather. Unlike the bitter cold here.'

The waiter brought our coffees and set them down in brown saucers. He then stepped back, eyeing us both.

'Any breakfast this morning?'

Midori tapped her cigarette in the ashtray and then looked up at him. 'Something local.'

The waiter moved closer to our table, taking the menus again and pointing at the breakfast dishes.

'We have a selection of morning sandwiches,' he said. 'The moonlight caper is our most popular - we top a Dausolli steak with

Rievas cheese and freshly powdered Aaoin; while lightly covering the bread in a spiced egg yolk sauce.'

I shrugged. 'Okay.'

Midori nodded to the waiter. 'We'll take those.'

The man took down the order and then pulled the menus off the table. As he turned, I reached out my hand, taking hold of his arm. He furrowed his brow at me, shocked for a moment.

'You mind leaving one of those menus here?' I said.

He took his hand out of my grip and handed me one back, slowly.

Midori watched me from across the table, bringing her smoke up underneath her lips.

I opened the menu and started to study the different items again. There were two markings at the end of each item, and one was clearly more expensive than the other.

Moonlight Caper: Dausolli steak topped with... (L)

Classic Trio: Three farm fresh eggs with three... (I/L)

The Bear's Mouth: A fresh cut of Terraian Salmon cooked to... (I)

I closed the menu shut. 'So what do the L's and I's stand for on the menu?' I tapped some ash from my cigarette into the tray.

'Local and Imported,' she said. 'People around here appreciate that kind of touch.'

'Yeah?'

'Why not? Other places do it.'

I paused a moment to have a sip of my coffee. It tasted strange. Still dark and bitter, but strange nonetheless.

I lowered it back to the table. 'So what's the draw to local or import?'

'Who knows? Another gimmick to drain more money out of people.'

'You seemed pretty intent on the local dishes, though?'

She took a puff of her cigarette and then set it back in the ashtray. 'That's because I don't enjoy imported food. I prefer some comforts from home.'

I paused a moment when I saw the table of businessmen all stand up at the same time. They glanced at us for a second and then continued on out the door. I snubbed my cigarette in the ashtray and took another sip of coffee. It was different from the others cups I'd had up Senturion or Kavius thus far.

'Do many tourists come into this joint?' I said.

She pursed her lips and shook her head a little. 'It's uncommon, but sometimes they make their way out here.'

I sipped some more coffee and put it back down. 'Why do you think that is?'

She wrapped her fingers around her mug and delayed her answer. The waiter had just arrived with our food and placed the two plates down on the table.

'Anything else?' he said.

'No, thanks.'

I turned my plate around, looking at the hot sandwich.

'So?'

'I can't imagine why any tourists would want to come here,' she said, organizing her silverware to eat. 'It's out of the way for them.'

I raised one of my eyebrows at her.

She picked up her fork as her eyes narrowed to slits. 'Well, it's not like they're disallowed. Anyone can come here if they really want to.'

'They're not invited, though?'

She snorted a laugh. 'I don't know of any tourists who would go out of their way to come here. What's so special on the menus that they can't get elsewhere? It's a place for the locals. And what's wrong with that?'

'Nothing really.'

'But you feel that way? That our businessmen can't find a nice place to relax before they go to work? Or that our students can't ease their minds before they hit the books for the entire day?'

'I never said that. You did.'

She shook her head, put the fork down, and reached for her sandwich, holding it up near her face.

'What are you really getting at, Mr. Gavelman? Is there something wrong with this restaurant? Because I'd like to know if that's the case.'

'You think too much.'

She bit her sandwich and turned her eyes away from me.

I did the same and looked at the other tables. They were filled with locals of a certain kind. Nice shirts and shoes on each of them. Even the college kids wore new clothes, bought by mom and dad most likely.

Midori sighed, placing her sandwich half down, and then lit another cigarette.

I took a bite of my sandwich and had another sip of coffee.

'Still overthinking?' I said.

She glared at me.

Oh well.

CHAPTER 25

I found a new hotel a little further up from my old one and slept most of the day, letting my head balance itself upright again. When dusk started to take over the skies, I called Serik from the night prior and asked if he could give me another ride.

I left the hotel and went across the street to wait for the car. It pulled up into a small alcove outside a shopping center. I opened the passenger door and slipped in. The driver had a grin that wrinkled every single scar upon his face.

'Well, aren't you lucky,' he said. 'Catch up with your friend?'

'No,' I said.

He chuckled a little and then clicked the gear into drive. 'What's next on your sightseeing tour?'

I licked my lips and looked out the windshield at the vacant street, dimming in fading lights.

'There's a port down the road I'd like to check out. You know it?'

He squinted out the window and leaned back in his seat. 'On the island?'

'No, on the way there.'

He made a hiss through his teeth that was meant to be a sigh. 'Shit.' He reached for a pack of thin cigars laying on his dash and offered me one.

I declined, taking one of my own out.

He lit it and lowered his window a crack. 'You came here to see the lights?' he said.

'That's right.'

'Filling up your time until then?'

'Why not?'

He laughed a vaunt of smoke. 'Why don't you just go up into the city then and wait there a little while longer? Or if you're looking for a whore, I'll take you to find some good ones.'

I shook my head and clamped my teeth on the fresh cigar. 'I love boats, is all. Can't get enough of them.'

'I hope you like swimming too.'

'From time to time.'

He laughed as he let his foot off the brake, rolling the car along the vacant street. Then, without any warning, he jammed his foot down on the pedal and raced the car onto the main stretch along the coast.

Serik turned the radio on, shifting the dials from static to static. Then, he paused on a faint station playing some pumped-up electronic music. After some time of gliding down the desolate roads, he turned off the radio and let the silence fill the void.

His face lit with the cigar hanging from his teeth, showing his mean scowl while he gripped both hands at the wheel.

'What's with the docks?'

'I told you I'm curious about boats.'

'All right.' He slowed the car down and pulled it alongside the curb. 'I'm not being any sort of accomplice.'

I brought the cigar down from my mouth. 'Fine. I've no problem walking.'

He tapped a clump of ash outside the window and then took another drag, speaking as he let it out.

'What do you want to find at these docks?'

'I was hoping to buy some fish.'

He growled. 'They don't drop their payload here. They dump 'em all on an island off the coast. That's where they get processed.'

I peered out the window across the shore. 'Seems kind of odd.'

Serik cleared his throat.

'What if I hired a boat out there to take me fishing for a while?'

The driver shook his head. 'Not allowed.'

'By who?'

'Government. It's their water. Their fish. No free rides in that aspect.'

I paused, smoking my cigar, and watching the waves break into white foam on the dark shore.

'You eat much fish?'

He bobbed his head to the side. 'Sure.'

'More than land animals?'

'Doesn't matter when meat is all the same.'

'What do you mean?'

He cracked his neck and spat outside the window. 'Everything tastes the same. Fry this one, bake that one, throw another in a furnace. What's the difference, and what does it matter to you? Tourists like you come in and have a bite and then leave first thing in the morning after the lights burn out. So what real difference does it make to you?'

I tapped my cigar outside, dropping some ash onto the pavement below. 'You ever heard of any diplomats going out to sea? Or getting too close to the fish supply?'

He turned off the car and looked out the windshield. 'Nope.' He then reached across my seat, opening my door for me. 'Sorry, but I can't be involved in this. If you walk down that way, you'll find the port.'

I sat in the car for some time, thinking to myself. Then another vehicle passed by, moving slowly along the coast.

Serik wouldn't make eye contact with me. He sat leaning into his side of the vehicle, studying the slow-moving car.

I stepped my foot outside and transferred him enough credits for his time.

'I'll see you around,' I said.

'Yeah. Sure.'

I closed the door behind me and walked the dark streets towards the port in the distance. It was some time before I heard his car screech to life as he swung into a u-turn, going by me in the opposite direction.

Now I really wanted to get my hands on some seafood. I walked alongside the buildings, keeping close to them with an eye on the shore, not caring to walk fully in the open anymore.

There were few cars that passed by me. The port was twenty meters away. It had a lonesome light shining outside the entrance like a faulty spotlight on an old abandoned theatre stage. I stood near the buildings for a moment, waiting to cross the street, when I saw another car passing.

It stopped right where I was at, and Serik hopped out and marched straight towards me. He slapped me hard, causing my head to swing, and then he grabbed me by my jacket and slammed me up against the wall.

'Stop being a damn fool! All right?'

I stood there breathing heavily. I touched my jawline and then spat some blood out to the side.

He pushed me against the wall even more and then turned back, pointing up into the sky. 'What's that mean to you up there?'

I followed his finger, looking at the moon shining in the black sky.

'Did you come up here to watch that thing light up or not?'

I stared at him and shook my head.

'Stop being an idiot. Yeah? Whatever you want - whatever you're after - let it go.'

'Not so easy,' I said with a grunt.

He slapped me again. 'Maybe she was your sister. I don't know, but things happen in this system. Things happen on this planet that you've gotta let go of! You got it?'

He shoved me up against the wall and released his hands from my collar. I dropped to my feet, crashing into one knee and outstretched hand. He murmured local swear words I'd never heard before. But I didn't have to understand him to guess at their meanings.

His eyes were glued to a car banking past us. His curses became even more virulent as it hit its brake lights and slowed ahead.

The driver lifted me, patting my shoulders and fixing my jacket. The car rolled an inch further, then stopped for a second, swinging its way into a quick u-turn and flashing blue and red lights atop.

The driver wiped the back of his mouth with his hand saying, 'Fuck.'

A set of blinding headlights roared in the darkness, shining over us both.

'You have anything on you?' said the driver.

'I'm clean.'

The car zoomed past, squealing its tires as it skidded another u-turn that set it right behind Serik's cab. Two stonewall officers peered through the windshield. The driver turned his back to them a moment and then fixed his jacket.

The two officers opened their doors and stepped out in unison with their shiny boots hitting the curb. The officer nearest us leaned his arm onto his door with a sneer on his face, like he was in pain and ready to unleash it on someone else.

'You boys okay out here?'

The second officer cut on his torchlight, shining it in both our faces. 'You want to talk about it down at the station?'

We shook our heads.

'Nah, no need to do that,' said the driver.

I put my hand up to break the light in my eyes. 'It's nothing, really.'

'Yeah? Didn't look that way from the street.'

The cab driver shrugged his shoulders and cocked his head to the side. 'You know we got a little heated, sure, but no broad is worth that kind of fuss.' He put his hand out towards me to shake it. I took it and nodded at him like I'd forgiven him or something.

'No hard feelings,' he said, patting me on the upper arm. 'She's your girl if you want.'

'Maybe we can share?'

The officers hung in their car doors for a moment longer and then slipped back inside and closed them shut. They talked into their radios while sizing up the both of us.

I backed a step towards the intersection.

The second officer opened his door and stepped out with his gun aimed at me. 'Hey! Who told you to move?'

I put my hands up near my head. 'All right. Nothing personal.'

'Watch yourself, punk.'

'Sorry.'

Slipping fully out of the car, he started to approach me, twisting his handgun into the side of his palm, giving him a strong grip on the barrel. When he reached me, he clocked me across the face with the side of the gun.

I dove into the cement, elbows first. Before I could nurse my bruised skin, he started to kick me in the ribs, then yanked me high enough from the ground to knee me in the chest. I rolled over on the floor wheezing, blood dripping out of my mouth.

The other officer stepped out from his side of the car.

'Hold on,' he said. 'I'm checking this guy out. Don't get him too bloody yet.'

The second officer turned back to his partner and snorted. 'For fuck's sakes. Can you hurry it up?'

Waving his hands in the air, the first officer remained glued to his radio as he slipped halfway back onto his seat.

The second officer returned his gaze to me on the ground. He knocked my hat off and grabbed a handful of my hair, tugging my head upwards to expose my throat. Clucking his tongue at me, he set the tip of his pistol under my chin, jabbing it into the soft area underneath my jaw.

'You look familiar,' he whispered. 'You a tourist?'

The first officer in the car talked over the radio, glancing at us with a pique in interest.

'Wanted to see the lights,' I said, with blood in my teeth.

'You're in the wrong district for that.'

The officer in the car put the radio away and opened his door. He lingered for some time and then motioned something to his partner.

The second officer took his gun off my throat and slowly put it away. He dragged out a pair of handcuffs while the other officer did the same, getting closer to the driver.

'Oh, come on,' said Serik. 'Just a little tiff. What's all this?'

The officer took hold of my wrist.

The driver began to back up against the wall. 'Come on, boys.'

'Sir, put your hands behind your back.'

The officer gripped my arm and clamped the first cuff on my wrist.

'Seriously,' said the driver.

'Sir. I'm going to have to ask you to-'

Cracking like whip, a gunshot hissed so fast that I didn't know where it came from. The first officer tumbled backward onto the street. Then the second officer let go of my wrists and fumbled for his pistol. He wasn't fast enough. Another shot ripped through his jaw, spraying it into bloody splinters along the pavement.

I bowed my face onto the cement and threw my hands atop my skull. The driver leaped over me and shot the second officer twice more in the head. I grit my teeth, listening to the explosions, and squinted my eyes at each flash of light, waiting for the next led bee to pierce through my flesh.

The driver stood exasperated above the dead officer. He tucked his gun away and then leaned down, grabbing hold of me. He tugged me to my feet for a second before he swiftly threw me into the back of his cab.

'Stay there,' he said, pointing his finger in my face.

I nodded.

He then raced to the police car and opened the doors, throwing the two dead officers inside the back. He drove it down the road, turning it onto an alleyway, and disappeared for a while. I still had one cuff on my wrist and blood on my face and jacket.

Serik walked back down the dark street with his hands in his pockets, as if on a casual stroll, minding his own business. He came to the driver's side of the cab and opened the door for himself. When he plopped down, the car trembled under his girth.

He opened his dash and snatched out a rag to wipe the blood from his hands and jacket.

'Fucking hell,' he whispered. 'God damn pieces of shit.'

I stayed in the back quietly with my hand resting on my gun.

He turned around and tossed the rag to me.

'Clean yourself up.'

I picked it up and wiped my face where the blood was already starting to dry. Sirens began to howl in the distance.

He cranked the engine and put the car into drive. 'Fucking hell. Fucking hell.'

I leaned in the back seat, keeping myself below the windows.

The sirens sounded closer. He shook his head and picked up a new thin cigar.

'Fucking hell. I got to deal with this shit again?'

I finished with the towel and rested it in the seat beside me.

The driver lit his cigar. 'Fucking hell. What kind of mess are you into here?'

'The lights-'

He slammed the brakes, rocketing me against the back of his seat. Then, just as fast, he slammed the gas again, throwing me back into my seat.

'Shut the fuck up! Those boys wanted to splatter our brains like we were a couple of crippled horses.' He turned the wheel quickly, squealing the tires on the asphalt and tossing me to the side. 'I swear to god. If you don't level with me, I'll drop your ass on their front doorstep with that bloody rag sewn inside your jacket.'

I sighed as we continued barreling through the streets.

'Come on,' he yelled.

'I was hired to find an old friend who disappeared, okay?'

He shook his head and gripped at the wheel until his knuckles turned white. 'Fucking hell.'

I nodded. 'Yeah?'

'They're wise to you ole boy. You're lucky I didn't feel like dying tonight. Otherwise, you'd be deep-sea fishing for the rest of your life.'

I glanced out the window, not recognizing our surroundings. 'Where are we going?'

He drove in silence, not answering my question.

I leaned back and took a cigarette out of my jacket, and lit it.

'You're gonna cost me some money tonight, you know?'

'I'll pay you back.'

He chewed on his cigar and kept mumbling to himself as he shook his head. The lights lessened outside, and the pavement grew rougher as the buildings grew sparse.

CHAPTER 26

It was a long time before either of us spoke. The car smelled of fresh blood, and our minds were both preoccupied with the ever-pressing necessity of our own survival. I thought about those cops for a while. The one putting cuffs on me and his jaw splitting open. That image didn't want to leave my mind right yet. It wanted to replay itself several more times, along with some old classics lingering inside the rattling brain of mine.

'I know some guys who can get you out of here,' he said. 'Get off this planet and think of it as a bad dream. You got that?'

I looked up at the rearview mirror as the driver kept his eyes out before him.

'What's hidden out there in the waves? You know, don't you?'

He fixed his hands on the steering wheel but didn't answer me.

'How about the foreigner that turned up on the shore the other day? You know what he was killed for? I talked with his wife. She said something about a factory. Any of this clicking upstairs?'

'Lay off it.' He turned over his shoulder to look at me. 'I'm serious, let it go. Take the ticket and get your ass out of here.'

'What about this, I went into someone's hideout and got knocked out, didn't get a dime stolen, and my gun was still loaded with all its bullets? What do you make of that?'

He snorted. 'It doesn't mean a damn thing.'

'You sure?'

'You got lucky.'

'Nah, I bet there was someone vouching for me. A lady I know.'

He turned the car down an unpaved road. 'So?'

'So what are all these tough guys doing, helping her out and doing her favors for?'

'Who knows?'

'I think you do know. It doesn't add up if you think about it. How is she so well connected here? Her husband died a few days ago, and then everyone starts rushing to her aide. Seems weird, no?'

We rolled up a hill to an abandoned cabin, overlooking a patch of dead grass and a small bay of water out back.

'I wouldn't read into it,' he said.

'I know you wouldn't. But I do.'

'Well, you shouldn't.'

'Why? These tough guys have something more up their sleeves? The whole charade is meant to throw us off from what's really going on?'

He stopped the car and turned off the lights, and our surroundings became completely dark. His cigar was still glowing enough under his face for me to see it in the mirror.

'I don't think you should be so concerned with them. Leave them alone. They've been working this business for a long time now.'

I took out my lighter and struck a flame. 'What business? Kidnapping junkies or putting widows on one-way ships home?'

He shook his head with a dead laugh. 'You don't know anything about this place.'

'I'm finding out pretty quick.'

'You're getting yourself lost while they've got a scope aimed at your head.'

'How'd you know what those cops were thinking? Everyone keeps talking about them like they're something bad. But I'm not sure either side is all that legit.'

'You saw the one hanging back in the car, talking on the radio? If you were a nobody tourist, he'd have sped off without another word.'

'All right. Then what made you come back and warn me about the port?'

He opened his door. 'I thought you were being stupid.' He stepped out of the car and shut the door behind him. He then opened my door from the outside. 'Bring that rag with you.'

I picked up the bloody rag and slid out of the car. He grabbed me by the shoulder and squeezed it tight as he led me towards the abandoned cabin.

The screen door was nearly rusted off its hinges as he creaked it open to a second door that was even worse and paper-thin. Jiggling a metal key in the handle, he wrestled for a time with the lock until it came loose, and he pushed into the house.

A pungent smell smacked me in the face as I stepped into the living area. The driver vanished in the dark house for a while. I stayed in the living area, trying to acclimatize to the lack of light.

I noticed some plastic curtains up ahead, the moon's glow slipping through space in between each of them as they swayed from the new energy settling in the darkness.

Then I heard a large thud in the back room that clicked on the lights. A lamp beside me had fallen over, its bulb smashed into shards long ago. I swept my feet away from the glass bits and shuffled along the brown carpeted floors towards the rear sliding doors.

Serik returned, holding a large wrench in his hands.

'Nice place.'

He scoffed. 'There're some clothes in the main bedroom there.' He pointed the wrench at a door behind me. 'We need to burn the ones we have on.'

'And our shoes?'

'Everything.'

I had a last glance at my black-tipped shoes. 'So long then.'

'There's some extra boots in there you can wear back into town.'

'Whose place is this?'

'Don't worry about that. Just get changed. We need to radio a signal in an hour or so.'

I opened my jacket lining and looked at it like an old friend.

'They're just clothes,' he said.

I let go of my jacket and looked at some dried blood under my fingernails. Then I stepped back, went into the main bedroom, turned on the lights, and shut the door. There was no bed, only cabinets and a giant wardrobe in the corner.

The wardrobe was packed full of clothes. None my style, but that wasn't the biggest concern at the time. I dragged out a long black coat, rotated it around two times, then checked to make sure it had a similar amount of pockets as my own.

After laying out my new outfit, I went about transferring my items to the different pockets and then noticed a wallet-sized tool kit in a sock drawer with various picks inside it. As I put on the new clothes, I made up my mind to snatch the tool kit and keep it with me.

On the way out, I caught a glimpse of myself in a dirty mirror on the wall. I felt like a seedy businessman or a gangster from a black and white film. If only I had a feather to put in my new hat.

'Lemoshe would be proud,' I mumbled to my reflection, then carried on into the living area.

Serik wasn't in the living room when I entered. But the backsliding doors lay wide open, the plastic blinds rustling as the chilly winds cooed through the opening. I stepped along, peering outward at the grassy knoll and the long stretch of water behind it.

Serik was busy snapping small twigs in his hands and throwing them into a dug-out fire pit. I went out to join him, my old clothes still pinned under my arm.

He stood up and pointed to a stack of logs up against a grey tree. 'Throw some of those in here. Not too much though; otherwise, it won't burn right.'

I set my clothes down beside the cement pit and went to get the small logs from the tree. Serik snapped his last twig and tossed it into the pit, and walked up into the house. I piled the logs inside, angling them at a rough slant to allow oxygen in to help them burn.

Serik was gone for a while, leaving me outside next to the cement fire pit. I looked out at the bay ahead of me, where the moon bounced off its calm surface. I crept down towards a small, broken pier, half-dragged in the water, the other half still hanging onto the land, trying not to drown. Then I noticed something near the shore, lapping in the soft waves.

Checking to my right and left showed me no other being; and the only lights were from the distant city, painted like a backdrop on the horizon. I stepped closer into the muddy sand and went near the floating items in the black waters.

There were about a dozen or so objects near me. I reached for the one closest to myself. It kept rolling in the soft waves, helpless as to whether it wanted to die on the land or sea. I picked up the slimy creature and felt sharp fins, poking into my skin.

It was a dead fish.

I reached into my new pockets with my other hand and pulled out a small torchlight, and shined it on the creature. It was a silver fish with red tumours growing around its mouth. I dropped it back into the water and then shined my light on the others floating along the shore.

They all had some kind of tumor on them. Some on their backs. Others on their eyes or in their mouths like cancerous sores. I scanned the soft waves and flashed my light on the water. There were countless fish floating belly-up on the surface.

'You happy now?' said Serik.

I turned back quickly, aiming my light on him like a gun.

'Come on. Help me with the fire.'

I remained in my spot. 'Do they sell these kinds of fish?'

He shrugged and cocked his head towards the fire pit. 'Come on. We still need to send out a transmission.'

I snapped a photo with my watch, then stepped up on the grassy knoll and followed him back to the fire pit.

He poured some petrol onto the logs and underneath the papers. Then he flicked a bundle of matches at once, dropping them into a gust of flames. The fire burned hot, charring the paper and singeing the fibrous ends of the broken twigs.

I pulled a cigarette out of my jacket and lit it. The driver did the same with the dead cigar hanging in his teeth.

We watched the fire consume the logs and then threw our clothes atop them. They took their time to burn, like they wanted to resist the whole process, refusing to cleanse the world of their presence.

'Most of our fish come from farms,' said Serik. 'They've got several locations in the sea along here and even more up on the moon. That's where the majority of our foods are sourced. That stupid orb up there.'

I took my cigarette down and eyed my jacket burning. 'I saw a lot of factories down here, though.'

He cocked his head to the side and looked around as if the wilderness might be hiding a microphone within them.

'Yeah, but those aren't foods and such. That's where most of our exports come from. Toys, electronics, car parts, and all the cheap crap you can think of.'

I took another drag of my cigarette and let out the smoke. 'And where does these factories' runoff go?'

He lifted his eyebrows as he nodded towards the bay.

'Of course,' I said. 'Where else.'

CHAPTER 27

I made a drink inside the house. A blend of whiskey left in one of the cabinets – no ice, though, but it didn't matter. Then I saw Serik prodding the fire pit with a metal rod moving the embers around meticulously, turning everything to dust, and starting another fire to leave no shred of evidence.

I went out to join him, sipping my drink and feeling warm inside my gut. He stood up from the fire and jabbed the metal rod into the ground beside his foot.

'So you've heard of a woman named Tsuki Kage?'

He rubbed his hands together and brushed some soot off the side of his jacket. The cold winds began to swell while the fire carried on, producing heat.

'So?'

'Sure. I've heard of her. Women and children's rights. She had enough sense to spout her mouth off about education and rights but never knew when to keep it shut.'

I took in a deep breath.

'There are ways of getting things done on Senturion. And making a big scene before god and everyone was the wrong way to go about it.'

'And what was the scene?'

He shrugged his shoulders. 'I can't remember to be honest. She was always in the news. The government hated her from the moment she stepped foot on this planet. They don't want a woman for a diplomat. And they especially don't want a stubborn one like her.'

'So much for human progress.'

He spat into the fire. 'Progress? By who's standard? Ceph? Give me a break.'

Flames licked above the charred logs.

'There's a reason people act this way on Senturion.'

I tapped some ash from my cigarette and took another long hit.

'Why then? I'm listening.'

He shook his head and picked up the metal rod, stabbing a log and breaking it into a mass of red-hot coals.

'You think it's cold now?'

I noted a tingling numbness at the tip of my nose.

'Ceph. There's a reason we resent you all. You guys had everything you needed to settle in nicely on your planet. Good weather. Plenty to eat, plenty to grow, plenty to hear. None of your frontiersmen had to endure the hardships they went through. Honestly, do you think it's cold now? Do you? Because this is nothing.'

He put his palm flat as if he were expecting to catch some rain in it. 'See, this right here is summer. This is as warm as it'll get for Senturion. And Kaivus is only a few degrees better.'

I flicked my cigarette butt into the fire and then took a sip of my whiskey. 'What's your point?'

'If we seem a little backward, it's because we are. We never had the pampered start you guys did. Things are still growing here, unstable, and even more uncertain given this planet's atmosphere.'

One of the logs cracked, shooting an ember from it out onto the grass. The ember waned and slowly died.

He jabbed the rod into the ground again and took a deep breath on his cigar. 'Tell me something. What did your parents do when you were young?'

I rubbed my eyebrow. 'What does it matter?'

'Come on. You want to talk. So let's talk.'

I licked my lips and had another sip of my drink. 'My mother was a social worker.'

He kept nodding. 'And your father?'

'Don't know. I was told the army. But I don't know.'

'Fair enough.'

I let out a big sigh and finished the glass.

'You know how rare it is for my parents' generation to have had a job like that?' He looked at me out of the corner of his eyes. 'Very rare. Most of us grew up with parents working in the factories or earning it off their backs.'

I turned the glass in my hand, looking at the bead of whiskey lingering at the bottom.

'Social planets like Ceph and those in the inner belt don't know what we've gone through and why we have things the way we do. It's not your place to come in here and tell us how life is supposed to be. Yeah, people like Miss Kage wanted to broaden minds, but in the end, all she managed to do was to find herself hung in the moonlight.'

'Didn't you guys take a seat in the United Council?' I said. 'Even asked to be let in at one point, so you could fall under its civil protections? Wasn't that part of the deal? Everyone chips in to help you out. Shouldn't we expect a bit of progress in return?'

He lifted his head with a nasal sigh. He stared at the moon shining white above. The fire crackled as a few more logs burst embers from their outer bark.

I swirled my empty glass and moved away from the pit and back into the house to refill my drink. I poured myself another glass and then added a drop of water in it. The driver came into the house with his lips pursed and his eyes down.

He went over to another room, opposite of the main one, and turned on the lights. I heard him pulling at something large and then a static noise after that. He was talking in code from then on. Nothing I understood.

I sat down on the old dusty couch and sipped my drink alone. I caught a few words and heard someone responding over the radio in the room behind me. I pat the couch, sending up a cloud of dust that burnt my nose.

Serik left his room and stood in the living area near me.

'It'll take them a day or so to collect us,' he said. 'The police have an image of the car but not of our faces.'

'That's lucky.'

'Doesn't mean they don't know who we are.'

I swished the brown liquid in my glass. 'I need to get back to the city. There's someone I need to talk with there.'

'It'll have to wait.'

I cleared my throat. 'Maybe you could do me a favor? You seem well connected.'

He crossed his arms and nodded his head a little – not saying yes, but merely nodding for me to continue.

I took a cigarette out of my jacket, one of the last ones, and clamped it between my curled lips. 'You know anything about the moon and how to get a ride there?' I brought the lighter up under my cigarette and flicked it into life.

Serik watched me, his face turning sour.

'Well?'

I knew he was clenching his teeth as his muscles pulsed along his jawline.

I held the cigarette between my fingers and my glass in the same hand. I took a final gulp of whiskey and set it on the floor beside me as I stood up.

'That's the key, isn't it?' I started to walk around him, circling him in the room. 'Name the cost, and I'll pay you twice over if you can land me up there.'

He kept his arms crossed and grit his teeth even more.

I smoked my cigarette, stopping now at his side. 'It's nothing you're involved in, is it?'

He cleared his throat and looked out the top of his eyes.

'I know you're not,' I said. 'And you know what I'm after. And if I'm not mistaken, it has little to do with you and your friends.'

He let out a nervous laugh.

'You wouldn't have let me go in that factory the other night if you thought I'd been after your crowd. Were you the one who told them I was in there? Asked them not to kill me?'

He opened his mouth and closed it back.

'You really thought I was just checking on my friend, right?'

'Yeah,' he said. 'She knew you as well.'

'So, you told them I was in there?'

He nodded.

'But whatever's on the moon has nothing to do with you and your friends. Same as tonight. At the port. If you had a stake in the fish, then you wouldn't have cared sending me out there to die. To keep me silent.'

He looked up, blinking a few deliberate winks, and then rubbed his face with the flat of his palm. He started to shake his head a bit.

'Listen,' he said. 'I know you're not from here. I've helped foreigners like yourself before. Most of them give me a nice tip for pointing them back to the safe areas of town.'

I took a drag of my cigarette. 'You want credits then?'

He looked around the room for a moment. 'Why don't you just get back to your home?'

'Can't do it. Not until I figure this out.'

He gave a dry laugh. 'Either you're dirt poor and desperate or worse dirt poor, and they're paying you something big.'

'It's not all about the money. I've got a nice track record. And I don't like to lose.'

He waved his hand at my jacket. I took out the cigarette pack and handed it to him. He pinched one out and gave it back. He then lit the cigarette with a small lighter in his big hands.

'I don't think this'll be worth it to you. Some things are better left a mystery.'

'Not in my books.'

'You're a fool then.'

'Okay.'

'Not even I know fully what goes on up there. We keep our eyes down and mind our own business. This is the way things are for most people. We have to turn a blind eye to keep alive.'

I threw a plume of smoke out of my nostrils and dropped some ash on the carpet below. 'Survival is all you want? Well, I'm not here to get in the way of your life or whatever it is you don't want to unsettle. I'm here for a reason. I need to find out why Miss Kage died. And when your cops are planning to shoot us both in the streets, that's a good indication I'm getting in someone's blind spot where I'm not supposed to be.'

He hissed through his teeth. 'The fuck am I helping you out for again?'

'Credits. And I'll pay you well if you transport me to Eroth.'

He stepped away, shaking his head, and went outside.

I followed him and stepped through the sliding doors. The winds were calm, but the air was still frigid.

'You want things to change?' I said.

He continued walking towards the fire pit.

I flicked my cigarette into the grass and followed him. 'For your mom? Your dad? You were talking about change. You want things to change, well, then you gotta take the risks involved.'

'You'll get killed.'

'I'm already dead. If you knew how many times that phantom brushed his scythe right up under my neck.'

He shook his head and looked down at the dwindling coals buried underneath a layer of grey ash.

'Your system's a part of the UC,' I said. 'If something gets back to them, then you've got their protection. The best group of forces will rush to your aide. That doesn't affect your work. So what if you're peddling drugs on the side or whoring out some women here and there? That happens everywhere. But they won't bother with your rackets if this thing is bigger than that.'

He left his mouth open, letting the smoke fall out through his teeth. He then looked up at the moon shining with a group of stars dispersed in the sky.

'Damn.' He laughed, still looking upwards. 'You're a fucking dick, you know?'

'Yeah. I know. But I think you're just as curious to find out where this leads, no?'

His sights lowered to the fire before us, saying nothing more on the topic.

CHAPTER 28

Two days passed in utter isolation. There was little more information I could pry out of Serik at that time. No amount of credits appeased him. Nor did my gentle nudging find me anywhere further along in meeting with Barbra one last time.

His most common reply was: 'It's out of my hands.'

We sat waiting for our ride to appear. The moment was more tense than I expected. He kept ejecting his pistol's clip, mentally calculating the bullets, then shoved it back inside the gun, waiting.

'I need to send out a signal,' he said. 'Keep an eye out for the car. If there's more than one, then we're in trouble.'

Duly noted.

Stirring restlessly, he stood from his seat and went into the side room to turn on the radio.

I scooted closer to the window, pushing the blinds down, staring into the dark woods.

Serik was talking in the other room.

'Stupid fucker thinks he's gonna get his way by acting like a…'

I turned over my shoulder, listening to the conversation for a few seconds, then I looked out the blinds again.

'Should've let him deal with the situation himself to see how tough he really is.'

There were headlights shining in the woods. They broke in and out as they passed by the black trees. I pressed the thin blinds down further to make sure there was only one car on its way. The lights slowly built and grew brighter as they edged closer to our cabin.

There were only two headlights and one car to hold them. The vehicle pulled into the dirt driveway and up onto the grass near the cabin.

I turned over my shoulder. 'We've got visitors.'

Serik barreled through the living room and peered out the blinds. He then went to the door and held his gun near his gut. I took my gun out as well, moving to the side.

There was a moment of silence before the screen door groaned, and a knock sounded from the others side.

'Got a few coppers out here,' said a raspy man's voice. 'Ready to blow your brains out. So what d'you say about letting us in for drinks first?'

Serik lowered his gun, then placed his hand atop mine, pushing it away. He then unlocked the door and wrenched it open. A large man wearing a snake-skin suit pushed inside, making way for a tall lady in a black suit behind himself. Their faces were shaded by the dark, but their statures remained daunting. In fact, the lady was a good head taller than the rest of us.

'This him?' said Snakeskin, jutting his chin at me.

'Yeah,' said Serik.

Their eyes fixed onto me. Snakeskin wagged his finger behind himself to the tall lady, who clicked on the faint lights. Two small eyes stared at me in a large and rotund face while a grin crept ear-to-ear. Lingering near the light switch, the tall lady stood impassive, her pointed hat hiding her eyes.

'This the same guy snooping around the factory?' said Snakeskin.

'You had a friend of mine there.'

The man touched his cuffs. 'Is that so?' His drooping cheeks jiggled as he chuckled.

The driver closed his eyes with annoyance.

Holding at her side, the tall lady clearly had her hand on a pistol. I shifted my sights between each of them. Taking in a deep breath, Snakeskin raised his brow and focused his tiny eyes on me.

'We want our pay upfront for getting you out of here.'

I returned the smile as I pulled a cigarette from my jacket.

Snapping his fingers, Snakeskin left his mouth open, then lay his hand flat in the air.

'That means now sugar.'

Lighting my cigarette, I blew smoke from the corner of my mouth and reached out my credit piece.

'I'll pay you. That's no problem. But I want to meet my friend one last time.'

Still motionless near the light, the tall lady titled her face upward, but not enough for me to see her eyes. Snakeskin laughed at me, his Adam's apple bobbing in his meaty throat. His smile melted slowly from his face.

'What friend? You've got no friends here.'

'Barbra,' I said. 'Married to the Cowboy they found floating around the beach not too long ago. The lady you had at your factory the other night. Can't remember?'

'Factory? Whose factory?'

'Barbra Velts.'

'Don't know her.'

I glanced at Serik and then back to Snakeskin in front of me.

'Right,' I said. 'How much extra to see her? Let's not be coy. You've a nice business trafficking people around, and I get the feeling it ain't because you've got a big heart.'

He smiled. 'Cute.'

I took a drag of my cigarette and let it out my nose. 'Name the price.'

He stared at me with his tiny eyes, nearly hidden in his large face. He put his head down a little as if looking at the floor and then probed a reaction from the tall lady behind himself. Serik focused on her as well.

My eyelid twitched as my hands grew clammy.

Moving one of her golden fingernails broke the spell in the room and caused both men to refocus on me.

'We want to pay upfront.'

'I already agreed to that.'

'I don't think you're hearing me properly.' Snakeskin cracked his neck. 'I said we want to pay upfront.'

My line of sight bounced from Snakeskin to Serik to the stern lady at the wall. No one moved. And I was pretty certain of the reason behind the standoff. Slowly, I lifted my credit piece and punched the number agreed upon on my holographic display.

'That's right,' he said. 'You're no dunce now, are you?'

I clicked the piece, transferring the credits.

Turning over his shoulder, Snakeskin nodded to the lady near the wall. She had her face tilted upward, allowing me a first glimpse at her painted white face. Then she lowered her head back down, once more concealing her eyes.

'Ready then?' said Snakeskin.

'What about Barbra?'

'Who?'

'Barbra. The lady you had at the factory the other night!'

'Keep your voice down,' he said. 'We're all in the same room, pal.'

Serik flashed me a cold glance. I shoved my credit piece back in my pocket and blew some air through my nose. Then the lady raised her painted face again. She stared at me; her face a mask with two pure black eyes, and deep rouge lips, betraying no emotion.

My cigarettes trembled between my fingers.

'Do you want to fuck her?' she said.

I shook my head. 'No.'

'Then you love her?' she said. 'You want to make love to her? Give her pussy a few licks?'

'No,' I whispered.

A slight crease pulled at one side of her lips. Her eyes could've been moving, but I had no way of telling without any pupils to gauge.

'An extra thousand will give you fifteen minutes with her.'

'A thousand? Credits?'

She nodded at me.

'Shit.'

'We're on a timetable,' she said. 'Better make up your mind fast.'

Fumbling for my credit piece, I pulled it back out and sent over another thousand credits.

Without any further word, she rounded out of the house.

Snakeskin continued to eye me.

I snorted at him. 'See, that wasn't so hard now.'

'You get your jaws popped often talking like that?'

I rubbed along my jawline. 'More than average.'

Snakeskin nodded to himself, then turned out the door following behind her. My heart ran apace in my chest. I knew they wouldn't think twice to bury me if those credits hadn't cleared.

I glanced at Serik, who said nothing and gave nothing in his vacant expression.

'Friends?' I said to him.

He simply cocked his head to the side at the open door.

Shuffling outside, I stayed on the tiny porch, examining the luxury car in the driveway and thinking how out of place it seemed. When Serik finished bolting the cabin's door, he gave me a harsh shove down the steps.

'Want me to hold your hand?' he said.

Brushing my jacket's sleeve, I whispered under my breath at him and made my way towards the luxury vehicle. Without the slightest warning, Serik threw his arm over my shoulders, nearly lifting me, as he changed my direction away from their car.

'You need a good deal of explaining, don't you?'

I dropped my cigarette and went to the cab, and settled in the passenger's seat. We both waited for a signal. Waited for something to tell us when to go. Then the car ahead turned on, its brake lights shining in our eyes, and as if on cue, Serik cranked the cab's ignition. The car in front peeled out of the driveway, and we drifted on behind them.

Stillness filled the void as we raced along a rocky path underneath a tunnel of dark foliage. The black forest showed no signs of life or any disturbance from our presence. We drove for an hour, never passing by anything other than motionless trees.

Then a break in the momentum eased our ride as the car ahead pulled to the side of the dirt road and parked. Serik slowed the cab behind them and shut off the engine. Hopping out, he came to my door and rapped his knuckle on the window, then waved a finger for me to leave.

I stepped outside and walked near the other car, where I caught wind of Snakeskin talking to an older man in coveralls. The driver tapped me on the shoulder to keep walking, but I wanted to hear what they were saying.

Coveralls rubbed the back of his head, leaving a wrench hanging at his side.

'In the middle of the night?'

Pausing to gaze at the side of the old man, Snakeskin made note of something in the dark woods.

'What type of trees are these?'

'Huh?'

'Trees. What kind are they?'

'I-I'm not so sure,' said the old man.

'Maybe oak?'

The old man's voice quivered as his hands started to twist about his wrench.

'I said I don't know.'

'You live amongst so many trees, and you don't take the time to learn their names?'

'I-I never - you see-'

'Try to figure it out then,' said Snakeskin. 'This is good knowledge to have when you've got disguised visitors knocking at your door.'

'Yes, sir.'

While digging an elbow at Serik, Snakeskin lifted his eyebrows an inch.

'Oi, what d'you think here? Have a look at this place?' he said. 'Tell me something, it's like this guy's got his own private Shady Oaks here in the woods, yeah?'

'Sure,' said Serik. 'Whatever you say.'

'People would pay big money for this kind of seclusion!'

The old man grimaced, flashing his crooked yellow teeth at the men.

'But if you don't want to help us out...' Snakeskin looked past the old man as if he were assessing the plot of land.

'Well, hold on a minute,' hissed the old man. 'Let's hold on a second. We can work something out.' He walked over to the luxury car, going near the hood. 'What exactly do you need done?'

Snakeskin turned to the side, pointing at the cab behind us. 'This is it back here,' he said. 'You know how to make these things seem brand new?'

The old man squinted in the cab's headlights, studying the vehicle a moment. He nodded his head and lowered the wrench to his side again.

'What'd you do to it?' he said.

Touching the back of his ear, Snakeskin looked confused at the old man. 'Excuse me?' he said. 'What did I ask you? I asked you if you could make this thing seem like brand new? Isn't that what I asked?'

'You did,' said the old man. 'Yes, sir, you did.'

'And?'

'I can,' he said. 'Yes, sir, if you give me a month, you won't be looking at the same cab anymore.'

Snakeskin smiled as he eyed the old man. 'That's fair.' He glanced at Serik beside himself. 'You think that's fair?'

'Sounds fair.'

'Fair is fair then,' he said. 'We'll swing by in a month or so to check in on you.'

The old man nodded fast. 'Yes, sir, I'll have it done by then.'

Giving him a pat on the back, Snakeskin laughed and slipped into his car, leaving the door ajar.

'You tell your wife and kid we said hello.'

Squeezing the wrench near his chest, the old man swallowed hard, while his face sank further.

Serik opened the car's back door and motioned for me to do the same. I followed his instructions and hopped inside.

'Your son should be pretty old by now, right?' said Snakeskin.

Unable to respond, the old man stood with his mouth wide open and the wrench slipping towards the ground.

'Oh, well, some kids don't want to go live in the big cities, do they? Too many bright lights and dark alleyways. No, some want to stay close to their parents. Real tight like. And don't think I can't respect that kind of wish. Especially in a secluded place such as this.'

The old man's face dragged down into heavy wrinkles, leaving a dark patch of fear to surround his white eyes.

'Let's meet them when we get back?'

The wrench dropped from his hands.

'Hope you don't lose your grip when fixing up the cab.'

'No, sir, I won't. I promise!'

'Then, we'll see you in a month?'

'Yes, sir.'

'See the wife and kid too?'

'Yes, sir,' the old man whispered.

'Good man. You're a good man.'

Bowing his head, the old man looked depressed as he stared at his wrench on the ground.

'You have a nice night now.'

'Thank you.'

Snapping his fingers, Snakeskin's door shut, and he rammed his foot onto the gas pedal. The car ripped onto the dirt road, flinging a trail of dust behind. I turned back and saw the cab growing farther away, its headlights shining through the thick cloudy veil. The old man faded, losing all shape in the darkness. I then fixed myself straight in my seat and watched the headlights guide the path ahead.

Snakeskin would chuckle to himself every so often and mumble words I couldn't decipher. Then he shifted in his seat and turned to glance me sidelong as he drove.

'Your face always that puffy?'

I dabbed a swell at the top of my forehead.

He scoffed to himself and then readjusted his position at the wheel. The bumpy road had little impact on the fancy car. We drove onward, gliding over the terrain in complete comfort, nestled in our giant seats.

The tall lady opened the center console near her elbow, pulling out a bar of chocolate that she snapped in half.

'You've backed yourself in a tight corner Mr. ?'

'Gavelman.'

'Right.'

'And you are?'

My words faltered as a giant hand squeezed the nerves in the back of my neck. After several seconds Serik retracted his hand to his lap and shot me a glare. I turned my sights out the window. Still surrounded by trees. Endless stretches of dark trees.

Then I felt the need to check my surroundings. I saw her black eyes linger over me in the rearview mirror as she took a bite of her chocolate bar.

'Who's sending you boys up here anyhow?' she said.

'Couldn't tell you.'

Reaching a square to Snakeskin, she fed it into his mouth, pushing it like a man force-feeding his dog a pill of medicine. He ate the chocolate without any fuss, though.

'Someone's curious about our planet,' she said, breaking another square. 'Very curious nowadays.'

'Why do you think that is?'

She chewed the square, delaying her answer for some time.

'What does it matter?' she said.

'Obviously, someone cares.'

The lady took hold of the rearview mirror and angled even more to put us eye to eye.

'Let me make something clear,' she said. 'I'm not fond of men like you. And I'm even less fond of men from other planets trying to pry apart my operations.'

'Didn't realize I was stepping on anyone's toes.'

'Then you're dumber than I thought.' She forced another square in Snakeskin's mouth. 'Stay out of our planet's affairs. Take whatever money they've paid you and tell them you spent it all getting back home.'

I glanced up into the rearview mirror at her black eyes.

'Is that a threat?'

She shifted the rearview mirror back and left us in silence for the rest of the ride.

Soon, the dark trees began to fade as new signs of life cropped up in the world passing by. A lone building stood on a flat plane of asphalt, with a neglected chain fence tangled in weeds and tall dead grass as we drove into the outskirts of civilization.

The car glided at its steady pace. I sat back in my seat and pulled a cigarette from my jacket.

There was a patch of houses up ahead. They had slanted roofs and the same kind of weeds growing around them. I lit the cigarette and closed my lighter. I took a deep breath and let it out as I spoke.

'You'll let me speak with Barbra, though?'

A golden fingernail lifted to where I could see it between the two front seats. 'Sure,' she said. 'The girl doesn't know anything.'

'Not why I asked.'

The car turned down a narrow street and began to weave through a few derelict buildings. We moved out from the tight maze into the open, where another large factory stood with a rusted barbed wire fence run around the perimeter.

The car drove through the open fence, right next to the factory. We waited outside for some time, just sitting there until the door opened wide enough to drive inside. There were some standing work-lights with people gathered near them, all seeming to be waiting for our arrival.

Our car stopped next to the other cars resting in the giant factory.

Snakeskin turned off the ignition and then killed the headlights. The tall lady stayed quiet in her seat and no one else dared to make any peep.

Then she tore into a second bar of chocolate and began to shove pieces into Snakeskin's mouth.

Eventually, she had a few squares herself and then crumpled the wrapper in her hands.

I opened my door a sliver to drop my cigarette before the embers reached my fingers. I closed it back again, waiting for any kind of movement.

She then took a final bite, dabbed her painted face with a cloth, and then angled the rearview mirror towards me.

'Get out,' she said. 'And don't ever let me find you on Senturion again.'

'Yes, ma'am.'

The door opened for me, and a thug grabbed my collar, yanking me outside. Serik exited himself; pushing the thug holding my collar away, and then squeezed the back of my neck to lead me through the factory.

A spotlight then shined upon us, causing me to flinch as I reflexively threw my hands over my eyes. When I had a chance to acclimate, I started to lower my arms, leaving my hand over my forehead like a visor at my forehead.

Serik tossed my neck out of his grip and disappeared, leaving me alone in the overbearing lights. Then in an instant, they shut off, and a large group of figures marched past me and into the various cars in the factory.

One by one, the cars purred to life, their headlights clicking on as they sped out from the factory. When the last one vanished, I stood in the vacant warehouse, with my hands raised near my head for some reason.

●　　　●　　　●　　　●　　　●

I stood in the center of the warehouse, smelling the fermented stench of worn oil and rusted metal. I then heard footsteps drawing closer. There was only one standing light left on at this point. I could see the figure getting closer. They were skinny whoever they were. Their suit was hanging off their bones, growing wide around the wrists.

The man carried his hand upwards as if he had something invisible he was carrying in it. He stared at me with his thin eyes, looking at me with the larger of the two and leaving the other half closed. His face was etched with lines and liver spots upon his forehead and a hat to cover his scraggly white hair.

'They told me to shoot you if you tried to get out.' He patted the breast of his jacket. 'But I don't want to do that, you know. So let's make it easy on each other.' He lifted one of his eyebrows.

I nodded with a smirk. 'Whatever you say, grandpa.'

He licked his lips with fervor. 'Prick.'

'When can we have a bathroom break?'

He measured me over with a squint and then patted his chest as he turned away. I cleared my throat as he continued to walk.

'And where's the lady?'

The man pointed to the back with a swish of his hand, without turning around to look at me. I patted my coat a few times and then went towards the back. There were offices lined in the brick walls. I opened the first door, nothing; second, nothing; and then third. She sat in there on a single bed with a work light standing in the corner of the room.

She sat up, grimacing as she rubbed her shaved head. I tipped my hat, showing her my eyes.

Her face relaxed. 'Vince?'

I nodded.

'Why are you wearing that?'

'Thought I'd join them.'

'Really?'

'No, I got in a bind like you.'

'Oh.' She sighed and then glanced at me with dark circles around her eyes. 'You too?' A tear slipped down her cheek. 'Oh, god, they say it'll be over soon but it never seems to end.'

I nodded, taking a thin cigar from my jacket.

She wiped her nose, using the back of her hand. 'I guess it's a common theme here?'

'They've got a whole business built around it.' I lit the cigar and clicked the lighter shut. 'How much are you paying them to send you home safely?'

She bit her lower lip a moment and then opened her mouth. 'Thirteen thousand?'

I laughed. 'Yeah. That's about right.' I blew some smoke out of my mouth. 'Seems like a nice way to make some money. Better than drugs.'

She peered over my shoulder towards the door, checking it before she continued talking. 'You don't think they did this to Oren, just to get money from us?'

'Who knows,' I said. 'They're pretty efficient at the whole process.'

Her face sank even more, a shade of horror growing in her eyes.

'You don't really think…'

'No, I don't,' I said. 'It doesn't add up.' Then I leveled my eyes upon hers. 'Barbara, how bad do you want some closure in this whole situation?'

'What?'

'You know what I'm saying. Now, how bad do you want it?'

'It's not possible.'

'Listen,' I said. 'I'm not here just for my own skin, all right? There is no such thing as a place called Sturdy's cars or any rubbish like that. You get me?'

'Okay. But what can either of us do here?'

'You leave that to me. What I need from you right now is the honest truth, all right? No half-truths or hiding anything you might feel uncomfortable saying, and just spit it out. Because a lot depends upon your answers.'

'What do you want to know?'

'A few things.'

She raised her eyes and nodded a little.

'Did Oren ever talk about going to Eroth?'

She was caught in a trance of thought for some time, searching her memories or lost in the situation at hand.

'The truth, Barbra.'

'Once,' she said. 'He recently told me about the idea. He said he wanted to visit Eroth to see their factories and plantations. To get a feel for the crops up there - maybe to think about it for a branch if he sold them on Silver Mists.'

I rubbed my face until it was warm and plenty red.

'Sounds about right.'

She gasped and then covered her mouth. 'You think?'

I licked the corner of my lips. 'I don't know, honestly. There's something else I need to check out before I could say. There are a lot of strings hanging loose at the moment.'

She eyed me from the cot. 'What are you?'

I rubbed some crud out of the corner of my eyes.

'Go home,' she said. 'Please don't get involved, Vince. No closure is worth your life.'

I then walked around the room, glancing at the old chairs and abandoned desks in the corner. There was one window at the side, but it had bars locking it in place. I stepped closer to the window, noticing how new the bars were compared to the rest of the building.

I opened the window and grabbed the bars, tugging them as hard as I could. They didn't budge.

'You can't get out,' she said. 'The whole place is locked down.'

I tapped the bar with my knuckle, listening to it thud.

'They're on all the windows.'

I stared at them for a moment longer. Then I stepped back and closed the window.

'Strange way to help someone out,' I said. 'Baring them in like animals.'

I flicked some ash from my cigar onto the ground. 'There was a bunch of people here earlier. Do you know what they were doing? Can't all be for one little girl.'

'They hold meetings in this place from what I've gathered.'

'Yeah? And what were those meetings about?'

She paused a moment. 'I couldn't catch much. But there's something about a place called Shady Oaks? They called it their bread and butter.'

I nodded, taking another drag from my cigar. 'You know the place?'

She pursed her lips and folded her hands atop her legs. 'No.'

'Come on, Barb.'

She slowly crossed her arms at her chest. 'I don't know.'

'Shady Oaks. I keep hearing about this place. Funny name, no?'

She gave a fake smile.

'Right. Your husband didn't know anything about it? How many years had he been coming to Senturion?'

'Don't...'

'Stop talking this way! You're not one of them!'

She put her hand over her mouth.

'You know better than this,' I said. 'I'm here to help, but I can only do so much without the truth.'

She paused to chew one of her bloody fingernails.

'Do you want some justice for what they did to your husband, or do you only want to save your own hide now?'

'I can't...'

'You're already home free,' I said. 'They'll set you on the ship and have you back to Ceph in no time. But beyond that, you have a choice to make. Whether you're going to let these forces abuse you, as they've done to others countless times before yourself, or whether you're going to level with me and start spitting out the truth.'

'There is no truth,' she whispered.

'You're talking like a coward,' I said. 'You're speaking as if you're stuck here for the rest of your life. Barb, don't you see, you've got nothing to lose by telling me.'

She released her bloody fingernail from her teeth and glared at me.

'Please?'

'How do I know you're not working for them?' she said. 'They have eyes and ears all over this world.'

'Me?' I said. 'Working for them?'

I clamped the cigar in my teeth and tugged at my jacket's lining out of frustration. My watch showed me that my fifteen minutes were soon to run dry.

'Then that's it,' I said. 'That's as far as this goes? We pack our bags and call it a bad day? Fuck Senturion. Fuck Kaivus. And fuck Eroth and any poor soul trapped in this system.'

She stared at me wide-eyed, scared to her wits, and on the brink of tears. Her mouth moved but wouldn't speak.

'I paid a grand to speak with you,' I said. 'For fifteen minutes, Barbra. But what's the point?'

She balled her hands on her legs and clamped her eyes shut.

'You're terrified, aren't you?'

Her eyes opened a slit.

'Then, stay that way. Fuck Senturion and every foreigner that's gone floating in their waters. Right?'

She clamped her eyes shut again.

I sighed, turning my face away and rubbed my temples. As I reached the door, I heard the bedsprings creak a little.

'It's some government place,' she said. 'I don't know what it is, though. We were told by a local never to ask.'

'That's all you know?'

'I've heard thugs using to threaten clients before.' She paused to bite her lip. 'There was another man in here the other day. A bit unstable. Talked like he had a swollen tongue, and he walked like his joints were too weak to hold him up.'

I nodded, stepping closer to her.

'I've heard of drugs that can do that to people,' she said. 'And I'm starting to think they might be the ones who got him hooked on it in the first place.'

'Black Death?'

'I don't know, Vince.'

I knelt down beside her. 'Why were they keeping him here then?'

She opened her mouth a little. 'I don't know,' she whispered. 'All I can think is that he might lead the cops back to their dens or say the wrong thing.'

I scratched the stubble underneath my chin and thought to myself for a second.

She met my eyes. 'He was looking for a dog,' she said. 'I heard him talking about it over and over again. I screamed at one point for him to shut up because he wouldn't stop talking about the same damn thing!'

I reached inside my jacket and offered her one of my last remaining cigarettes. She put her hand on the pack, closing them, and then gently left her fingers on mine. I glanced from the pack up into her eyes.

She moved her fingers further over mine.

'Vince,' she said. 'Please don't let me end up like Oren.'

'You'll be fine.'

'And if you fled back to Ceph the way I am,' she said. 'I wouldn't blame you. Please know that. I'm not asking you or anyone else to bring me justice.'

I nodded with a dry smile.

There was a sudden clank at the door behind us. I moved my hands away from hers and slipped the cigarettes back inside my jacket. The door opened up, and the old man stood with his loose suit dangling off his body and large eyes probing the both of us.

I turned towards him. 'Room service?'

He licked his lips and then snorted with disgust. 'You girl,' he said, pointing at her. 'Let's go. They're moving you. Say bye-bye to your lover boy and get your tail outside.' He jerked his thumb back over his shoulder.

She looked at me, and I gave her a faint nod. She then stood up with a weighted sigh.

I nabbed hold of her wrist before she left and tapped our watches together. They transferred our contact information to each other.

'I'll meet you back on Ceph,' I said.

She nodded with her eyes down and an uncertain smile on her lips. I stood and held her by the hand.

'Can you make it quick?' said the old man. 'There are people waiting out here?'

She let go of my fingers with a final squeeze and slowly went to the door, and turned around to give me a wink before she left.

The old man shook his head at me, still patting the breast of his jacket where I assume he kept his firearm. I patted my jacket as well and gave him a smile. He shut the door and left me to myself.

CHAPTER 29

I sat in the backroom for most of the night, drifting in and out of sleep, hearing odd noises outside that perked my adrenalin from time to time. And then the door screeched open to my room. The same old guy stood on the threshold.

'You made bail,' he said.

'Yeah? But what if I wanted to stay? I'm kind of fond of the place now. Especially having you as my new chum.'

'Get outside.'

I cracked my neck and then stretched my arms before standing. I brushed the sleeves of my jacket and looked around the room a moment. The old man hummed at me and then took a deep breath, letting it out with disgust.

I walked through the door and past him as he shut it behind us. I saw a familiar face waiting for me beside a nice black car. Serik rested his arms on his open door, the same scars on his face and a new cigar in his teeth. He didn't move as I walked towards him. Just drew on his cigar as he watched me.

I stepped to the passenger side and opened the door. He moved out of his stance and slid into the front seat. We shut the doors in unison like we'd been working together for years. He cranked the car and lit the headlights. The factory door started to open. Serik put the car in reverse, backing into a ray of moonlight.

'You almost missed the lights,' he said. 'What a shame coming all the way out here for nothing.'

'Yeah. Would've been a pity.'

The car drifted out from the factory, along the moonlit asphalt, and past the barbwire fence into a weed-infested ghost town. Serik weaved smoothly down several tight alleyways, rumbling over a patch of unpaved road at one point and then banked out onto a familiar stretch. We cruised alongside the coastline, whipping past the small fishing port and eventually the pink hotel.

'Do you understand what it took to keep you alive?' he said.

'Credits.'

'She told me to leave you at the lake house. To keep your bones warm in the fire pit.' He pulled the cigar down in between his fingers and left his hand on top of the steering wheel. 'And I thought about it too.'

'Then why didn't you?'

'Because you're quite popular,' he said. 'The authorities want to get their hands on you pretty badly, you know? My brother told me they've been watching you like a hawk, ever since you stepped foot on Senturion... And they're searching even more now that you've vanished.'

I swallowed my breath and rubbed my damp palms together.

'Your brother,' I said. 'He's the fat one that picked us up at the lake house?'

'He's big-boned.'

'You look similar. Except for the eyes. I guess his never fully opened after birth.'

'You're an uncomfortable man to be around.'

I touched the cigarette pack in my jacket. There was one smoke left to my name. And she kept on beaconing to me.

'You've got some options here, Vince,' he said. 'We can ride for a while until the ferry services open and put you on the first ship to Kaivus... Or we can ride around even more and see how long you can keep up this gig before they wrap a noose about your neck.'

'Don't you care?' I said. 'This isn't even my planet and yet...'

The driver cleared his throat and turned the wheel down a new stretch of road. I searched my jacket for one of my thin cigars. There was one left. I took it out and lit it.

'So your brother told you to come pick me up at the factory and send me on my way?'

'No, his wife asked him to sink a thing of lead in the back of your head tonight, but I happened to catch wind before they left their house.'

'Nice couple.'

The driver exhaled and turned the wheel again.

'You ever feel helpless to your situation in life?' he said. 'Like you know too much about shit you can do a damn thing about?'

'All the time.'

'It's what keeps you playing this game?'

'Yeah.'

'I don't think you're something noble,' he said. 'You think you deserve pain, I bet. Who knows where you got that notion, but my guess is that it's stuck inside you fairly deep.'

I glanced outside my window.

'You know how I know this?' he said. 'Because I got that same thing inside me too. Only difference is, I'm not stupid enough to pass it up, when I see an opportunity to change these things.'

'And what exactly do you want to see change?'

He chuckled a little. 'There's a friend of mine who transports cargo between here and the moon.'

We turned down another narrow street that was lined with a few more cars, and a couple of homeless folks gathered in coarse blankets on the sidewalk.

'He told me they have a strict code for working those transports,' he said. 'If they catch you breaking ranks, they whack your legs with a sledgehammer. If they see you peeping where you ought not be peeping, they gouge your eyes out and mail them to your parents. You need me to keep going?'

'No. I follow.'

'And if you were able to sneak on a passage, risk and all, you'd still want to go?'

'It's not just for me anymore. Is it?'

'Right.' He took a drag of his cigar and gripped his hands back on the wheel. 'My friend might be able to put you on that ship.' He turned to glance at me. 'Need a uniform, though. Can't go there dressed like you work for my sister-in-law.'

My face went numb. My hands trembled uncontrollably on my lap.

'I don't know you after this,' he said. 'And you sure as hell don't know me. If anything happens, you're an asshole that snuck on the ship without anyone's help. Not even my friend. Got it?'

I nodded, trying to swallow the cold lump in my throat.

'You hear me?'

'Fine,' I said. 'That's fine.'

He sighed and turned down another dim street. 'He doesn't fly for a couple of hours. We have some time to kill. You hungry?'

I thought to myself for a moment and then looked out the window along the dark sidewalk where a man stumbled up ahead.

'Shady Oaks,' I said. 'I keep hearing about this place. It's up there, isn't it?'

The driver pulled the car slowly along the street and laughed. 'Shady Oaks. Shaded Oaks is the real name.' He started to slow down the car as we approached a wobbly man on the pavement. 'It's a place for guys like him.' He nodded towards the man on the sidewalk.

I glanced over Serik and out the window at the hobbling guy.

'Stop the car!'

He slammed the brakes. I opened the door and rushed out to meet Dogman. I turned over my shoulder to make sure no one else was in the area and then went up beside him.

'Saw a dog that went up the hill, big black dog, with furry ears,' he said to himself.

I took him by the arm. 'Champ. You're looking for a dog, right?'

He stopped to look at me. His eyes couldn't focus in one place for long. They twitched back and forth like they were broken in his sockets.

'You seen a big black dog with furry ears?'

I spied over my shoulder at the driver sitting in the car.

'Yeah,' I said. 'We found him over there. You come ride with us, and I'll take you to him.'

Dogman tried to focus on the car, but his eyes kept moving. I looked at Serik, cocking my head to the side, gesturing for him to move closer. The car drifted up next to us. I took hold of the man's arm and dragged him to the back seat. I put him in, shut the door, then went around to the passenger's side and got in myself.

Serik stared at me. 'You're catching on, aren't you?'

'I need to meet with a friend of mine - real quick. Let's keep moving.'

The driver moved ahead, spitting faint laughs to himself.

I put my wrist up under my mouth. 'Ju,' I said. 'Listen. It's important that we meet tonight. I need to see you. I can't meet you at the hotel, but maybe there's somewhere else we could catch each other? Has to be quiet. I mean dead silent. You feel me?'

I then lowered my wrist and turned back to the man in the back.

'There was a dog that went up the hill.'

I nodded but then interrupted him. 'What's your name?'

'Gabe.'

I kept nodding. 'Gabe. All right. You have any family? Sister, brother, mom, dad?'

'I don't have a brother.'

'Where's your sis then?'

'She left with my mom,' he said. 'They went to go find my dad. He left when I was young, and it was all my fault.'

I took a drag of my thin cigar and let it out.

'Why is it your fault?'

'Because I let the dog out. If I hadn't done that, dad wouldn't be out searching for him now. He went to find him and never came back.'

I rubbed my eyebrow and glanced at Serik. He pursed his lips and refused to look at me.

'And your mom and sis, they're searching for that dog too?'

'Me too,' he said. 'If I can find him, then I'm sure they'll come home. I didn't mean to let him out. He had to pee, and I didn't want to get smacked.'

I turned back around in my seat and let out a sigh. 'Fuck,' I whispered to myself.

'I always look for him. Sometimes the men come and get me and tell me to hide, but I don't want to. They say I'll go to Shady Oaks if I'm bad and keep looking for him...'

I got a message from Ju: *I hope everything's okay? There's a place that no one ever goes. I can send you the coordinates if you'd want to meet there. Bring your own sheets if you have that in mind. The cot's pretty old.*

I saw the coordinates come through and then clicked it on my wrist. I then glanced over to Serik, nudging him with my elbow.

'Take us here?'

He glanced at the map. 'Send it to me.'

I sent it to him.

'...saw a big one going up the hill. If I can get back there, it might be him. They don't like me to go up the hill, though. Every time I escape, they get mad and put me somewhere else...'

I started to rub my eyebrows again. 'Does the name Sycamore mean anything to you?'

Gabe paused in the back. 'That's the apartment I used to live in. Before my mom and sis left.'

I nodded and clenched my teeth. 'I'm sure it is.'

We continued driving through the dark city, passing by a few cops and even fewer pedestrians on the walk. The car ride was silent for some time before we reached the destination. The driver pulled up into an abandoned complex with three buildings stacked atop each other, unevenly at that, with most areas left unfinished. Serik turned off his lights and sat behind the wheel, scanning the place for a while.

'You sure she's in there?'

I glanced around, seeing even more uncompleted buildings like a stretch of construction abandoned overnight. I gazed up at the rough complex and tipped open my door.

'I'll check it out first. Stay here until I get back.'

The driver looked at his wrist, tapping it with his large forefinger. 'Clock is ticking,' he said. 'Remember, we've got some cargo to deliver in a few hours.'

I nodded. 'We'll make it. Just keep cool.' I closed the door and pulled the gun out from my side, dropping my cigar onto the gravel as I walked towards the complex. There was a main door at the front with no handle. I gave it a push that swung it open with little effort.

I aimed the gun out ahead of me and stepped inside the room, keeping my eyes near the stairwell. There was a creaking sound in the floor above me. Like someone was moving gingerly upstairs. I put my back against the wall and slid towards the steps.

The movement grew louder upstairs.

I put my foot on the first step and climbed slowly with my gun leading the way. I passed by the first landing and saw three doors, with one cracked open in the middle. I stepped with care towards it, not making a sound, and nudged it open with my barrel.

There was someone inside. A girl.

I aimed the gun at her.

'Evening,' I said.

The lady turned around. Her arm twitched at her side, and her head clicked the same.

'Vince?' she said.

The room was bare with cement floors, an old broken cabinet to the side, and a cot next to a steel bed frame that laid unassembled on the floor. I kept my gun trained on her. She blinked a rapid flutter and then twitched.

'Vince? What's going on?'

'How'd you get here?'

She blinked again. 'I had someone drive me. For my own safety.'

'They're still around?'

She opened her mouth as her arm twitched at her side. 'Well - yes, but not at this complex.'

I nodded as I licked my cold lips. 'Who drove you?'

She blinked a flutter and looked as if she were out of breath. Her lips started to quiver.

'A man from the bar,' she said. 'You didn't see him the night you came, but he takes me everywhere.'

'Is he working in a pinstripe suit?'

She shuddered her entire body. 'No, he does it on his own - or I mean through the bar. The owner's his uncle.'

I started to lower my gun. 'How long have you known him?'

'Five or six years?'

I put my gun down. 'Has he ever worked with the cops?'

Her arm twitched, and her eyelids fluttered. 'No, he hates them. And the pinstripes.'

I sighed and then put my gun away.

'What's happened?'

I shook my head and rubbed my eyebrow. 'Nothing. Just needed to be sure.'

She gulped, and then her head twitched. I looked up at her and breathed a hiss through my teeth.

'You didn't get that spaz from any drugs, did you?'

She shook her head, blinking her eyes. 'I've never done them. I was born like this.' Her lips were shaking as she spoke.

I walked closer to her with my head down. 'There's a lot of people born with similar ailments on Senturion?'

'More than you know.'

I nodded as I exhaled through my clenched teeth. 'Your planet's a bit poisonous, no?'

She licked her lips as her shoulder moved.

'I saw what kind of fish you're eating here. Tumors spread along their mouths, and even more, growing on their backs. Can't be safe, can it?'

She opened her lips and made a noise as if she'd lost her voice. I tipped my hat up and eyed her.

'It was during the industrialization,' she said. 'They had so many factories in this city. Pouring waste in the waters. Clouding the skies with haze. We never outgrew that damage, either. That's why we keep the tourists away from these areas.'

I nodded at her. 'And Shady Oaks?'

She shook her head, putting her fingers on her bottom lip.

'To keep people like you out of sight?'

A tear ran down her face. Her eyelids blinked out of control as her nose began to run. I reached inside my jacket and pulled an old handkerchief from it. She took it and wiped her eyes and then her nose. Her arm twitched again. I then took the handkerchief from her and wiped a blotch of makeup running down her cheek.

'I saw something funny in one of those posh diners,' I said, holding her shoulder. 'There were these markings beside each individual item in their menus.' I moved the handkerchief to her other cheek and wiped the make-up clean. 'They had letters at the end of every one of them. Indicating whether the food was Imported or Local.'

She sniffed, and her eyes fluttered. I finished wiping the make-up and put the handkerchief back in her hand. She lifted it to her nose and continued to sniff.

'I looked around at the tables, taking note of what everyone ordered. There were some wealthy men and women there, and not one of them eating a local dish, and it got me thinking. Why would it matter? If all their food is cooked well enough. Then why would a rich customer want to know?'

She lowered the handkerchief and looked at me with her red eyes. 'We can't afford to eat imported foods. Not the real people in this city. And yet our kids keep turning out like...' She paused as her arm jerked to the side.

I exhaled through my nose and nodded.

She came closer to me and fell into my chest. 'I'm sorry, Vince. I didn't mean to unload this on you, I know it's not your job...'

I wrapped my arms around her and stroked her hair as she cried. The moon shined bright through the window, tapping me on the shoulder, reminding me there was still one more place to go.

CHAPTER 30

I put Gabe into the car with Ju and her driver and sent them on their way. I then went back to the cab and hopped in at the side, closing the door with a quick sigh. Serik turned on the engine and left his hands near the air vents, waiting for them to warm. I rubbed my eyes up to the bridge of my nose.

'We still have time to make it to the ferries. Next stop Kaivus?'

I didn't answer him.

He pulled the shifter down and brought the gear into drive. We rolled out of the complex and continued down the moonlit stretch of road.

I took my cigarette pack out and opened it, looking at the final smoke in there. I closed it back up and growled a little. The driver continued on down the road, paying no attention to me. I balled my fist and hit the center console without thinking.

The driver put his elbow on the console, knocking my fist off it.

'Gentle now,' he said. 'This ain't even my car.'

I nodded, looking at the dash and touching the vents with my finger. 'Your brother lent this one to you?'

'Yeah.'

'Fascinating guy.' I let out a breath. 'He owns that shabby pink hotel on the beachfront?'

The driver cleared his throat. 'Not him. His wife.'

'I figured. Strange place they've got there. Hard to piece it together all at once.'

We pulled onto a highway, driving alongside some other vehicles. There was a hovercraft jetting through the skies above us. The driver relaxed his posture and leaned into the seat, holding the bottom of the steering wheel as he drove.

'The first guy I saw was Gabe when I reached this town. He was being watched by a few of your brother's friends. I thought it was odd. What did they care so much about a junkie like him? The government can't be all that strict on drugs. Right?'

The driver didn't say anything.

'Then I found Barbra at the hotel. Or rather, she found me. But your brother's gang didn't kill her husband. Not from what she said.'

'They only do it when they have to,' said Serik.

'Sure, I thought that much. But what kind of mix-up is this with a lady like Barbra and Gabe in the same company?'

The driver moved in his seat, readjusting himself.

'You can't tell me yourself, can you? That's their business, right? Some drugs here and there, but most of it comes from hiding people from your government. Am I right?'

He put his head up a bit and then down to look out the windshield. He pointed out a transport station with his thick finger.

'That's the place there,' he said. 'It's the only way to reach the moon. There's no spaceport on Eroth. Just these stupid ferries.'

I saw a ship taking off into the sky at a relentless pace. I opened my mouth to speak again, but he cut me off before I could.

'Crazy things those ships,' he said. 'Zoom right up in the air. Hell, I'll never know how they got them to work like that, but they did.' He shook his head. 'They did. And who's thinking we had any smarts left on this planet. People with real brains don't exist here anymore. And if they do, they're either rich, or they're dead.'

I watched another ship take off.

'There's a uniform in the trunk,' he said. 'If you pull the back seat up, you can reach it. Might want to change before we arrive.'

'How do these smart folks die?' I said. 'More accidents? And unnaturally black veins when they're found?'

He chuckled. 'You're a strange guy.'

I started to tap my thumb up and down.

'You know about the Black Death, don't you?'

'Nope.'

'Your brother ever sell any?'

'Not on purpose.'

'I see,' I said. 'And Shady Oaks is…'

'Shaded Oaks. If there were no Shaded Oaks, there'd be nobody for my brother to hide. You know, when the government finds out you've got a Gabe on your hands, they come knocking with a signed letter to ship 'em out, to receive a fine education.'

I left my hand over my stomach. I felt queasy all of a sudden. I needed a smoked. There were no more cigars left, though, and I couldn't break for the last Silver Mist just yet.

'They make the parents loads of promises, saying those kids will get proper education they can't find in the cities and that they'll take good care of them, but no one's ever seen the Shady Oaks. So how would any of us know what really goes on?'

We were getting closer to the shipyard.

'Better get that uniform on. Otherwise, you're staying down here with me.'

I nodded a few times before I went to the back.

• • • • •

The driver stopped across the street and waited for a while. I was dressed in a black uniform with leather gloves and military boots on my feet. There was also a helmet I was meant to wear, but I didn't put it on right yet. Instead, we watched the entrance where the employees, all in their identical uniforms, marched single-file inside the shipyard.

I tucked my gun at my side, pushing it up near my ribs, within the uniform. A man walked by our vehicle and waited there for a moment, looking across the street at the entrance.

The driver cleared his throat and opened his hand towards me. The man was still standing in front of us, gazing across the street. The driver cleared his throat again and jiggled his open hand. I sighed and pulled the gun out from my side, slapping it in his palm. The man hadn't moved from his position in front of our car.

Serik then gave me a push. 'That's your friend there. Don't talk to him, just follow what he does and keep your head down.'

I pursed my lips and pulled at my tight collar. 'Right.'

He looked at my helmet and then at his wrist. 'Don't be late for your shift.'

I put the helmet on and stepped outside. I went up near the man standing on the sidewalk and stood quietly beside him. He turned his head towards me and then continued walking across the street. I followed close beside him.

We queued up with the other workers and waited for our turns to be cleared inside. I tried to keep myself calm as I walked through. I know I had all the verifications on me, but it still didn't give me a great deal of comfort.

The person in front of me went up into the clearance section. He lifted his hand, and a machine scanned his wrist. It turned blue when it was finished and let him pass through. I followed and allowed the scanner to check me the same. It lagged a couple of seconds, skipping my heart, then shined blue, letting me pass.

I moved quickly to keep up with my new friend. He was hanging back, waiting for me to join while a river of others moved past him. I jogged alongside him and nodded a bit. He didn't return it, he merely kept walking.

I followed him as we weaved through some narrow gates that herded us workers, like cattle ready for the day's slaughter. I squeezed between the tall metal gate and reached the opposite end, keeping an eye on the guy ahead of me.

We moved into a large hanger, scanning our hands in another queue and pushing by the armed guards in the corner. The hanger was filled with people unloading crates out of the gravitational transport ships and loading empty containers on the empty vessels. There were other people walking around the vessels using large metal rods to examine them. Some ships were being worked on by mechanics erupting sparks across their noses, while other mechanics opened their underbellies, checking the core reactors while wearing thick silver suits.

I lost my attention for a second and had to scan the hanger in panic, looking for my new friend. He was waiting near the side of the base. I rushed to catch up with him. We continued walking towards an empty ship being loaded at the moment.

A small ground car pulled nearby, and high-ranking workers stepped out with scanners in their hands and rifles on their backs. I felt my heart bounce off my ribs like a wild ape thrashing at its cage. The officials put their hands out, stopping me and my new friend. They put the scanners up, and we both lifted our palms to them. They scanned us and then drew their machines back, looking at them for some time.

I had nothing else to do other than stand there and sweat like a pig. The officials nodded their heads and then waved us to the ship. The guy beside me gave a little bow, I quickly did the same, and we moved past them.

My friend climbed the ship's ramp, then down a thin ladder to a small hold inside. We ended up in a dark room filled with meaty creatures squirming all around us.

My friend went to the wall nearby while I watched the fleshy beings drip and ooze from their orifices, slowly crawling towards us like we might be a nice snack for them to feast upon. My friend opened the wall and took out a few prod-like devices, and handed me one. He gave his a twist, and a violet-blue spark appeared at the end of it. I took hold of the forked prod and twisted it quickly, and violet-blue sparks flew out of the end of my device as well.

My friend jabbed his prod into the ceiling, hitting one of the meaty beings. It dropped to the floor, and my friend stabbed it, then gave it a shock, killing the pest. I followed his lead and jabbed one of the fleshy creatures getting closer to me. I stabbed it when it fell to the floor, electrocuting it till it stopped moving.

My friend was going at a much faster pace than myself. He was frantically jabbing into the dark ceiling and shocking them quickly on the ground as if they might overtake us if we didn't make their deaths fast.

I felt something on my shoulder and then whipped around, trying to pull the creature off me. It had clamped its mouth onto my shoulder with an immense amount of pressure. I felt it through my leather jacket, digging into my shoulder bone as if it were nothing.

My friend jabbed it quickly and then killed it on the floor. He looked up and pointed above me. There was another creature there. I was quick to stab this one. It squealed as it hit the ground, and then I shocked it with a final whimper.

We kept going through the dark room, jabbing at the creatures and shocking them to death. Then after some time, I felt the ship moving. My friend stopped a moment and pointed towards the ladder. I climbed up quickly and stood there waiting for him to join me.

He stepped through and pointed at two gravitational seats being drawn out from the wall as we arrived. We sat in them as the restraints automatically fixed over us. My friend turned off his forked prod and put it into the wall beside himself. I did the same.

The ship began to rumble. Then, in an instant, it shot us into the sky, up towards the moon. I closed my eyes when the ride became too intense, stretching my flesh around my bones and smearing my eyes back into my brains. I don't know if I passed out or not, but I awoke all of a sudden, looking up at my friend who was kicking my shins.

He handed me my prod. I took it and released myself from the constraints. I then stood and saw the cargo door being lowered at the back of the ship. My friend went through the giant containers stacked inside the dock, finding meaty creatures to kill. I joined alongside him.

I could hear some heavy machinery crawling into the ship's cargo bay. It was a huge tractor with a crane at its side and a massive tow platform on its back. Using the crane, it grabbed the first metal container and swung it onto its back.

I slid a little further down towards the exit, catching a glimpse of the moon's surface. It was filled with yellow and black sand and endless rows of scraggly trees growing upwards like twisted nails mis-hammered by a shoddy carpenter.

I went a bit further, unnoticed by anyone, as the commotion of unloading took up so much attention. There was a river running through the land with tall grass alongside it and factories covering the rest of the expanse farther than my eyes could see.

I'm sure the skies were blue at one point. Or clear, at least. But now, a dark fog hung over the land while burning smokestacks puffed a continuous stream of black smoke. I stalked down the landing dock, moving close alongside the massive ground transport vehicle, remaining hidden at its side from the rest of the workers.

Branching away from the machine, I crept on towards the closest factory across the river. There were other uniformed workers walking from the different factories – some helping to direct the vehicles, others swarming about the caravans on roaring motorbikes, while one aerial craft zipped overhead on a patrol.

Hiding beneath the scraggly trees, I put more distance between myself and the ship and neared closer to the tall stalks of grass at the river's edge. When I glanced over my shoulder, I saw no bout of frantic motion nor heard any emergency signals shrieking yet.

The aerial craft thrummed over the river and hovered gradually in my direction. Tucking my body into a wide opening at the tree's base, I panicked as the machine rustled the sand and lingered overtop the patch of scraggly trees.

The craft swept onwards, probing the lands, and in time moving closer to the recently grounded spacecraft. When I saw the craft monitoring over the workers buzzing across the bridge, I dashed to the river's edge and hid myself in the tall grass.

I sat amongst the stalks watching the workers move back and forth for what seemed hours. At one point, I compacted the electric prod and found a leather strap at my side that held it perfectly.

The machines dropped cargo loudly in the distance. Kneeling deeper beneath the tall grass, I stopped to wait for what might come next, but nothing happened, the hammering sounds were just a part of normal operations.

Taking my helmet off my head for a second allowed me to breathe some fresh air and gave my face a break from the confined space. The keyword was fresh though, besides the comfort of being out of the mask, it did little for my lungs in the noxious atmosphere, leaving a metallic taste on the back of my tongue and burning sharp pains in my chest.

I put the helmet back on and gazed at the sun above. I couldn't guess how fast or slow it would rise and set on this planet, but it would eventually go dark and give me a chance to have a better look at the world without walking in broad daylight.

Sliding lower along the river's bank, my foot slipped into the water, and if I hadn't reacted quick enough, the rest of me might've fallen in as well. When I resettled, I checked my leg and saw my foot covered in slimy grime.

I peered across the water's surfaces and saw an oily glisten atop the stream. A little further beyond near the other side, I caught sight of a type of clog stuck on a large broken tree branch, gathering rubbish and collecting a thick foam over itself.

While the sun was bright, I removed my glove and tried to snap a couple of photos of the scene. My watch failed to capture any images, flashing a holographic error message that threatened to set off an alarm if the same action occurred again.

Rubbing the top of my helmet did little in the way of an answer, but upon removing my second glove, an illuminating suspicion roused within me. I went about taking off the entire suit, leaving it in the grass, as I started crawling in my underwear along the muddy bank far enough from the uniform.

The winds were bitter cold, inserting tiny pinpricks into my skin, and plaguing goose flesh down the back of my neck. Around fifty meters from the uniform, I pushed some of the tall grass aside and snapped another picture with my watch.

This time, it snapped and saved the holographic image. I laughed to myself, shivering uncontrollably in the process, then crawled back fast to my uniform. The suits were well designed to keep their secrets safe. No photos could be taken within proximity of the uniforms, and if a person tried more than once, apparently, it would set off an alarm.

Throwing my uniform back on warmed me slightly, and scared me even more. As I sat in the grass, waiting for the sun to set, I knew no one could see me in passing, but that didn't make me feel any safer.

CHAPTER 31

I awoke with a startle as the ship blasted off into the sky. Watching the vessel soar through the air, I noted the fading sun's position as it now touched the edge of the horizon. I sat up from the tall grass and gazed across the river at the clogged mass still stuck in the flowing water.

Not a soul moved across the lands. The factories were radiating a stillness that was quite the opposite of the daylights operations. Then the lights went out in the factory, and the other buildings surrounding it cut to black as well.

That was a good enough cue for me to move. I slipped into the frigid waters and walked towards that floating object on the opposite side. The waters rose up to my neck in the center of the river, and the current kept asking me to follow it downstream. I plowed through faster, wanting to escape the cold and the flowing stream yanking at my ankles.

Kicking my knees up higher, I legged myself to the other end and instantly knew what the clog was, as soon as I reached. I wiped some of the rubbish off the person's back and flipped them upwards to see their face. It was a woman, recently dead, with water lodged in her throat up to her bulging eyes.

I dragged the woman up through the bank and laid her in the tall grass. She wore rags for clothes and possibly no shoes while she was alive. Removing my uniform, I set my things twenty meters away, then came back and tried to take another photo. It snapped and saved without a hitch.

Before leaving, I shut her eyes down, pushed her tongue into her mouth, and retrieved my clothes. I moved as far as I could through the tall grass, then peered out at the main factory. Several armed guards marched the perimeter and shone bright torch lights before their feet.

They checked the main factory, making sure the giant doors were well locked, then moved on to the next factory. I waited a moment before stepping out to check the area once more. When the coast was clear, I started my jog towards the main factory. I rushed quickly to the shadows, keeping near the walls as I drew nearer to the entrance.

I reached the building and pulled at the locked doors just to make sure. An aerial vehicle stormed fast in the night sky. The machine raced over the factory and lingered near the river, shining a spotlight onto its surface.

Not stopping to watch, I darted around the building, where I saw a stack of containers piled high atop each other and close enough to the factory's roof. The area was vacant. I couldn't hear anyone or see any figures lurking at the corners.

Rocketing through the air, the flying vehicle circled a factory, three buildings away, shining its bright spotlight for ten seconds before it zipped away, and this time far enough out of sight.

Voices echoed from around the corner.

Jogging fast, I swept beside the stacked containers and double-checked the area, then jumped, catching the top of the first container and pulled myself onto it. I struggled to get my legs up over the roof but eventually managed by grabbing one of the handlebars running down its side.

The voices were getting louder.

Standing exposed atop the first box left me little time to catch my breath, as I climbed up the second container along an indented foothold. Then without breaking my momentum, I scaled the third container, putting me a few meters over the factory's roof. I glanced down at the steep drop below and then to the rooftop where I needed to be.

Loud voices barked from the ground. I crouched down near the middle of the container, frozen in place. The aerial craft's green blinking light caught my attention in the distance. It would only take a few seconds for it to reach me. One zip and a blue spotlight would leave me bare to the world.

I could hear two heavily booted soldiers marching in the gravel road nearby. Pieces of rock cracked as they stepped in the gap between the factory and piled containers.

I stayed flat for some time, waiting to be sure they'd gone. Then I slid down on my chest and peered over the edges to check that they'd left.

The blinking green light flew across the dark skies, then blasted a bright spotlight onto a smokestack, perhaps half a kilometer away. I stood to my feet and reevaluated my jump onto the roof. There was no time to muck about. So, I rubbed my hands together and then made a quick dash, launching from the containers and plummeting in the air towards the factory.

My toe caught the edge of the building, tripping me mid-air and slamming my helmet onto the factory's roof. Even though I had my hands outstretched to catch myself, I still had the wind knocked out of me like a solid kick to the gut. Rolling away from the steep edge, I tried to keep my coughs quiet as I didn't want to draw any attention to myself.

The blinking green light seemed to be drawing closer to me. Its spotlight ripping through the dark and evaporating just as fast.

When I regained my breath, I stood to my feet and felt a dull pain throbbing through my left wrist. I rubbed my ulna bone and hissed at the tender spot on my arm. Minor fracture, I assumed. Better than my helmet cracking and smashing glass into my face.

I stumbled on along the rooftop to a brick hatch in the center, leading down into the factory. Leaning my shoulder onto the hatch, I lifted up a padlock bound to a thick chain wrapped about the door's handle.

A second and third blinking green light appeared from the horizon. Three different spotlights snapped on and off, while the machines hummed, like hornets, searching for something in the night. I could hear them drawing closer. Could feel the winds changing around me.

I glanced quickly at the electric slot in the bottom of the lock's figure.

There was a tricky method to open these things. I had to learn that the hard way in one of my first freelance cases. Getting it wrong will give you one hell of shock you don't soon forget. I rubbed the crease in my right hand between my thumb and forefinger, where I had an old scar burnt across my skin.

I reached into my uniform and pulled out my metal lighter and the small wallet-shaped kit that held different picks of varied sizes. I clicked the lighter on and left the fire underneath the electric slot for some time.

One of the air crafts narrowed its light on a factory less than fifty meters away. I grit my teeth, waiting for the sign, keeping the fire burning on the electric slot. Then as the aerial craft moved to the next factory, whirring closer, the lock began to fizz at the end with sparks spewing outward.

I closed the lighter and put it down to cool and took out one of the larger picks, and shoved it into the lock. I then worked the second-largest pick inside, making a triangular point with it. Finally, I grabbed a thin metal piece with a magnetic pole at its end and dug it into the lock, twisting until it was unlatched.

The aircraft darted to a factory two buildings down from mine. Bright lights lit the roof and surrounding permitter. It only took a second for the craft to change direction and see me weaseling my way into the roof's hatch.

Carefully, I slithered the chains out from the door's handle, making as little sound as I could, while keeping my ears piqued to the humming aircraft nearby. The chains loosened their grips and coiled neatly onto the ground without making too much ruckus.

Opening the hatch door, I pushed inside, grabbing the coiled chains, and closing the door shut. Dust wafted through the air. I toed slowly down the steps and onward to the main floor.

At the bottom, I emerged into a dark corridor full of metal doors with tiny square windows in their frames, and digital locks at their sides. I shut the staircase door behind me, leaving the chains within, and continued through the hall to another intersection that led me deeper inside the building.

The place was a maze of corridors. After a long time of weaving and retracing my steps down the same halls over and over again, I finally found a new wing that seemed promising. There was a reception area, like what you might find in prison, and some showerheads in a white-tiled chamber.

I took off my helmet, gloves, and uniform, placing them on the ground while keeping hold of my torchlight. Behind a lobby desk, I found a pile of discarded jackets, scarves, pants, and gloves lying in a mess. Pulling out a trench coat and some loose trousers, I slipped them on and transferred my things into the pockets.

Stalking along the wall, I found a lone door at the back of the reception area, with an old-fashioned handle and a single padlock holding it together.

I kicked the door inward, splintering its frame and illuminating the darkroom with my portable torchlight. The room was filled with giant filing cabinets and shelves crammed with paperwork – old paperwork – not a single electronic file. I swept through the room, went to the nearest cabinet, opened it, and pulled out a file.

I put my light in my mouth and kept it shining on the paper. There was a picture of a young boy, paper-clipped in the top corner, like a passport photo and a profile written in black and white on the document.

It read:

Arthur Gaelii Soulden - Faust-Hymes Disorder DL-IV - High Functioning - Factory Line for the first three years, then promote to Mechanical Lifts. Send progression report.

I closed the chart and pulled out another. My heart began to race. There was a similar picture at the top of the new chart – a girl with pigtails, thick-rimmed glasses, and teeth protruding out her mouth. She was in a wheelchair with ribbons tied to the back of it.

I read the document:

Carrie Mirabilis Jalapa - Bergchild's Syndrome - Low Functioning - Dispose of and send The Letter to family...

I slowly lay the chart atop the file cabinet and rubbed my eyes. The air was stifling in the room. I thought of that lone cigarette left in my pack of Silver Mists. Thought hard and long on it.

As I moved my hand, I caused a sheet of paper to tumble from the file and to the ground.

Taking a knee, I picked up the fallen sheet and proceeded to examine it. It was a copy of the original letter they must've sent to this little girl's parents. Carrie's picture was pinned at the top corner of the letter as she stood against a fun blue background with a rainbow arch behind her.

Dear Mom and Dad,

I'm having a great time at Shaded Oaks. We are learning so many things each day. I hope that, at some point, I will be able to return home to see you and give you all a big hug. Until then, I must focus on my own development so that I can become a healthy and well-functioning member of society. Don't worry about me too much. They're feeding me good food and giving me lots of sun. I hope you are both doing well.

Lots of Love,
Carrie.

I put the letter and the girl's information into my jacket and stepped away from the cabinet. I snapped more photos of other files, letters, case descriptions, and plenty of classified documents. I then aimed my light through the rest of the spacious room. It was all the same. Walls of cabinets and files inside them with stolen children's names.

I moved away and slipped out the door, going towards the showers. There was a place right before the showers with a blue-painted backdrop and a fun rainbow arch between two white clouds. I shone my light on it for some time, snapped a picture, and then continued walking into the showers.

As I walked through them, I saw some pamphlets on the ground and picked one of them up. It had the name Shaded Oaks printed across the top with some copywriting and tagline scrawled across the rest.

I opened it up:

Shaded Oaks is an institution for children with unique qualities that require special tailored attention from our team of professionals. We are a government-funded program with help from taxpayers' money as well as funds from other charitable investors. Our goal is to help defray rehabilitation costs for our citizens who struggle to afford customized care and education for their children.

Shaded Oaks has reached out to help millions of children across Senturion, giving them real world skills to help them function in our society and at no cost to their parents, who need to focus on their own contributions.

We will never ask a parent to pay for this service as long as we are in operation, and we will always stand by our pledge to give their children the best opportunities they might have in life...

I took the pamphlet and continued walking.

Soon I reached a large chamber where it forked into two different routes: *Dormitories* and *Playground.* I kept my light on both the signs, moving back and forth between them, deciding which to follow. I chose the Playground, as I highly doubted it existed.

I marched down the open hall and entered into an industrial room with cold metal chairs spread throughout. Each chair had its own restraints near the ankles and armrests and some at the necks and chests. I walked along the chairs, shining my light on each, casting a shadow behind them. I wondered how many children sat in these chairs.

My body shuddered. My throat felt cold and dry.

I kept walking and touching the metal chairs when I saw a huge vat in the back. It was filled halfway with a murky blue liquid inside, like a giant dunking tank you might see at a local carnival.

I walked closer to it, thinking that it looked familiar. It shone in such a fascinating way, one that I'd seen before, but where? I graced the cold vat with my bare hand. It seemed to permeate through me like a poison that didn't need to touch your flesh to radiate its power.

'For those, we can't use,' I heard behind me.

I whipped around, shining my light in the voice's direction and backing up against the cold vat. There was no one to be seen.

'You know this brand, don't you? People on Ceph are calling it the Black Death? Isn't that right?'

Making a sidelong glance around the vat caused a tingling numbness to ripple through my head down to the base of my spine.

'We have our workers harvest it themselves from the plants we grow up on Eroth,' she said. 'It's become a very popular crop recently. We've been planting new fields every day and exporting more and more of it to the highest bidder.'

'You're poisoning other planets.'

'We're not the one's spreading the Black Death,' she said. 'We grow it here, but we don't make the drugs filling your streets on Ceph. That's some other thrill seeker making that deadly adventure. You see, you're looking at a very concentrated dose in that vat there. The way we've always made it in this planetary system. A few CC and you've got a recipe for instant death.'

My teeth clenched tight to a dull throbbing pain. 'You treat your own people like cattle?'

'What else can we do though, really?' she said. 'At least the drug is painless for our *unsuitable* visitors to Shaded Oaks. We made it that way; to be humane.'

I saw her green eyes emerging from the darkness and her red hair tied in a ponytail at the back of her neck. I then spotted the silver gun in her hand, pointed right at me.

'Mr. Sturgis. Private dick, no?'

A growl escaped my lips.

'Don't be so hard on yourself. For a bumbling nut, you've made it very far. Much further than your sophisticated friend before you. He only made it to the fisheries before we caught up with him. But you've made it here to Eroth. And I have to say I'm impressed. Almost impressed enough to hire you for a few tasks of my own.'

I backed against the vat, trying to slip around the side a bit.

'But you're too moral, aren't you? You'd tell me no or slip away if I set you to a mission?'

I tried to edge further to the side.

'Don't move!' she said. 'Did I say you could move?'

I put my hands up. 'You set me up Midori?'

'Set you up?' She scoffed at me. 'You set yourself up. I was just there to watch you unravel.'

I slipped another inch around the vat. 'You've been keeping an eye on me the whole time?' I said.

She laughed. 'Of course, Vince. Going straight to the pink hotel like you knew what you were looking for? Asking locals about the Black Death. Of course I kept an eye on you! You big dummy. That metal case of cigarettes I gave you let me trace your locations and hear everything you said. But you kept listening to that damn radio of yours. I couldn't make a definite move with so much static masking your words.'

The back of my skull prickled colder.

She shook her head, keeping the gun aimed at me, clicking her heels slowly across the floor.

'I wanted to kill you the first time I pick you up near the docks,' she said. 'I thought I'd hear your conversation and leave you faced down, but again that damn radio of yours. I couldn't kill you just yet. I had to make sure you weren't a real tourist. Don't you know that's why I brought you to that fancy restaurant and ordered some local fish? If you knew about our rivers, then you wouldn't have eaten it. Would you?'

'No.'

'God! You were so confusing, Vince.'

I nodded my head, leaving my hands visible in the air. 'How'd you find me here?'

'I knew you wouldn't stay on Senturion,' she said. 'While everyone searched the town for you, I felt I had to pay Eroth a visit. Just to be sure. But I was right, wasn't I? Of course, it's impossible to tell any worker from another in these uniforms, but when I noticed you creep away from the cargo bay slowly but surely, I knew I had you, even if we lost track of you in the trees.'

I chewed my upper lip until it started to bleed.

'How did you do it, Vince? How'd you get this far? Obviously, you had help. Right?'

'I did it myself. Knocked out a worker and took his uniform.'

She walked closer to me, standing a distance away, narrowing her gun at my neck. She clicked the hammer back.

'You're such a bad liar,' she said. 'Oh well, maybe you'll believe it when I say, sweet dreams Mr. Sturgis.'

'Hold on,' I said, lowering my hands. 'Hold on. For one second. Please?'

'Awww,' she said. 'Need to pee your pants first, big boy?'

'Hold on, Midori.'

'Sorry, hun.' She leveled the gun at my heart.

'You've already got me, though! It's checkmate, game over, right?'

She hesitated, letting me continue.

'You can end me. However you please. But I've made it this far. Don't I deserve the whole story, to know what I'm about to die for?'

'No.'

'Come on, Sweetheart?'

I then winked at her and smooched my lips in the air.

She snorted. 'Vile.'

I lowered my hands all the way, clicking the recorder on my watch. 'Why the kids?' I said. 'Free labor and no questions from the parents?'

She paused, allowing her mental cogs to whir. Then she squint at me.

'That's right,' she said. 'A free education for their children, at no expense to the parents' meager bank accounts.'

'And you don't have any plans to fix this problem anytime soon?'

She grinned. 'Not when we can make so much profit off it. Why should we clean up the rivers or stop our factories from pouring into our seas? They give us the perfect citizens at birth – people who are more than willing to work up in this toxic planet for nothing.'

'The parents have little choice in the matter then?'

She smirked. 'Shaded Oaks is compulsory, yes, if that's what you mean?'

I lowered my hands even more. 'Your husband was in on it?'

She moved the gun in her hand to the side of her waist as she spoke. 'I never had one, dipshit. It was my dad who helped build this government! You're so fucking stupid.'

'Fair enough.'

'It is fair!'

I tensed up as she waved the gun in the air.

'Why shouldn't I be living like royalty? My father built this place. Factory after factory down there, raising Senturion out of filth and poverty. So why should I or anyone else give up what we've earned? What do we owe the common sheeple? The lazy fucks.'

I put my hands to my side. 'You killed Oren, didn't you? Your government would never let an outside business in on the deal. Not when they could find out how your exports really work?'

Her face turned to a vicious sneer, and without thinking, she dropped the gun's barrel. 'Your friend was getting too pushy about his stupid cigarettes,' she said. 'We don't mind having foreigners work in our companies at higher salaries to keep their mouths shut, but not when they want to set up their own gig on our lands...'

I glanced to the side of the vat and grunted.

She lifted the gun at me again with a big smile. 'Happy Vince?'

I shook my head. 'One more thing. Miss Kage. Tsuki. She knew what was going on here. Didn't she?'

She squinted her eyes and snorted a condescending breath. 'Stupid bitch. Miss holier than thou? You know her family is quite wealthy too? You think she's perfect because she's from Terra-Seven? That she doesn't have skeletons in her closet too?'

'I never implied - '

'Shut the fuck up!' she barked. 'People like her go around shooting themselves in the foot, you know? I asked her nicely over tea to tone it down. We tried to handle that situation by taking the high road. But she wouldn't stop with all her asinine rights.'

'Women's rights aren't a real threat to your operation though?'

'We had informants sitting in her private meetings. She was only starting with women's rights. Then gays and queers. But her final blow was aimed squarely at the way we do our business here. She knew what she was doing.'

'So you pumped her full of this Black Death and roped her neck to the ceiling rafters?'

'Yes! Yes! Yes!'

'Because you know she's better than you? Because you know what she's saying is the truth and worse - she might be just as rich as yourself!'

Midori's face twisted into a mean scowl as she glared to the side, lowering her gun, and erupted a foul shrill.

In a sudden flood of determination, I jumped around the vat before she regained her composure and aimed the gun back at my chest.

While shrieking, she fired two shots, nicking at the floor, barely missing my ankles. I scurried toward a dark corner and turned off my torchlight, crouching behind one of the chairs.

She turned on a light and started to search the walls.

'Vincent? Get out here, you fool! They won't let you back aboard the ship without me dragging you there! You hear me? You're already dead. I have my soldiers waiting for me right outside this factory, so get your ass out here and take it like a man!'

Swinging the chair in a twirl, I rushed out from hiding and dove into another darkened corner. Her torchlight lit the spinning chair, and three bullets ricocheted off its metal back.

Midori ducked fast as the lead pelted on the floor near her feet, then up on the ceilings, before calming down.

I kept running, going past her along the wall.

'Oh, stop being so sentimental, you prick. What harm are we really doing? Taking dopes from their parents and putting them to good use? Don't get soppy. They're useless, Vince. We all know it!'

I then turned on my light and chucked it in the opposite direction. She followed the light, aiming her gun at it the torch, while I rushed up behind her; pulling out the electric prod from my trousers and lifting it high over my head.

She careened back, catching my eyes, as I shoved the sharp end of the prod into her neck. A fat spurt of blood slapped onto my face as a gunshot rang out near my foot. She tried to raise the pistol to my head, but I clicked on the electricity, giving her a nice shock and tossing the weapon from her hands.

Her eyes convulsed wide in her head as she tried to yell. I turned the voltage even higher and sizzled her some more, watching her shake out of control until she bit off her tongue and shat herself.

When smoke emanated from her neck wound and her eyes had long since fried, I ripped the prod out from her collarbone and let her fall dead to the floor. Her feet kept twitching as a pool of urine pooled beneath her body.

Stepping back, I spat on her face and growled in frustration.

'Useless bitch.' I dropped the prod beside me and fell down as my knees gave way underneath me. I reached into my jacket and pulled out my lighter and the last Silver Mist from my pack.

The lighter shook in my trembling hands as the cigarette wobbled unsteadily in my lips. Eventually, I got it lit, and felt a surge of nicotine rushing through my veins. I couldn't stop shaking, never quit the shakes for what seemed an eternity.

•　　　•　　　•　　　•　　　•

There was nothing left to my smoke when I came out of my trance. I'd puffed my cigarette down to the butt, burning a small mark on my fingers without noticing.

I glanced down at Midori, wide-eyed and smelling like shit. I spat at her again and stood up, going towards the blue vat in the room. Its shimmering blue glow reflected in my eyes.

Carrie, I thought. *Which chair did they put you in before they did it?* I closed my eyes and saw the little girl from the file I'd found earlier. She was sitting in one of the cold metal seats with a masked doctor standing over her, holding a syringe-tube that connected to the murky vat of poison beside me.

The needle drew closer to her arm, and the doctor whispered something to her. 'It's only a pinch and then a bit of sleepy liquid that'll help your brain grow properly from now on.' I opened my eyes and looked at one of the chairs near me.

I don't remember how long I sat there, but at one point, I found myself in that chair, rubbing its armrest over and over without much thought.

•   •   •   •   •

I took my time getting all the pictures and samples I needed then returned to the death chamber. I kneeled down to the ground with a boxcutter I'd found and turned Midori's face to the side. I pulled her head up, grabbed her red ponytail, cut it off near the back of her skull, and set it down beside me. Next, I took off her right glove, wristwatch, and a tag-like necklace up at her neck and switched them with mine (except for my own personal watch, I kept that with all my other valuables tucked at my side).

No soldiers rushed into the factory. Nor did any sort of official bother me. As I sifted through her belongings further, I found a metal case of cigarettes in her jacket and laughed as I tossed it aside. There was another case out there, likely being chewed by rats or in Ju's possession, complete with a tracking device and some two-way radio.

Not that I would ever know, the signal wouldn't reach between planets, and I didn't care to test the thing out. To tidy everything up, I shoved my helmet over her head and my glove onto her hands and plopped her body into a wheelchair I found near the showers.

And for the final touch, I put her cut ponytail inside my helmet, letting it peek underneath the back, just enough to let the others see it. I took hold of her wheelchair and tried my best to walk like a bitchy woman out of place.

CHAPTER 32

I waited for the next ship to land before I went out with the wheelchair. Two guards were quick to take notice of me. They rushed along with their rifles in hands and then paused when they saw the red hair poking out from under my helmet. The nearest guard pulled out a scanner and held it up to me.

I put my hand in the air gently, as if I were some dolphin surfacing through the water.

The guard scanned my hand then bowed his head. The other did the same. The second guard came around me and took hold of the wheelchair, and walked it down the path toward the cargo ship that was being unloaded. When we reached the ship, I regained control of the wheelchair and took it up the ramp, past all the heavy machines and busy workers.

No one bothered me as I wheeled Midori straight into the airlock. I left her inside and closed the door shut. A guard patrolling the ship saw me working on this task and came over to help. He scanned my hand and then went to the side of the airlock, setting a timer so that it would open mid-flight, and its contents would fall out into space.

He bowed to me when this was done and walked away in silence.

•   •   •   •   •

I sat inside my reserved seat in my private room aboard the ship, feeling the gravity more than anyone else. Then I thought I heard something, like the airlock opening. I don't know if it was my imagination, but I heard something and felt something in my chest.

After a while, I lay back, face smeared with the rush of speed, and closed my eyes for the rest of the trip.

•   •   •   •   •

I exited the shipyard, scanned my hand, and threw my hips out with exaggeration as I walked free from work. There was a fancy car sitting up near the curb with a rich man behind the wheel, eyeing all the uniformed workers, hoping to meet someone at the exit.

Lowering my head down, I tucked the ponytail further up into my helmet and walked across the street through the tall buildings near the business district. There was a cab driver waiting inside his vehicle with a nasty scowl on his face. I went over toward him and asked him to take me to the transport station headed for Kaivus.

He cocked his head to the side, telling me to get in. We got to the station when the skies were turning dark. I got out and gave him some extra credits for his troubles, to which he grumbled a thanks.

Using Midori's credits, I purchased a first-class ticket, no questions asked, and waited for the intercom to announce when it would be my chance to board.

I lingered in the station for a while, getting nervous, thinking the whole operation seemed off; that there must be a reason for the ship's delay. The workers started to rush outside as if there was a fire across the street. I sat up curiously and followed them. Then I peered my head out the doorway, looking at everyone craning their necks upwards to the skies.

I stepped out and took the helmet off, gazing at the moon with them. Brilliant streaks of light covered the moon as if they were melting across the surface with an electric current raining inside. The night sky erupted in a magnificent display of lights. I was lost for words at the almost unnatural colors, and even more how everyone on Senturion stared right at the problem.

How many citizens were wondering about their children right then as they looked into the skies, distracted by the lights?

And there it was. Right before our eyes. But we're blind to it most of the time.

'The lights over the Senturion moon,' I said to myself as I watched them burn.

EPILOGUE

Six months later...

I sat in a cafe drinking a hot cup of coffee as the winter snow hit our desert lands. It wasn't uncommon. I didn't make much of it. It's a big planet anyhow.

The waitress came by with a reuben sandwich and some purple fries, and a bit of vinegar for them. I picked up my food and took a bite, thinking to myself about the moon. Not the one in my sky, no, not that one.

I thought about the children up there. The plants they were forced to grow and harvest. And the unwanted souls.

You see, the Black Death taking lives every so often now. We still can't get rid of the stuff.

I took another bite of my sandwich and shook my head loose of that moon. I had other things to think about now. How in the hell a man was killed in his own bedroom with multiple security cameras failing all at once. That's what I needed to be thinking about. Ceph. The present moment.

The door opened in the diner, and a lady with thick curly hair walked in with a scrawny man jittering at her side. I put my sandwich down and stared at her with a blank expression.

She scanned the diner until she made eye contact with me. She nodded a few times and then came over with the jittery kid at her side.

'Can I?' she said.

I nodded.

She put the kid in the booth first and then herself next.

I knew this guy with her. I'd seen him before. But I couldn't place his face.

She opened her mouth to talk, but nothing came out.

I sighed as I raised my hand up to get the waitress's attention. The lady with mounds of heavy makeup on her face came over to our table. 'Yeah?'

'Two coffees and some sandwiches.'

The lady opened her mouth. 'What sandwiches?'

'Reuben. Doesn't matter.'

'Fine.' She walked back toward the kitchen.

I started to rub my eyebrow and then picked up my coffee to take a sip.

'I – I...' she said.

'What's your real name?' I asked.

'Nyadinn.'

I smiled. 'And the apartment you grew up in was called?'

She took in a deep breath. 'Sycamore Court. I've always liked the name Sycamore so...'

I looked at the kid across the table and felt it slowly coming back to me.

'Everything's changing now,' she said. 'You know Ceph is giving out more visas to us, well, after... you heard, right?'

'I read about it.'

She put her hands on the table, rubbing them anxiously. 'There were even a handful of investors here who put up some homes for the refugees to stay while everything is being sorted.'

I licked my lips and sipped my coffee again.

She looked around the table a bit unsure and then spoke again. 'I was hoping you might help me find an old friend of mine?'

I laughed, holding the mug up under my lips. 'Looking for your brother Gabe?'

Her expression froze.

'I already found him.'

She moved her hands closer to me along the table.

'You found him?'

I nodded. 'He's well taken care of on Senturion. The pinstripe boys seem to think he's worth it anyhow.'

She smiled with a small tear rolling down her cheek.

I looked at the twitching kid again. *That's it,* I thought. *That's got to be him.*

'I didn't think they'd keep their word,' she said with a quiver. 'Dad used to work for them, smuggling cargo from the moon. When he died in service, they promised to take care of Gabe for us, but I didn't think they really would.'

I licked my lips. 'And they smuggled you and your mom to a safer place?'

She was reluctant to nod.

'He's still looking for that black dog of yours,' I said. 'He thinks if he can find it, your family will come back to him.'

She touched her lips as her eyes began to well.

I put the coffee back down and looked at the guy across the table and then back to Sycamore. 'I guess you'll want to bring Gabe here, like the other immigrants?'

She nodded with a tear in her eye.

'I can give you some contacts that will help you find him,' I said. 'You'll be safer now with the UC army base there.'

The coffees found their way to the table and steamed thick in the winter air. I took another bite of my sandwich. Then I paused to look at the kid.

'The kid trying to sell me drugs on the ship?' I said, looking at Sycamore - Nyadinn. 'How'd this happen?'

Sycamore took a sip of her coffee and then looked at him. 'He reminded me of my brother,' she said. 'And I couldn't let them take him to the airlock, so I faked his death that night when you were walking around, smoking in the halls.'

I put my head down and gazed at my coffee. She looked at him for a moment, still with a slight grimace.

'I couldn't sneak out when we landed on Ceph,' he said. 'So I had to ride it back to Kaivus once more.'

'Ah.'

'I've been smuggling people for some time,' she said. 'Often hoping one of them might be Gabe.'

'I see.'

'You think I left my brother?' she said.

'No.'

'We had to escape to Kaivus when my father died,' she said. 'My mother told me he would join us later. That my father's friends would take care of him for a while, then send him to us. But maybe they never did, because he was too much of a risk.'

'I see.'

'Things never should've gotten to this point,' she said.

I sighed and then picked up my hat from the booth. 'Yeah, I agree.'

'We should all be able to-'

I slid out of the booth and put a cigarette in my mouth.

'Good luck with your visas. I'll send you my friend's information to help you find your brother.'

She looked at me, her red eyes wide in confusion. 'Vince? Is everything okay?'

I nodded and then clicked to pay the bill on the table.

'Yeah, fine, I've got some big things on my mind right now, is all. Don't take it personally.'

My heart slugged in my chest. The pain was growing worse these days. I had to see a doctor or someone about it at some point.

'Vince?'

I lit my cigarette and exhaled. My heart kept acting up. So, I pivoted towards the door but hesitated a moment when I reached the exit and turned back to her.

'Give me a call in a month or so,' I said, touching my chest. 'We'll get a coffee then. Just not right now. Is that all right?'

She nodded with confusion. 'Did I do something?' she said.

I opened my mouth to say something but stopped and continued out the door. The snow was falling softly on the ground, and my car was gathering a thin film atop its roof. I stood on the steps smoking my cigarette, watching the slow cars trickle past.

Another kick sliced inside my chest. I grimaced the pain away. Wanting to ignore it. I think it's better that way. Ignoring things. Pretending it's not there. Pretending it never happened.

I couldn't walk for some time. So I watched the cars. Smoking. Thinking and not thinking at all. Like a bad dream that refused to leave my headspace.

THE END

ABOUT THE AUTHOR

Jon Vassa is a Singapore-based Science Fiction writer who specializes in dystopian horrors. When he's not editing scripts for Asian Cinema Entertainment, he's out writing his own original works or reading a nice book. His works have appeared in Crimson Street's Magazine, the No Sleep Podcast and Black Rose Writing.

NOTE FROM THE AUTHOR

Word-of-mouth is crucial for any author to succeed. If you enjoyed *Lights Over the Senturion Moon*, please leave a review online—anywhere you are able. Even if it's just a sentence or two. It would make all the difference and would be very much appreciated.

Thanks!
Jon Vassa

We hope you enjoyed reading this title from:

BLACK ❦ ROSE
writing™

www.blackrosewriting.com

Subscribe to our mailing list – *The Rosevine* – and receive **FREE** books, daily deals, and stay current with news about upcoming releases and our hottest authors. Scan the QR code below to sign up.

Already a subscriber? Please accept a sincere thank you for being a fan of Black Rose Writing authors.

View other Black Rose Writing titles at www.blackrosewriting.com/books and use promo code **PRINT** to receive a **20% discount** when purchasing.

www.ingramcontent.com/pod-product-compliance
Lightning Source LLC
Chambersburg PA
CBHW010729100726
47899CB00009B/2993